He gaze
generos

She smiled back.

All that wattage made his knees even weaker.

He cleared his throat to introduce the girls. "This is Harper, and this is Piper, but she likes Pippa better because it's easier to say," Lawson said.

"I have a bunny," Harper said. "Pippa has a dog. They have beds, too."

Stuffed, he mouthed.

"I can't wait to meet them," Clara said. "Pippa, do you like real dogs? I have a small one. I left him inside in case one of you didn't like dog kisses. And my friend Matias has a big one. You can meet them soon if you like."

Tugging on the ends of her pigtails, Pippa nodded.

Clara's grin was as big as her heart, the size of which he'd grossly underestimated. She was flipping perfect with the twins, and he could kiss her for it.

Kissing Clara...

What would it be like to taste those plush lips as pale pink as the roses blooming along the sunny side of the house?

Shaking his head, he chalked up the brief curiosity to exhaustion. Since when did he daydream about kissing his tenant?

Dear Reader,

What better place for a fresh start than a tenacious, close-knit island that survives the Pacific's battering storms and swells? The small community of Hideaway Wharf represents different beginnings for Lawson and Clara. Lawson is on a quest to mend the harm he caused five years ago when he jilted his fiancée and walked out on his business partner. Clara, a newcomer who's renting the other half of Lawson's beachfront duplex, is facing being an empty nester at thirty-nine. Oyster Island is her opportunity to say *yes* to herself. But all her *yeses* draw her into the path of the island's prodigal brewmaster and the two preschoolers suddenly in his care.

As the new guardian to his college roommate's twin daughters, Lawson is determined to build a solid foundation for his instant family. For him, that will mean remaining single—a necessary sacrifice to establish the stability the grieving twins need. But Clara shakes up his determination to shelve romance indefinitely. Her kind generosity fills his emotional well while he fumbles with the basics of raising children he never expected to have. And with all their island adventures come his ultimate opportunity for redemption and her biggest possibility of *yes*—a chance at love!

Keep up-to-date on my next rugged heroes and adventurous heroines at www.laurelgreer.com, where you'll find extras, news and a link to my newsletter. You can also find me on Facebook or Instagram. I'm @laurelgreerauthor on both.

Happy reading!

Laurel

A SEASON OF
SECOND CHANCES

LAUREL GREER

SPECIAL EDITION

If you purchased this book without a cover you should be aware that this book is stolen property. It was reported as "unsold and destroyed" to the publisher, and neither the author nor the publisher has received any payment for this "stripped book."

Harlequin®
SPECIAL EDITION™

Recycling programs for this product may not exist in your area.

ISBN-13: 978-1-335-18006-3

A Season of Second Chances

Copyright © 2025 by Lindsay Macgowan

All rights reserved. No part of this book may be used or reproduced in any manner whatsoever without written permission.

Without limiting the author's and publisher's exclusive rights, any unauthorized use of this publication to train generative artificial intelligence (AI) technologies is expressly prohibited.

This is a work of fiction. Names, characters, places and incidents are either the product of the author's imagination or are used fictitiously. Any resemblance to actual persons, living or dead, businesses, companies, events or locales is entirely coincidental.

For questions and comments about the quality of this book, please contact us at CustomerService@Harlequin.com.

TM and ® are trademarks of Harlequin Enterprises ULC.

 Harlequin Enterprises ULC
22 Adelaide St. West, 41st Floor
Toronto, Ontario M5H 4E3, Canada
www.Harlequin.com

Printed in Lithuania

MIX
Paper | Supporting responsible forestry
FSC® C021394

USA TODAY bestselling author **Laurel Greer** loves writing about all the ways love can change people for the better, especially when messy families and charming small towns are involved. She lives outside Vancouver, BC, with her law-talking husband and two daughters, and is never far from a cup of tea, a good book or the ocean—preferably all three. Find her at www.laurelgreer.com.

Books by Laurel Greer

Montana Mavericks: The Tenacity Social Club

A Maverick Worth Waiting For

Harlequin Special Edition

Love at Hideaway Wharf

Diving into Forever
A Hideaway Wharf Holiday
Their Unexpected Forever
A Season of Second Chances

Sutter Creek, Montana

From Exes to Expecting
A Father for Her Child
Holiday by Candlelight
Their Nine-Month Surprise
In Service of Love
Snowbound with the Sheriff
Twelve Dates of Christmas
Lights, Camera...Wedding?
What to Expect When She's Expecting

Visit the Author Profile page
at Harlequin.com for more titles.

For anyone starting out or starting over.
You've got this.

Chapter One

Clara Martinez tucked a plastic sandwich container into the small cooler. Did making her newly college-age son's lunch violate the principles of the Year of Yes she began last month?

Probably. The whole point of the challenge she'd set out was to focus on herself, and hauling herself out of bed to mess around in the kitchen in the wee hours of the morning wasn't prioritizing her own sleep. Even her French bulldog was still sacked out on the bed in her room, having refused to get up and join the breakfast brigade.

But she felt no guilt over the small gesture.

For one, Daniel being finished with high school still threw her.

Somehow, her baby boy was the proud earner of the diploma sitting framed on the living room mantel of their rented duplex, and had big dreams for his future.

And two, those big dreams involved spending as much time as he could underwater, which meant Clara needed to protect him somehow. Even if it was with an extra BLT, carrot sticks and a tiny container of ranch dressing.

The food wouldn't actually keep him from danger, especially today when he was going to explore a deep artificial reef, but maybe the reminder she loved him would prompt him to think twice about safety.

She added his water bottle and a can of Coke to the cooler, and carried it out to the front porch with her coffee, ready to curl up in one of the two Adirondack chairs overlooking the lawn, and beyond it, the Salish Sea. With any luck, the otters would be out this morning, eager to show off for their audience of one.

A small prickle of awareness twinged at the base of her neck, a little electrical zap of awareness of another human nearby.

Never mind then, the otters had an audience of two.

A wall of faux greenery divided her half of the wraparound porch from her landlord's side. She usually had the whole stretch to herself before 8:00 a.m., but this morning, she could feel his presence on the other side of the screen. She felt the prickle at night sometimes, too, knowing he was on the other side of her bedroom wall, lying in his bed. The units mirrored each other, and only one wall in the primary bedroom was big enough to fit a headboard.

She'd been sleeping three feet away from Lawson Thorne since the Memorial Day weekend. On the nights when the air was still, she'd lie there, legs sticky from the lack of breeze through the window and sheets already in a tangle, wondering about the creaks and thunks against the wall. Nothing ever sounded frisky, but it was enough to know another person was simultaneously nearby and out of reach.

It was beyond her why there weren't any frisky sounds. He was…really attractive.

In a tousled, thick-framed-glasses kind of way, anyway.

And that way is right up my alley.

She wouldn't let herself go there. In working for closely linked businesses, they were almost coworkers. She was the summer manager at The Cannery on the harbor, in charge of the staff during the busy season for the local pub, owned by Matias Kahale. The brawny publican, an island fixture, also owned the island's brand-new brewery, located in the same building complex as the pub. Hauʻoli Brewing was Lawson's domain—he was Matias's sidekick these days, strutting around the converted warehouse like a chemistry professor with a penchant for beer-pun T-shirts.

Whenever he was pouring in the tasting room, the sales doubled, mainly from people coming to the bar for extra orders, just for the chance to stare into his eyes.

But from what she could tell, no one got invited back to his bed.

Clara sighed. Oh, to have the option. Until Daniel left for college at the end of the summer, she was an itty bit hampered by her darling roommate.

Any squeaks from her side of the wall were solely self-induced.

She took a swig of coffee and settled into the view. An incredible swath of ocean fronted the duplex, the angle allowing a glimpse of the mainland and the Cascades in the distance. Six a.m. on what would turn into a sunny, early July day was one of the best moments of the year to enjoy it. God, the colors. How was it possible for the human eye to see so many shades of blue and green all at once? Her perch looked over the cedar gazebo in the center of the yard. A row of fir trees stood sentry between the grass and the driftwood washed up on the beach. Beyond the trunks, the tide lapped against the rocks. The vista was far removed from the Portland suburb she and Daniel had left behind after the school year had ended.

Chair legs scraped on the wood on the other side of the privacy screen, followed by the sound of a suppressed sniffle and a gently blowing nose.

She was about to call through the fake foliage to ask Lawson if he had a cold when her son barreled out of the front door, a large duffel bag slung over his lanky shoulder. His mile-wide smile was worth every minute of sleep she'd lost last night. Today's dive of a scuttled ship involved a higher degree of difficulty than the shallower plunges he'd taken to date.

If Eduardo had been alive, he'd be the one taking their son

out, teaching him the ropes. Instead, Daniel's training was in the competent hands of his godfather, Archer Frost.

Her husband had been gone for five years. These days, more of her grief was focused on remembering the wonderful memories, rather than dwelling on the ones they'd lost the chance to make. Even so, Daniel's decision to log the hours he'd need to train as a scuba instructor was testing her limits.

Tucking her blanket around herself and returning her son's smile, she drank her coffee and tried to breathe in another inch of air. She could say goodbye to him this morning without him noticing how nervous she was.

She pointed at the cooler. "Don't forget your lunch."

His cheeks reddened. "Aw, Mom, you didn't have to. I was going to grab something from the bakery."

"Save your money," she said. "You're going to need it once you're covering your own social budget in the fall."

The healthy flush slid away, his light brown skin paling a few shades.

His nerves about going to college seemed stronger than any he felt when he dove, even though the sport had had a hand in his father's death. His love of being underwater despite the risk… It was healthy, to be honest. She didn't want Daniel to live his life in fear or pain.

But she did wish he was more excited about starting his biology degree in the fall. Clara's college experience hadn't been typical. She'd fit in the degrees she'd needed to become a home economics teacher around being a young mom and wife to a Coast Guard member. She wanted desperately for her son to have more of the excitement and freedom of living on campus and less of the stress and juggling.

"Stop reminding me about 'the fall.' I want to enjoy the summer, first," he said under his breath.

He took the small cooler in his free hand and came over to give her a quick hug. When he was fresh out of bed like this, his dark curls messy and eyes still heavy with sleep, she could still catch a hint of little-boy smell, and it punched through her nostalgia centers like a boxing glove on a spring.

Daniel was his father's duplicate in so many ways—living for the sights below the surface. Clara was more about watching things from shore. The occasional glimpses of whales and porpoises, and the more frequent harbor seals. The animals somehow managed to live their whole lives underwater without getting the bends and having a fatal heart attack.

Everyone assumed Eduardo had died from the explosion. She'd corrected people about his cause of death so many times, she could usually be matter-of-fact about it.

Today, though, with Daniel upping the difficulty on his own dive, the details had her heart creeping up to her throat.

"Triple-check your math today, okay?" she said.

He made a face. "Your hovering sucks, Mom. Don't you trust Archer? If you're overprotective, he's not going to believe you don't blame him for the accident, no matter what you say."

Yet another moment where her kid was smarter than she was. Not sure if it reflected how Eddy and she had raised him, or Daniel's own innate EQ, but truth dominated his words. In no way did she want Archer to think she held him at fault for the chain of events ending with Eduardo's death. He'd been Eduardo's best friend and coworker, and was now one of Clara's best friends, not to mention a hell of a role model for Daniel. The new father deserved to live an unencumbered life, and her son was right—if she got too nervous about Daniel's diving, Archer *would* think she didn't trust him.

She shot her son a guilty-as-charged look.

If Daniel'd had a tail, he would be wagging it, for sure. "My first wreck dive, Mom. It's going to be wicked."

"I know you'll make safe choices."

He rolled his eyes and headed for the car.

He'd been borrowing it more lately, which was fine, provided he was willing to come get her after work. She walked to her shifts at the pub, and Oyster Island was safe enough that even at night she'd probably have more likelihood of running into a wild animal than another person, but she'd spent too much of her life in urban places to feel comfortable wandering around in the dark.

"My shift ends at eleven," she called out as he chucked his gear in the trunk of the small SUV.

"I know. I'm on the hook for taxi service," he grumbled, as if Clara hadn't spent the majority of her weekday afternoons ferrying him to soccer and lacrosse and swimming lessons.

He settled in the driver's seat and gave her one last wave.

She forced away the memory of last time she saw his father toss her a kiss and a casual wave on his way to work. He'd assumed the munitions sweep with his Coast Guard dive team would be routine.

Dwelling on it only hurt, both her and her son. Daniel would be fine. In six short hours, he'd have logged a precious experience, a stepping stone toward his goal, and would be full of stories of the amazing new things he saw.

She returned her son's wave and tossed back the rest of her quickly cooling coffee. She was about to go back into the kitchen for a refill when the creak of someone shifting in a chair split the silence.

"If you need a ride home on Fridays, you could catch one with me." Lawson spoke in his usual measured syllables, but congestion muffled the offer. "It's my weekly tasting room shift."

Then another sniffle.

"Maybe not today," she said, knowing she didn't have to raise her voice to be heard through the privacy screen. "If you're sick, you should stay home."

His laugh was disbelieving, edgy.

"Give me a few hours and I'll be fine," he said.

She grimaced into her mug. "You aren't one of those people who loads themselves full of decongestants and then goes about their day, are you? Haven't we all learned cold medicine doesn't make the germs go away? Matias won't want you snotting all over the brewing equipment."

"I said I'll be fine." He sniffed again, but this time it came out ragged. Vulnerable.

She wasn't used to that kind of emotion escaping his guarded exterior.

His curt, whispered profanity was unexpected, too.

Something tugged at her through the privacy screen.

Prior to moving to Oyster Island last month, she'd only known *of* Lawson. The storied, often disparaged ex-fiancé of Archer's sister Violet, long moved off-island to build his fame in the brewing world elsewhere.

But for whatever reason, he was back. And seemed to have mended ties with Violet. With Violet's fiancé, too, who happened to be Clara's boss, Matias.

Honestly, it made her head hurt a little when she tried to connect all the ties binding the residents of Oyster Island, so she just went on about her life, committed to taking on as many adventures this year as her son intended to check off his own list. On land, of course, for her.

And given Violet and Matias seemed okay with Lawson, she'd assumed renting the other side of his duplex wasn't taboo. He was giving her a heck of a deal on rent, something she couldn't turn down, given her leave of absence from teaching for the time being.

He was quiet, private… Hard to picture him as the bad guy of all Violet's post-breakup stories. He seemed content to keep his interactions with Clara to brief hellos when passing each other in the corridor linking the brewery to the pub, or the occasional conversation over splitting the yard work. Not standoffish, but not inviting friendship. A boundary she should respect.

She *would*. Neighborly concern had limits.

Another jagged gasp broke the morning silence. Footsteps rattled the floorboards. He burst onto the short lawn, barefoot and in shorts and a T-shirt, his back to Clara. Hands digging into his hair, he stalked toward the beach.

Well, now he was in public space. No longer behind the illusion of privacy. Checking on him was only right.

She wrapped her thin blanket around her shoulders. She was wearing a lined tank and cropped pajama pants, not exactly company clothes, but covered enough. Her flip-flops slapped her heels as she traversed the yard.

The beach was painted in the morning pastels of sky and water. A few birds bobbed on the surface, ducking under for their breakfast.

And a rigid-shouldered man, toes scuffing a small patch of sand breaking up the predominantly rocky shore, stared out at the pale horizon.

"Lawson? Do you need something?"

His stiff posture was all the answer she needed. *I need to be alone.*

She shouldn't have followed.

But when he turned, his eyes red around the edges behind his thick-framed glasses, his hair a skewed mess from either sleep or his hands, he didn't send her away. He stumbled back a step, landing on his ass on a log. He stared up at her, lips stiff.

"Sorry, I shouldn't have intruded." She turned to leave.

"Wait," he said, then patted the log next to him.

Hugging the blanket tighter, she wobbled over the rocks and sat, careful to leave a foot of space between them. She'd already intruded enough, and it was barely six in the morning.

Minutes ticked by, with only the gentle, crinkling rattle of waves over pebbles to fill the silence.

Something had shaken his world this morning. He was trying to hold it in.

She knew the routine well.

She also knew what it was like to lose her hold on an overwhelming feeling. To have it ooze out of her pores and spill from her chest, leaving her desperate to gather it up, only to have it run through the finger-cracks in her cupped hands. And in those moments, she'd needed someone else to gather *her* up, until she was able to hold herself together unaided.

So, she waited.

He leaned forward, bracing his elbows on his knees. His shoulders shook once, twice. His T-shirt stretched tight enough for her to see his rib cage fighting his lungs.

Damn it, she didn't have it in her not to do something. But she couldn't touch him, couldn't put a comforting hand over the taut muscle and hard blade. Not unless invited, and nothing about him welcomed closeness.

Whatever was coursing through him right now was making him vibrate.

"Do you need part of my blanket?" she offered.

He shook his head.

"Want to talk about it?" she asked.

"Have you ever..." His voice cracked and he cleared his throat. "Have you ever had something happen, and it feels like as long as you don't put words to it, don't say it out loud, there might be a chance it didn't happen at all?"

She barked out a dry laugh, unable to stop the sound.

He peered at her, one of his tawny eyebrows lifting. Either in curiosity, or maybe her laugh had seemed too dismissive.

"I... Yeah. I've had that happen. Or waking up and thinking something is a bad dream, and then climbing out of bed and having my world crash down on me again."

He nodded and stared at his feet, digging into the sand with one of his big toes. His sigh swirled around them both, drifting with the wind. "One of my college roommates called me an hour ago."

"Early," she said mildly.

"He's on the east coast. And he...he found out one of our other roommates... My best friend..."

He hung his head.

"You don't have to tell me," she said. News at this time of

the morning tended to be either death or illness. If he needed to keep it inside to mute the pain for a little while longer, she wouldn't force it. "I'm sure you have people you're closer to who would want to listen. Matias, or your sister…"

"Not sure if you've noticed, but Mati and I aren't exactly back to confidant status yet. And my sister…" He groaned. "To use a crappy metaphor, I disconnected all my sounding boards years ago, and I need to wait for everyone else to plug them back in. Just because I've been trying—" He held the heels of his hands to his eyes and swore again. "They don't owe me their time."

Surely the people in his life would want to support him if they saw him like this. Then again, she didn't know him well enough to be sure.

"You can have mine," she said.

"What?"

"My time."

"Oh." A breath left him in a gush. "That's…nice, Clara."

"Bare minimum for someone in a crisis, Lawson. Seriously."

He coughed and wiped at his eyes with the back of a hand.

His shoulders shook for long, silent minutes. Tears dripped onto the sand. Her kingdom for a Kleenex, but at thirty-eight, she hadn't reached the stuff-a-tissue-in-her-cleavage stage of cronedom yet. Instead, she lifted a corner of her drooping blanket.

He took it and wiped his eyes. "Car accident. His w-wife, too. Almost…unimaginable." A sob twisted the word. "I can't believe he's gone."

Ah. *Gone.* Awful to think she'd been crossing her fingers for illness, but at least it would have left room for hope.

"It's never the same from one person to another, so please don't take this as an 'I know how you're feeling,' but…" She paused. "I've had that exact thought before. Many times."

He jerked and launched himself to his feet. "You…you…Goddamn it. I forgot about your… I'm sorry."

She cocked her head, not entirely sure what he was apologizing for. "For forgetting I'm a widow? Um, you've had a fair amount on your mind this morning."

Raking his hands through his already messy hair, he said, "I shouldn't be unloading on you. Not when you've lost someone far more—"

"Or maybe I'm the exact person." Sensing he'd hit his limit for company, she rose from the log and readjusted the blanket. "If you want to talk, or not to talk, you know where I live."

"I'll be okay," he said, voice gritty.

"You will. But it's also okay that you aren't right now. Text if you need anything. Or call." She smirked at him. "Or tap out SOS in Morse code on the wall between our bedrooms."

He chuckled. It sounded like it hurt, but he also looked a little lighter for having done it.

One small thing she could do.

And she needed to do more. If Lawson Thorne didn't feel he could open up to the other people in his life, she was going to make sure he could open up to her.

Something was missing.

Given the phone call Lawson Thorne had gotten this morning, it was the fricking understatement of the year, but puzzling over Hauʻoli's projected beer releases was easier than imagining a life suddenly absent of Quentin, his college roommate and one of his best friends, and Quentin's wife, Kiera.

Lawson stared at the desk blotter–size calendar spread out on one of the long, rough-hewn tables in the tasting space. Sketches of labels and a dog-eared notebook of recipes surrounded the large, laminated rectangle. Usually nothing got Lawson more excited than splashy, colorful brewery branding, and the sketches of different Oyster Island scenes Matias had chosen for his labels were some of the best designs Lawson had come across in years. But with how crowded the market was these days, he wasn't sure beautiful art was going to be enough for Hau'oli to stick out.

He rubbed his temples and wandered to the other side. A different angle might shake something loose.

Opposite him, Matias crossed his thick arms, and narrowed his eyes. "It's good. A good starting lineup."

"Will 'good' be enough?" Lawson asked.

He wanted nothing but happiness and success for Matias and Violet, both at the brewery and with their engagement and impending parenthood. They were already years behind schedule because of the decision he'd made years ago to abandon his life on Oyster Island. He was itchy to clean up the fallout, as fast as he could.

Problem was, after the news about the car accident, Lawson's brain was less than functional. His friend had kids. Twin girls, not even four years old yet.

One of the bright spots of Lawson having worked for a major brewing conglomerate in Vancouver, Washington, was the fact his college roommate had lived there, too, and Lawson had gotten to be an honorary uncle to those precious twins.

His heart tore a little more. Somewhere, in one of the boxes he still hadn't bothered to unpack, was a series of four Christmas cards. Different designs, the same two shining faces with their tiny progeny at two months, one year, two years, three. What would next Christmas look like for his nieces?

Hell, what would next *week* look like?

The inside corners of his eyes stung, and he pinched the bridge of his nose. Hopefully, Matias wouldn't notice his tears. Lawson had explained what had happened when he'd arrived this morning, and Matias had offered to give him time off.

Lawson didn't want to accept the offer. His personal life could stay firmly outside of the warehouse doors.

The man who would have been his business partner was busy staring at the loose collection of plans on the table. The plans should have been *theirs*, but any joint ownership had ended when Lawson walked out on both Violet and his agreement with Matias.

Matias let out a low, disgruntled noise. "You're right. It isn't perfect."

"Almost, but not quite."

Dark eyes peered at him, narrowing. "You sure you don't need to take the day, man?"

Lawson laughed. The sound was rusty against his raw throat. "We can't afford for me not to be here. We're in the middle of a seasonal rollout."

He needed to work more, to figure out the missing element. Matias was resting part of Hauʻoli's success on Lawson, a level of forgiveness and trust he wasn't sure he deserved. Plus, what would he do at home? Mope? Sit on the beach more?

Reduce myself to another puddle of emotions in front of my tenant?

Clara had known what to say in a crisis. Had prevented him from falling apart worse, really. Without her kind words and calm presence, he might not have made it off that log and into work today.

He'd been spending most of June trying not to notice her, let alone connecting with her. But this morning, the only place in the world he'd wanted to be was next to Clara Martinez.

"Seriously, Law. Some things come before work," Matias said.

"I need to stay busy," he said honestly. Maybe if he gave his hands something to do, they'd stop shaking.

Matias nodded and went back to glaring at the lineup. "We'll figure it out. If something special, attention-getting comes to mind, I'm all ears."

"I know," Lawson said. Problem was, there was no shortage of craft brewers trying their hand at wild and wacky experiments. Name even a marginally palatable flavor, and you'd find a brewery that'd tried to market it the past few years.

Lawson hated to say they needed to trade on the name he'd built working for Mill Plain Brewers, but he was thinking they were going to need to get attention based on the quality of their product, not by chasing a fad. Having his name involved would help, no matter how much Hau'oli was Matias's baby, not Lawson's. However, he felt like a jerk pointing out how his name carried some clout since he'd put Mill Plain's craft branch on the map.

"In the meantime, pilsner," Matias grumbled.

Lawson nodded. It'd been selling well, so they were brewing another batch.

His phone had buzzed in his pocket a few times while they were working, but he hadn't recognized the number, so he had let it go to voicemail.

After an hour, it buzzed again, and this time, a text followed, from a different, but still unfamiliar, number.

Mr. Thorne, this is Quentin and Kiera Singer's lawyer, Gurpreet Sarai. Please call me as soon as possible, on my office line.

The following number was the same one from which he'd received the two calls.

His heart tripped. They wouldn't be dealing with bequests to friends yet, would they? Was everything okay with the twins? They'd be with their grandparents, Kiera's parents, no doubt.

"My friends' lawyer texted. I need to follow up," Lawson said, making an apologetic face and heading past the ropes dividing the brewing space from the tasting area. Like usual, the big warehouse doors were raised, open to the wooden boardwalk and the harbor beyond. He leaned against one side of the broad opening.

It took a minute of talking to a receptionist and waiting on hold before he was talking to Ms. Sarai, who was giving him a rundown of Washington estate law. She spoke in a caring manner, and it was plain she was excellent at her job, but the minute she got into the reason for her call, Lawson's brain started tripping over her words.

"Maternal grandparents were primary guardians…also in the accident…"

"I'm sorry, *what*?"

He managed to get the words out before his throat was closing over. Nausea roiled in his belly. A long-ago conversation was coming back to him, when he'd still been engaged to Violet and they'd thought they were going to be parents themselves. He'd agreed to something that should never have been necessary to enact, and…

"You were named as the second guardian in the will."

"I remember," he whispered.

There were details. So many damned details, and none of them were sinking in beyond those two little faces. What was an honorary uncle in the face of the loss of their parents *and* grandparents? Oh, God. Their entire support system was gone. Well, not *entire*—he wouldn't desert them, not on his life—but he hadn't seen them in months.

Immeasurable guilt corroded his insides. Would Harper and Pippa feel as close to him as they had before he left Vancouver? Even if they did, how could he provide even a fraction of what they'd lost?

"Are you still there, Mr. Thorne?"

He jolted back to the conversation. "Of course. I… I'm sorry. You lost me at the point you were talking about a judge needing to sign paperwork of some kind."

"Yes," she said gently, then repeated the details on the legal necessities, as well as where his nieces would be living until he could get down to Vancouver. Temporary approval was in place for them to stay with their day care provider.

"I assume you'll keep them in the area?" she said. "Ms. Thompson seemed to know you, and said you picked them up from day care from time to time. She's under the impression you have a house in the area?"

Of all the things the lawyer had mentioned, this threw him the most, a 360-degree loop on a verbal rollercoaster.

"But… I have a new job. On Oyster Island. Where—my sister is here." The bond with Isla, one he was working on to restore, was still tender and fragile. However, she would never take the lingering hurt from his desertion out on two sweet preschoolers. The girls would essentially become her nieces. He and Isla would need to act like a real family again.

"Hmm," the lawyer intoned.

"Is there anyone who will fight me on that?"

"No. Kiera was an only child, and I'm sure you're familiar with Quentin's family. They aren't eligible for guardianship—his emancipation from his parents is on record, and a guardian needs a clear criminal record, which his brother doesn't have. And you were named in the will. The parents' wishes are paramount."

"I will be in Vancouver tomorrow," he promised. "I'll drive down tonight, in fact."

"It may take days for everything to be processed, Mr. Thorne."

"I want to be there the minute I'm allowed to take them into my care."

They discussed the process for a few more minutes and then signed off. He turned and faced the warehouse. His stomach sank. How was he going to tell his partner—no, not his partner anymore, his employer—he was going to need an immediate leave? Every day between now and the end of the tourist season was critical for building Hau'oli. Beyond it, too. They had big plans to focus on liquor store distribution this winter.

They were already having to adjust for time off for Matias when his and Violet's baby arrived in November. The pair were so right for each other. He wished them the absolute best, but Christ, watching them glitter together was painful some days.

Not that he'd allowed himself "it should be me" moments. He'd lost the chance to even hope for a family with Violet the minute he got his results from the fertility clinic. When he'd panicked, walking out right before their wedding instead? It was a hell of a thing, facing his own cowardice. He'd regretted not sticking around and having the hard conversation every day since.

Lesson learned, both about not letting fear make his decisions for him, as well as realizing that some decisions couldn't be undone.

He could only make better ones going forward.

So as much as the conversation he'd had with Gurpreet Sarai was terrifying to the point of it being hard to believe it happened, he couldn't run away from it.

He walked back toward the brewhouse system Matias had earmarked for the pilsner, nearly colliding with one of the long tasting room benches. His legs weren't working quite right.

Matias's near-black eyebrows knitted into a line. "You look like you're going to faint, Thorne."

"Uh… Yeah." Lawson gripped the back of a chair and locked his knees, rolling around the words he'd assumed he'd lost the chance to say. "Seems like I'm going to be a parent."

Chapter Two

Clara locked her front door, ready to walk into town for her shift, when she heard a crash and a curse word from the driveway parallel to hers. She rushed over to the noise.

Lawson stood next to the red pickup he drove now and again. The white logo on the side proudly announced Nanny Goats Gruff Farm, the name of his sister's popular cheese business on the other side of the island. A trailer was attached to the back.

The remains of a plate and a batch of bakery-bought brownies dotted with chunks of white chocolate decorated the ground. Had to be the monthly special from Hideaway Bakery. Clara had never tried them—her celiac disease meant avoiding the baked goods at the popular establishment—but the chocolate scent was still delicious.

She'd eaten her fair share of wheat-based bakery treats before her diagnosis. And exploring how to keep baking with ingredients that didn't make her sick was one of her favorite hobbies.

"That's a shame," she said. "Those look like they were made with love. Need help?"

She had enough time to give him a hand if he needed one. She doubted his day had improved much after the awful news to which he'd woken up.

His eyes shuttered closed, mouth a haggard twist.

The man was shook.

"Not all the days will be as bad as this one," she said quietly.

He let out a disbelieving sound.

"Give me a sec," she said, and then darted into her house. She returned with one of the paper bags Daniel kept getting from the grocery store whenever she sent him there to fetch something, and he invariably forgot the reusable shopping bags. She brought it over to Lawson, who was still standing with his head hung and fists clenched at his sides. Kneeling, Clara started picking up shards of pottery and chunks of fresh brownie.

"Can't you not touch flour products?" he asked.

He remembered, then. She'd mentioned having the disease when she'd moved in, making sure the kitchen was properly cleaned to be considered gluten-free. "As long as I wash my hands before I eat or cook anything, I'll be fine. And I like staying busy."

"Right." He coughed. "Question—do you still have the third bedroom upstairs free of furniture?"

"Mostly." She stood, handing him the paper bag. "I have some boxes and a couple of armchairs in there."

He took it with a shaking hand. "Mind if I move a bed and dresser in there temporarily?"

She lifted a shoulder. With staying on the island for a year, a whole stretch of twelve months to sort out her own priorities and desires, she'd been thinking of turning the space into an office of sorts. "Sure. For now, I'm using it for storage. Are you redecorating?"

"Of a sort."

Cocking her head, she took a step back and waited for him to elaborate.

The fingers of his free hand dug into his thick hair. A frequent habit, each time making her curious how good those strands would feel through her own fingers.

"I'll… I'll have to do it when I get back," he said. "I need to catch the ferry."

"For—" She winced. "The funeral?"

"Maybe. But it's more… Their daughters. They have—had—twin girls. They'll turn four in the fall. They need to be with family. They don't have much left, now. Their parents, grandparents—" He was turning gray, as if he was going to be sick. "All they have is—" his voice cracked "—me."

Her stomach churned for whatever the little girls were going to face. "Are you helping them transition to state care?"

A feral anger lit his eyes. "No. Hell no."

"I'm sorry. When you said they didn't have family, I assumed…"

"Quent and Kiera never changed their will," he said. "Not after Violet and I split."

She winced. "Lots of people forget about updating."

He shook his head. "No, that's the thing. They did update it. Recently. And kept me as the secondary guardian. The girls are coming to stay with me."

Her jaw dropped.

He laughed, raw, harsh. "I know."

"It must be what they'd truly wanted, then," she said quietly. "But as far as I know, if it isn't what you want, you can decline."

Horror slackened the muscles in his face. "Are you kidding? I love those kids. I'd never let them go to someone they didn't know."

"Probably part of the reason their parents stuck with you, then."

Stumbling back a step, he slumped against the side of the truck. "I love them, but I have no idea how to be a parent." Another raw laugh. "A few years back, it was all I wanted."

"It isn't anymore?"

"I—" He released a long breath. "It's not in the cards for me. Nor is this a situation I can rightly feel excited about."

"Excited, no. Of course not."

"Back when I thought fatherhood was a possibility, I always assumed I'd be taking on a newborn. Feed, snuggle, nap and slowly learn their personality. Preschoolers, though... Dropping in as the fun uncle is nothing close to raising them every day."

She snorted. "You say that as if any of us feel like we've got parenting figured out."

"You seem to have done a good job. Daniel's a good kid."

"He is, and he's all the more resilient for the mistakes Eduardo and I made." Wringing her hands, she asked, "Can I do anything to help before you go?"

Yet another moment where she contemplated offering a hug, but his withdrawn posture suggested he needed space. She didn't want to offer one and risk him feeling awkward for declining.

"Any brilliant advice?" he mumbled.

Images of Daniel's face bolted through her mind, his anguish and anger after Eddy's death. And Danny had been close to thirteen, not four, and had had a surviving parent to support him. Clara wished she had specific answers for Lawson. "You're bringing them back here to live?"

"I have to." Guilt raked over his tone. "My job is here, now."

That explained the truck and trailer. "You borrowed this from your sister?"

He nodded. "She would have come with me, but can't leave the goats on such short notice. My mom got an emergency week off work though. She's flying from St. Louis. She'll meet me in Vancouver, help with the legal stuff."

At least he wouldn't be alone. "Leave me your key. I'll get the furniture moved."

"Thank you." Gratitude, but aching.

"As for advice, bring as many of their own things as you can back with you. Find a good counselor. Have weekly appointments—at least—set up for your return. Whatever social work supports you're given—take them. Take support of *any* kind. Including mine. Text me. Any time of day." It took every ounce of her effort not to wrap her arms around him. "And with the girls, Lawson... Start with love."

Lawson's side of the duplex was silent with him gone. Absurd to expect anything different, but the empty energy of the place struck her as she and Daniel schlepped furniture from Lawson's spare room over to their own.

Clara had never realized how often she sensed her landlord's presence in the duplex until he wasn't there. It was odd not to hear his sink running while she made coffee in the morning, or watching TV at night and catching the occasional sound from whatever show he was watching himself. His heavy steps on the staircase. The odd whine of his electric car when he reversed out of his carport in the morning. And worst of all, silence on their text thread, too.

She'd been silly to think he might reach out for emotional support, given they usually only talked about house-related things, like if he was good with her tending to the raspberries and sprucing up the planter boxes, or him giving her a heads-up when he planned to clean the gutters.

But he had accepted her advice before he'd left, so she'd held out hope he might lean on her again.

He'd been gone seven days. Each one, she'd waited for her phone to buzz, and then, disappointed it hadn't, went to bed wondering what wall he was lying on the other side of. Was he staying in his own house in Vancouver, still? Or had the judge's order gone through, allowing him access to his friends' home to stay with the girls while he packed up their things?

Hopefully, he'd be home soon, and with him, the little reminders of him on the other side of the wall they shared. She wouldn't let herself get carried away, though. She and her son had been at their task for over an hour, and during that time, she'd managed to control herself and hadn't snooped for the confirmation her headboard mirrored Lawson's.

His privacy mattered to her.

She wished the verdant Hideaway Wharf grapevine would extend him the same courtesy. The number of people who'd come through The Cannery to get the scoop on his quick departure nearly equaled the population of the small island. The nosiness was certainly nothing like what she was used to from her Portland neighbors.

Now, having finished the furniture favor, she stared at the empty room Lawson had earmarked for his nieces. The small gesture of clearing out the space wasn't enough. What preschool-age girl wanted pale gray walls?

"This color is blah," she said to her son.

Daniel grimaced as he hauled one last box labeled CHRIST-MAS DECORATIONS from the closet. "Yeah, it's like… sweatpants gray. Should we order some of those wall stickers or something? Like the flowery ones in the living room back home?"

She studied the blank walls and frowned. "Maybe."

"We could offer to paint," he said.

His thoughtfulness pulled the corners of her mouth up. *My sweet kid.* He had his dad's sense of generosity. "You want to spend your weekend covered in pastel flecks?"

His eyes darkened further. "They lost their mom and dad. And they're so little. I doubt paint can help, but…"

"It can't hurt." And it was something concrete, instead of aimless brainstorming.

She pulled out her phone and found Lawson's number. If he wasn't going to reach out to her, she'd have to be the one to text first. When it came down to it, though, she had no idea what to say. *How's your grief? How's theirs? What are their names?*

He'd left so fast, she hadn't even gotten that detail from him. Better not to overthink it and stick to the basics.

Hey. Thinking of you. What color is the girls' room at home?

He replied with a picture so garishly bubblegum pink, it hurt her eyes.

She showed her son. "Sure you want freckles this bright?"

"I look good in any color," he said with a smirk.

Rolling her eyes at Daniel's healthy ego, she replied to Lawson with a shot of the empty room.

Three dots popped up, then his answer. A bit of a letdown from what they have.

Then: I'll have to throw some paint on the walls once I'm home.

Excellent, he was almost on the same page as her.

Want me to see if I can liven it up?

You don't have to.

I won't go overboard, she promised.

Visions of unicorns danced in her head.

"What did he say?" Daniel asked.

"He agrees the paint is a little womp womp," she replied. "But it's not a problem we're going to fix tonight. We might as well get going. You have a party to get to."

He grimaced, as if struck by sudden indigestion.

"Come on, honey. You need to agonize over your clothes for at least a half hour before you'll be ready to go," she said, leading the way to the main floor.

"It's just a bonfire," Daniel grumbled, following her out the door to the back porch.

His boss at the dive shop, who was around Clara's age, had a much younger sister, Charlotte, who was only a year older than Daniel. Charlotte had invited him to join her and a group of her friends for a beach party this evening.

Clara had thought her son was looking forward to it, but maybe she'd read him wrong.

He'd always been the kind of kid who needed a good

amount of time to process his feelings, so she knew if she pried, she'd get a nonanswer.

Later that afternoon, though, as he pulled the car into The Cannery's rectangular parking lot to drop her off for her shift, his face was still screwed into a nervous frown.

Hmm.

"Will the party go late tonight?" she asked.

"Maybe, but I won't stay. I'll come get you at eleven."

"Want me to make other arrangements to get home? I don't want you to have to leave right when things are getting good. I'm glad you're making friends," she said.

"I'm going to have to do it all over again when I get to college."

Oh, there it was.

Why did he have to be dreading something she'd loved so much?

"You never know, Daniel. Even if the friends you make here are just summer friends, they might be excellent people."

"Charlotte seems okay," he admitted, the glint back in his eye.

"Got a condom on you?" she asked bluntly.

"Mom!"

Excellent. Hopefully his "you are the most cringe" reaction would mean he was extra careful when the time came.

Clara hadn't been much older than Daniel was now when she and Eduardo had conceived their son. She wouldn't trade Daniel for the world, especially given how much he reminded her of Eddy, but finishing school before becoming a mom would have been easier.

"There's a box in the glove compartment," she said.

"Are they *yours*?"

"No. It's unopened." She tried to keep the regret out of her voice when she gave him the assurance. In her five years since Eddy, she'd dated a couple of guys, very casually and never for more than a couple of months. She'd appreciated the physical relationship with both of them but hadn't been ready to connect emotionally yet. Nor had she been interested in introducing either of them to Daniel. And in the last year or so, she hadn't even managed to go on a date in Portland. She hated using apps, and her last set-up had been the friend of a colleague. Kind enough, considerate, too, but hadn't blown her socks off. And something about her Year of Yes begged for some spicy decision-making. Nothing she needed to fill her son in on, though.

"When you're ready—when your partner is, too, of course—use as many as you need. *One at a time*," she cautioned. "Doubling up is a myth—"

"Mom!" He pointed at the door. "Out. Out!"

"Ordering me from my own car, young Jedi. Bold move." She winked at him and made her exit.

He drove off, leaving her on the asphalt in the brilliant July sun.

With a wave and a fervent thought for his safety, she watched him go and breathed deeply. She'd been filling her lungs with the sea air since the minute she had disembarked from the ferry on the Memorial Day weekend. She loved the smell in the parking lot of the pub. Clean ocean breeze and the bite of seaweed, the warmth of needles off a nearby thicket of evergreens.

Except the minute she turned on a heel, she was mentally back in the empty gray room in Lawson's house. In the very adult kitchen and living room, with all the unshielded electrical sockets. In the equally gray-walled bathroom, and the tub with no bottle of bubble bath or stack of plastic cups to play with.

Gah. She was pitching toward obsession. The need to help him was growing by the minute. Her happy-hour-to-closing shift wasn't going to be enough to keep her mind occupied today.

After a week of interrupted sleeps, she was somehow managing to be full of yawns at the same time she was buzzing.

She checked her phone and saw she'd missed a text from Lawson.

Don't feel obligated.

She laughed. Should have expected that. I insist.

Whatever you want to do is fine.

She could almost hear his sigh. A smile crept onto her face. Aye, aye. Do I have a deadline?

I'll let you know as soon as I have the guardianship's legalities in place enough to bring them home. Early next week?

She felt for him. No doubt he was having to deal with a mile-long paper trail. Need to talk about it?

No.

Humph. Liar. Directly asking wasn't getting her anywhere, though.

In other news, now that I've seen your fancy-schmancy espresso machine, you are totally on the hook for making my morning coffee.

Oh god, oh god... Had her fingers really needed to go there? It had sounded teasing when she first typed it, but after she pressed Send, it looked so...forward. She and Lawson were not close enough for her to be inviting herself over. And definitely not enough to imply they'd spend mornings together.

Thoughts spiraling into chaos, she typed the next thing that came to mind: What do you call a dog magician?

Oh, good God.

It was official. She'd gone from a thinly veiled come-on to absurd in about three seconds.

He replied with a question mark.

A labracadabrador. Try it on the girls. Trust me.

Oof, she'd at least managed to give a plausible reason for the ridiculous joke.

An answer popped up right away. I'll give it a go

And then: Thanks

And: This is hard

She didn't even have time to reply before more bubbles appeared.

I keep coming back to you saying not all days will be this hard

It's the only thing that's kept me level since I got here

So yeah

Thx for knowing what to say and for the silly joke

Been a while since I laughed

Sorry, I better go

Her chest was knotted for him. His was probably ten times as tangled, like a piece of macramé wall art.

At least she'd managed to reach him, to provide him with a few seconds of brightness.

With any luck, by the time he got home, he'd have forgotten about the espresso machine comment. And if she kept busy enough with work and with getting the twins' room ready, she might be able to forget about it, too.

Getting Lawson's half of the duplex ready seemed like an all-hands-on-deck job, though. She was going to need more than Daniel's assistance.

Matias. He knew everyone on the island. He'd know what to do.

She sped through the door next to the loading bay and headed to his office, located off the hallway that separated the pub from the brewery. The whole complex used to be an old fish cannery, and she had to give it to Matias—he'd managed to take something industrial and make it welcoming.

The guy was community-minded, always. Once he learned about her celiac disease, he'd gone so far as to designate one of the fryers as gluten-free, and had created a GF prep space that they used for any menu items that could be labeled GF.

Given how far he'd gone to accommodate her needs, it wasn't out of the question that he'd do the same for Lawson's. Maybe he'd be interested in helping her improve Lawson's girls' room.

As she approached the open door, two laughs rang out, one alto, one much deeper.

"Everyone decent?" Clara called out.

"We're at work, Clara," Matias said dryly as she rounded the corner and leaned against the doorframe.

"As if that's stopped you before," she said.

Though the couple weathered a fair amount of teasing for all the heart eyes they directed at each other whenever Violet visited Matias at work, the pair weren't snuggled up to each other today. Matias sat at his desk with a selection of menus in front of him. Violet, Oyster Island's midwife, stretched out on the old couch, with one hand on her pregnant belly and one draped over the side of the couch. On the floor, their dozy black lab accepted Violet's lackluster ear rubs.

"I heard from Lawson," Clara said carefully. "And I think he needs our help."

She knew Violet and Matias's history with Lawson was complicated. Lawson himself had confirmed it, with his comment about no longer having Matias as a sounding board. But was there really that much of a divide, still? Matias had hired Lawson to work for Hau'oli, after all. Enough healing must have taken place for the couple to feel invested in Lawson's well-being.

Matias lifted a dark eyebrow. "I'm glad he's made contact. He's been radio silent on my end. No scuttlebutt, either, so I don't know if he's even been talking to his sister. Or if he has been, she's being quiet about it."

"I saw Isla at the bakery yesterday. She knows," Violet said. "But no one else said anything."

The lack of bakery gossip surprised Clara. It hadn't taken her more than a week on Oyster Island to realize Rachel and Winnie, the middle-aged couple who owned the delicious-smelling Hideaway Bakery located a half block from The Cannery, were a key part of the axle that turned the wheels of the small community.

"I take it his parents aren't close by?" she asked. "He said his mom was meeting him in Vancouver."

Violet shook her head. "His father passed away over a decade ago. His mom's remarried, lives in the Midwest."

Oh. Clara had to catch her breath. Like Daniel, Lawson had lost his dad too young.

"I wonder if his family is going to pitch in with his house," she said. "I was in his place, and it's really adult oriented. Not exactly welcoming to a pair of preschoolers. I don't even know what his plan is for beds. Maybe he's bringing theirs?"

"If he needed anything, he'd ask," Matias said.

Violet rose up to a sitting position. She was around five months pregnant, enough for the movement to look a little awkward.

Clara's heart panged. She wasn't anywhere near wanting a baby anymore, but she still had flashes of missing parts of pregnancy and the early days of parenthood.

"I don't think he would, Mati," Violet said quietly.

"He was the one who made overtures with us. Don't you think that means he'd be willing to reach out for his own sake?" Matias said.

Violet shook her head.

Clara did, too. "I'm not sure he'd be comfortable asking for something for himself."

She didn't want to go into more detail—doing so would feel like breaking a confidence—but it was important for people to understand he was putting up a good front.

"Okay, so what should we do?" Matias asked.

"We need to make his house more child friendly, for the sake of his—" Clara was about to say *kids*, but the description didn't feel quite right. "Nieces," she finished. "Twins will be tough. Grieving twins, even more so. He told me I could do what I wanted in their room, and I want to paint it. Other preparations, too. Finding him plastic dishes and bath mats and plug covers, maybe some outdoor toys. It could save him some steps. A meal train, even."

"Of course," Violet said.

Matias nodded in agreement.

"Is there a way to put out the call and see what people have to contribute? Rachel and Winnie, maybe?"

Clara nodded. Of anyone on the island, the owners of the Hideaway Bakery, one of whom was Daniel's boss's mom, had their fingers on the pulse of the island. They could probably start up a phone tree in their sleep.

"It's the perfect job for them. They can use their powers for good," Violet said. "They've collected meals for people in a bind before."

"Excellent. I'll head over there and talk to them on my break."

"I'll come with you," she said, trading a glance with her fiancé. "Lawson needs to not be alone through this. We might not be close anymore, but I don't like the thought of him struggling."

Clara nodded, happy for the teamwork. She didn't like the thought of him struggling, either.

But unlike Violet, she didn't mind the possibility of being close with him. Not at all.

Chapter Three

Guardian screwup number one: trying to fit a five-hour drive and a ferry ride into one travel day. By the time Lawson steered his sister's truck off the ferry, he had two little storm clouds strapped into their booster seats behind him in the crew cab.

Rookie mistakes are to be expected.

He was more than a rookie.

Even so, he should have listened to his mom's gentle suggestion to break the trip up somehow. He bet Clara would have given him the same advice. She would have been able to better estimate a child's tolerance for car rides, had he summoned the courage to ask her.

He needed one of her silly jokes, stat. She'd been texting him a few daily.

"I want Goldfish!" Pippa. She hadn't been willing to eat anything else, and he was trying to be patient.

"I don't wanna be in my car seat!" Harper, who'd been on the verge of motion sickness all day.

"Meow."

And then a hiss and a wail.

"Unca Sonny, Felina was mean to me!"

His temples throbbed. He glanced in the rearview mirror, making sure the cat hadn't actually scratched Harper.

"We're so close to home, sweethearts," he said soothingly.

"Look, there's the ice-cream shop, and the bakery where they make cakes, and—"

"We get cake and ice cream?" Harper said brightly.

"Well, not today, they're already closed, but—"

Another wail.

Way to go, Thorne.

"I might have something at home, but first we need dinner," he said, turning off Harbor Street in the direction of his place.

"Chicka nuggies!"

"More fishy crackers!"

"I was thinking spaghetti." He was pretty sure he had some sauce in the freezer. It would heat up quickly, at least.

"I hate geggy doodles."

Right. Damn it. "Okay, girls. What do you call a sleeping dinosaur?"

"A dino-snore. You told us," Pippa complained.

Get a new joke, in other words.

They bickered with each other until he pulled the truck in the driveway next to the plastic playhouse.

He braked too hard. The playhouse? And was that a swing set on the other side of the lawn? Confusion stirred.

The girls needed help out of the truck. He'd promised himself he'd go at their pace, so when they both stopped to stare at the yard and the house, he waited with them, a small, clammy hand in each of his. Or maybe his hands were the damp ones.

"See, girls? Just like the pictures," he said.

"You got swings," Harper said

"I did." *Somehow.*

"And a pink house," Pippa added, her little face screwed up. "Do the fairies live there?"

"Would you like there to be fairies in the yard, sweetheart?" he asked.

She nodded solemnly. "Fairies are magic. They could save Mommy and Daddy."

Harper peered up at him, too. "Can they?"

Oh God. A bomb went off in his chest. He was pulp inside. How was he going to support them through this? Legs shaking, he sat on the edge of the lawn and held his arms out. A second later, crooked pigtails and sniffles filled his lap. The girls smelled like Goldfish crackers and agitated cat, and he mentally added *bath* to the to-do list before bed.

He couldn't answer Harper's question. Repeating *they can't come back, honey* every time one of them asked only went so far. "Maybe we can find some chicken nuggets, yeah? And then we'll set up foam mattresses on the floor. It'll be like we're camping in your new room. And in the morning, we'll unload your beds, and you can decide where all your stuffies go."

He heard Clara's door creak and a few seconds later, Matias, Daniel and his interfering tenant were making their way across the stretch of grass.

"I hear I have new neighbors, and I'm betting they like cookies," Clara said, voice cheerful.

"That's a nice offer," he said, "but I'm thinking we'll stick close to our half of the duplex tonight."

"Of course. I already put them in your breakfast nook. FYI, I baked them in your kitchen to add a little homey aroma." She gave him a meaningful look. "It's the recipe I eat myself, and Daniel swears he can't tell the difference. I have it perfected."

The girls scrambled off his lap and stood, holding hands. They lifted their chins and studied their audience.

"I want cookies, not dinner," Pippa announced.

"Well, you have a lot of choices," Clara said gently before looking at him. "Your fridge is full, Lawson."

He shot her a questioning look as he rose to his feet. "Why?"

"Because people care," she murmured before kneeling. "Hi. I'm Clara. I'm your neighbor. And that guy right there—" she pointed at her son "—is Daniel. He's excellent at doing underdogs on swing sets. And that man—" it was Matias's turn to be under the microscope "—works with your Uncle Lawson and owns his very own restaurant. He makes the best cheesy noodles in the whole wide world."

"I like *cheesy* doodles," Harper whispered around the thumb in her mouth.

"Terrific. There are some in your oven, waiting for you to eat them with your uncle. And while the three of you have dinner and a cookie—" Clara wiggled her blond eyebrows "—Daniel, Matias and I are going to move your beds inside. I'm betting you'd like to sleep in them tonight."

Lawson swayed on his feet, trying to keep up. His fridge was full? Dinner was made? And his neighbors and Mati were planning to move furniture?

Matias clapped a steadying hand on his shoulder. "Deep breath, Law."

"Right. *Right.* I just wasn't expecting…" *Anything.*

"You forgot what things are like here," Matias said.

He had. But he also bet Clara had spearheaded everything, and she could still count the number of weeks she'd been living on the island on one hand.

He gazed at her, bowled over by her generosity.

She smiled back.

All that wattage made his knees even weaker.

He cleared his throat to introduce the girls. "This is Harper, and this is Piper, but she likes *Pippa* better," Lawson said.

"I have a bunny," Pippa said. "Harper has a dog. They have beds, too."

Stuffed, he mouthed.

"I can't wait to meet them," Clara said. "Harper, do you like real dogs? I have a small one. I left him inside in case one of you didn't like dog kisses. And Matias has a big one. You can meet them soon if you like."

Tugging on the ends of her pigtails, Harper nodded.

Clara's grin was as big as her heart, the size of which he'd grossly underestimated. She was flipping perfect with the twins, and he could kiss her for it.

Kissing Clara...

What would it be like to taste those plush lips, dusky pink like the roses blooming along the sunny side of the house?

Shaking his head, he chalked up the brief curiosity to exhaustion. Since when did he daydream about kissing his tenant? Especially in the middle of bringing his nieces home. He needed to get his head on straight.

Blinking, he refocused on the conversation.

She and the twins were speculating about whether Harper's stuffed dog would like Français the Frenchie or Otter the black Labrador better.

Her big heart had Lawson's swelling, too, stretching, pulling at the aches and scratches of the last two weeks. He'd never thought of himself as a grinch, with his heart needing to grow at all, let alone two sizes. More like the prodigal son, coming back to the island to beg forgiveness of the many people he'd wronged, starting with the mountain of a dude who he now called his boss. Matias stood behind Clara with his hands in his pockets, expression gentle and welcoming.

It felt like family. Something he hadn't done enough to earn yet, himself. But he'd do everything in his power to make sure it existed for these children.

Clara was sitting on her half of the lawn on the ocean side of the duplex. The remains of a large cardboard box surrounded her, along with an unassembled paddle and foot pump and a stand-up paddleboard ready to be inflated. With always having Mondays off—her other day off rotated from week to week—she'd committed to trying a new island activity every week until she found something that stuck.

Me Monday.

Two weeks ago, it had been a pottery class put on by a local artist. Clara's attempt at a mug was displayed on the kitchen windowsill, too lopsided to ever hold coffee. Last week, Matias and Violet had taken her sailing, which had been fun, but not something she could do alone.

Today, she planned to master the waves to make sure she didn't embarrass herself at the local stand-up paddling club.

Her Year of Yes wasn't about big things. It was about breaking the mindset of her needs always having to come second.

She didn't regret having formed the habit. She'd chosen it when she decided to have Daniel young. Parenting at any age wasn't for the selfish—not good parenting, anyway. And all through her twenties, when her friends were going to music festivals in the desert or sleeping in until three or driving to Canada for midnight doughnuts, she'd been doing her best to make a life with Eddy and Daniel and scrambling to fit in her schooling and then her job. Really, she'd done herself no favors by picking a career that demanded selflessness. The school bell might ring at three, but God knew no teacher was done with work at that early hour.

But with her leave of absence and Daniel's exodus to college, independence fluttered on the horizon, an amazing proposition given how young she still was to have a graduated son.

Unease rippled like static along her skin.

From the anticipation of her SUP adventure, of course. Not from the prospect of being alone in the world. She *wouldn't* be alone. She had friends, and Daniel would only be a phone call away.

"And I have you, right, buddy?" she said.

Their dog, sacked out on the grass next to the board, opened one eyelid but didn't even lift his head.

"Thanks for the enthusiasm, Frank."

Continued disinterest.

She chuckled, and then assembled the foot pump. She was about to inflate the board when Français deigned to stand. He stayed right by her, but his stubby little tail wiggled, and he whined in the direction of the house.

She turned. A small face stared through the slats of Lawson's side of the porch.

"Hi, there," Clara said.

Little fingers waved in an open-close-open-close style.

Clara waved back.

God. How had Harper's and Pippa's first few days on Oyster Island gone? Clara had seen Lawson with his nieces in passing, but hadn't gotten the chance to ask after them. Each time she'd seen the trio, Lawson had been chasing after the girls and in a hurry.

Still, they'd been on Clara's mind. She had doubled a batch of gluten-free blueberry muffins yesterday trying out a new blend of GF flour the grocery store had just started to carry. She intended to take her neighbors a dozen this afternoon, provided she survived her paddle.

"What are you doing?" a curious voice called. The door was open behind the twin at the railing. Clara hadn't learned their faces well enough to tell them apart, so it could be Harper or Pippa. The child being alone had her mom alarm pealing.

"Can I say hi to the puppy?" came the small voice.

"Are you supposed to be outside alone, sweetie?" Clara asked, glancing at her dog. Français scooched closer to the house and the girl. "Sit, Français."

He did, but glared over his shoulder at her.

"Uncle Sonny is braiding Harper's hair," Pippa complained, not looking much happier than the dog. "I only got pigtails."

Sonny? She'd have to ask him about that.

"And does he know you're out here?" Clara asked, trying to get the girl back on track.

"He said I got braids yesterday and can have them tomorrow."

"Gotcha," Clara said, not wanting to comment on whatever hairstyling system was going on. Also, her questions were being skirted with wild abandon, which could only mean Pippa was supposed to be inside. "I don't think your uncle would want you outside alone."

"I'm with you," Pippa said. "And he said you're a safe grown-up."

"Okay." Clara smiled. "I still don't think he'd want you outside without knowing where you are."

"Pippa? Piiiiiii-ppaaaaa. *Piper?*" The name grew louder with each repetition, and then Lawson rushed out of the house. He wore a threadbare T-shirt and gym shorts. The panicked mask twisting his full mouth slid off, replaced by a second of relief. Then his brows drew together, and his jaw tightened.

For a brief moment, Clara wondered if he was going to lose his temper. She knew the feeling, how irritation so often masked fear when a child did something they weren't supposed to. She cocked an eyebrow at him, trying to wordlessly suggest he take a deep breath. Letting the feeling out never ended up being the outlet needed, not in her experience, anyway.

He inhaled, and anything resembling anger melted into an earnest seriousness. He knelt in front of the child, gently palming her head and then dropping his hand to her shoulder.

"Pippa, sweetheart, it's not okay to leave the house without me."

"My pigtails are done. And the puppy wants to say hi."

"All true things. But safety first, okay? Come back inside, and maybe we can say hi to François after I'm done with Harper's hair. *If* Clara isn't busy." He glanced at the assortment of equipment scattered on the lawn. "She looks busy."

"I could wait, if the girls want to help me blow up my paddleboard," Clara suggested.

The offer earned a grateful smile from Lawson. "Give us five minutes."

She almost suggested Pippa could stay outside with her, but she didn't want to contradict the instructions Lawson had already given.

She killed the time until the girls were ready by playing

fetch with Français, tossing the stuffed baguette her best friend in Portland had found for him.

A few minutes later, the girls barreled out, followed by their broad-shouldered guardian. The twins were cute in denim shorts and cotton tops with tiny flutter sleeves, Pippa's in a pretty turquoise and Harper's in a sunshiny yellow. But while the Frenchie's attention was focused on being smothered by childlike love, Clara couldn't tear her eyes off the rumpled brewer behind them.

Affection glinted in his eyes as he watched the tangle of limbs, both furred and not.

"Can't underestimate the therapeutic value of a dog," Clara said.

He nodded, pushing his glasses up his nose. The thick-rimmed tortoiseshell pair lit the spark of all Clara's English-professor fantasies.

She swallowed, mouth suddenly dry.

His rueful smile did nothing to lessen her reaction.

"Their cat's still hiding behind the couch, so she hasn't been providing much affection," he said.

"Anytime I'm home, they can borrow Français. He's a glutton for scritches." Not something she needed to point out. The dog sprawled on his back in the grass, tummy jiggling like a jellyfish washed up on the sand.

"I don't want to impose, Clara." His voice was rough, the strain of change pulling at his vocal cords. He waved a hand at the playground equipment. "All the things you collected, my overflowing fridge… Please don't feel obligated to do more."

She tilted her head. He really didn't expect his neighbors would help out? Clara had visited Archer many times since the accident. The underwater explosion had left Archer with a leg amputation, and both the adjustment to living with a disability and settling into retirement from the Coast Guard had been challenging for her friend. But every time she'd come to stay, she'd seen how the Hideaway Wharf community worked together when needed. The closeness had been one of the major factors convincing her to spend her gap year on Oyster Island. And after all her time being married to someone in the Coast Guard and teaching in large high schools, she understood she needed to take part in creating community if she wanted to be a part of one.

Add to that, something about this man touched her heart. Not only the situation he'd found himself in, but the way his tilted smile lit up his eyes when a bit of humor shone through his burdens. She was drawn to him, and as much as he seemed resistant to being lent a hand, she couldn't help but keep a figurative arm extended toward him to see if he'd reach back.

"These are small things," she assured him. She had time to bring a smile to two small faces who'd had their world turned upside down. She did, however, want to get out for her inaugural paddle eventually. With the dog demanding lavish quantities of belly rubs, the girls were occupied enough. She didn't want to interrupt, so started inflating the board herself.

Pippa and Harper stayed on the grass, snuggled up to an elated Français, who Clara staunchly believed had been a French aristocrat in another life. He had a hell of a penchant for lounging on chaise longues and eating the doggy equivalent of petits fours.

"Girls, you were going to give Clara a hand," Lawson reminded them.

"Dog cuddles always win over literal manual labor," Clara said, bracing her feet on the base to be able to raise and lower the handle as fast as possible.

"It's good for them to help," he said. "Or I could do it."

"No, no. I need to practice."

She tried a few tentative ups and downs. *Hmm.* Stiffer than she'd expected.

It looked like it physically pained Lawson not to take over. "Let me know if you want to switch off."

"Okay. It's only supposed to take six minutes, though." Surely, her underworked muscles could handle the task.

Checking out Lawson's rock-solid arms, she guessed he didn't share her aversion to exercise for the sake of exercise. Even covered by a soft, faded gray T-shirt, the lines and dips of his shoulders and biceps begged to be traced with a finger.

Maybe his strength came from turning valves at work. Or maybe he did some sort of weight training, in addition to all the times she'd noticed him going out for runs.

Whatever the reason, she was happy to have the glory of his arms to focus on instead of how her own triceps were burning like she had road rash.

Looking uncomfortable at standing around doing nothing, he started to unwrap the two parts of the paddle, and once he had them free of their plastic, screwed them together.

Not a tricky task, but still, something about his ease while assembling suggested he was the kind of guy who could put together an IKEA shelf without even looking at the directions.

Up down. Up down. Two minutes, max, and sweat already dotted her forehead.

"So, where does 'Uncle Sonny' come from?" she asked.

"Harper's always struggled with 'Lawson,'" he said. "It started closer to 'Una-Son' and evolved from there."

"Cute," she said. "Daniel used to muddle his r-sounds. 'Archer' was impossible. Came out more like 'Itchy.'"

He laughed.

She did, too. Wheezed, rather.

"Maybe I need an electric pump," she huffed, though she knew she wouldn't spend money on it when she had a perfectly functional, simpler option available.

Thanks to scrimping and Eduardo's healthy life insurance policy, as well as money Eddy's parents had put aside for Daniel's schooling, Clara had enough to be comfortable working seasonal jobs during her leave of absence. Still, she had to be choosy about treats and extras.

"I wish I had one to lend you," Lawson said, holding the paddle two-handed, like a hockey player waiting around to participate in a drill. "I'd suggest asking Sam if they have a spare down at the dive shop, but I think all their boards are foam core."

"That's okay."

She'd known Sam, the owner of the dive shop, for years now, given he was Archer's boss at Otter Marine Tours. And now with Daniel's part-time job there, along with all her son's diving, she was becoming friends with the expert diver on her own terms, rather than through their friend-of-a-friend connection. Even so, asking for a freebie from a small-business owner chafed.

"Maybe someone in the SUP club will have one I can borrow," she continued. "I have my first group paddle on Wednesday afternoon."

"Sounds like fun. Can anyone join?"

"Far as I know. You should come."

His face fell, his knuckles turning white on the paddle shaft. He glanced at his nieces. "Clara?"

"Yeah?"

"How the hell—" he cleared his throat "—*heck* do single parents manage any time to themselves?"

Yikes. She'd asked herself that question, oh, a million times since Eddy had died. The guardianship hadn't only turned the girls' worlds upside down. Lawson had gone from being a freewheeling bachelor to a man with two car seats in the back of his car in a matter of days.

"Well," she said, matching his quiet tone. "Early bedtime can mean a couple of hours to yourself. Or you rely on the generosity of family and friends. And a reliable babysitter is worth their weight in gold."

He winced. "I don't even know what I'm going to do about their care while I'm at work, let alone to do anything social without them."

He lifted the paddle over his head, bracing it on the back of his neck and shoulders and slinging his arms over the shaft.

Hold the phone.

What were *those* muscles called? The movement pulled his T-shirt against his abs, too, and *wow*. Did he really make beer for a living?

Focus, silly. On his problem, not his physique, however mouthwatering.

"I can't imagine day care spots are plentiful on the island," she sympathized.

"Two are opening up when school starts, which is a life-saver," he said. "But until then, we're wait-listed. I don't know what to do. I can't take them with me to work."

"I'd offer to help, but our schedules overlap too often," she said. "Nor would Daniel be a reliable option."

"Of course. I need someone who isn't working another job and can commit to all the days. With the upheaval Pippa and Harper have already dealt with, I don't want to bring in more than one babysitter for the first month or two. The counselor I spoke to recommended as consistent a schedule as I can manage." His mouth flattened and he raked a hand through his already-messy waves. "If I can help it. I might not have a choice. But I also have to get back to work sooner rather than later. Matias has been more than generous with my time off."

"He understands."

Sweat trickled down her neck and she doubled down on her hand-pump efforts.

His eyes glinted as he watched her. Appreciation?

Warmth trickled through her belly. His gaze was magnetic, and she couldn't look away.

"Mom?" Daniel called from somewhere behind her.

She jolted, her hand slipping on the pump. Her thighs were already tired from being crouched and the extra momentum was enough to throw her off-balance and sideways onto the grass.

Her face burned, an entirely different heat from the hint of appreciation she'd felt while noticing Lawson's strong frame.

"Damn, sorry," her son said, jogging down the porch steps.

"You okay?" Lawson put the paddle down and reached for her.

She nodded and slid her fingers into his grip. His hand was warm, solid, a little rough.

Yes, please.

Having his palm against hers was almost worth the embarrassment of losing her footing.

A little pull, and she was on her feet.

"I'm such a klutz," she said. "I'm not even *on* the board yet, and I'm falling."

He didn't let go. His thumb ran along hers, those gray eyes pulling at her own gaze for a long second. With his other hand, he enveloped the back of hers. A two-palm squeeze so gentle, it erased the burn from her cheeks.

When he let go, it took every last ounce of her will not to reach out and reconnect.

Daniel stopped a few feet away, rubbing the back of his neck and wincing. "My bad, Mom."

Frenchie, mouth full of stuffed baguette, abandoned the twins and darted over to Daniel. The hero worship from her dog to her son would never get old, though the girls' smiles turned to sulking, no doubt due to no longer being the main attraction.

"Oh, you get to play with me all the time," Daniel chided. He wrestled the toy from slobbery jaws and tossed it back toward Pippa and Harper. "Play chase with him, and he won't care about me."

Her son was a good kid. She knew this but was never disappointed to witness the small reminders of his kind soul.

"Are you going out paddling now, Mom?"

"If I can stop making a fool of myself inflating it, yeah."

"Do you need the car?" he asked.

"I can walk to the store later—where are you going?"

His cheeks reddened. "Charlotte invited me to the beach."

"Just the two of you?"

"Yeah." He looked like he was trying to be cool, but the twitch of his nose gave away his excitement.

"Keys are in my purse," she said. "Have fun. Text me if you want in on dinner or not."

"Thanks, Mom."

Lawson tilted his head. His eyes narrowed a little. "Sam's youngest sister, right? Is she your age?"

"No, she's a year older." Daniel's forehead knitted, as if he was wondering why their neighbor was taking an interest in his dating life.

"Can you ask her if she knows anyone who's looking for full-time nanny work this summer? Someone college-aged?" Lawson continued.

Understanding dawned on Daniel's face, and he glanced over at the twins, who were whispering to each other and walking toward the swing set. "Yeah, no problem. They're pretty cute. I bet someone is looking for work."

With a wave, her son rushed back to the house.

"I hope he's right," Lawson said quietly. "I'm ten days into parenting and I'm already being pulled between it and my job. I know Matias said to take the time I needed, but I know I'm letting him down. Something I should be well familiar with."

Clara mulled over how the hell to respond. Somewhere, she was missing some context. "I don't know every detail of what happened between you and Matias and Violet, but I don't think this is anything similar."

He glanced over at Pippa and Harper. "I guess not, but still…"

"He won't see it as letting him down. We had a staff meeting while you were gone, where he moved some shifts around between the pub and the tasting room, and nothing he said implied he was upset or angry."

"I appreciate the encouragement, but I can't help but feel that the promises I made Quentin and Kiera are going to mean I can't follow through on the promises I made to Matias and Hau'oli."

His eyes were getting a little watery.

"Of anyone, Mati believes family comes first," Clara said.

"Yeah, I know. The Kahales are a tight-knit crew. I mean, look how they've taken Violet in." He cleared his throat. "I'm glad she's part of their family now. She deserves all the love."

So do you.

Deep grooves framed the corners of his mouth.

She reached for his hand.

Maybe one day, she'd get his side of the story about what had happened when he had broken off his engagement to Violet.

She kept her curiosity to herself and gripped his hand instead.

He clutched her fingers and stared at the ground. "Vi would have known what to do with Pippa and Harper. She's a natural with kids."

"You don't need to be a natural to parent lovingly. Find ways to laugh with them. Care about what they care about. Set clear expectations. Expect they'll miss and twist and ignore those rules, and be gracious in creating consequences. You just need to love them and want the best for them."

"The 'best' doesn't exist anymore." His words were gritty, grief laden and bitter. "The 'best' was their parents. How can I replace them? I'll never be their actual dad."

Echoes of her own anguished questions after she had lost Eddy dwelled in his pain. She'd anguished over her inability to fill the role of two parents, the enormous gap left behind by a truly remarkable husband and father.

Was Lawson's situation too fresh for her to explain to him how filling that crevasse was impossible?

"I'm limited to my own experience," she said.

"I'll take anything," he said

"Sometimes, it's about not feeling alone." She studied him. "Feel free to say no, of course, but do you want a hug?"

He nodded. His gaze was fixed on the two pairs of feet swinging side by side. The girls' bellies pressed into the seats instead of their bums.

Clara was short enough there was no way she'd block his view of his nieces. She wrapped her arms around his ribs and pressed her cheek to his chest.

He clung to her, smelling of fresh air and laundry detergent. She wanted to wear that smell like a shawl. God, he was delicious.

Delicious and hurting.

"You can only be you, Lawson," she assured him. "Whether or not they see you as their uncle, or grow to view you as a father, you'll be their parent and their biggest advocate. You'll learn what they need."

Strangled doubt escaped his throat, rumbling against her ear.

"Thank you," he whispered, his hands wide and firm on her back.

With him finally in her arms, she did not want to let go.

"Unca Sonny! Come push me!" came a small but mighty voice.

"See, most of the time, they'll tell you what they need," Clara added.

"Be right there!" he called back, before letting Clara go and fixing her with an anxious look. "Pushing them on the swings isn't exactly the important stuff."

"Yeah, it is. I promise."

Skepticism tilted his lips. "I'll bow to your expertise."

"Pshhh," she said, sloughing off the implication she was

at all an expert. "My best advice? Always pack snacks and wet wipes."

He laughed.

And for today, that was good enough.

Chapter Four

Lawson woke up Tuesday morning with a crick in his neck. Sleeping on the floor would do that to a nearly forty-year-old spine. Yes, he had a thin foam mattress under him, so it wasn't like he was lying directly on the hardwood between the girls' beds, but still—his body wasn't made for this abuse anymore.

Had he'd been able to roll from side to side, it might have been more tolerable, but at some point in the night, both Pippa and Harper had ended up snuggled next to him, one under each of his arms. They were finally, *finally* conked out after a night of tears and unanswerable questions. He breathed in the silence, desperately hoping he wouldn't wake them.

His bladder was barking at him, though, so with as much care as he could manage, he shifted his arm out from under Harper, then Pippa, and thanked his lucky stars he could do a roll-up to standing to avoid jarring them further. He left them on the floor, covering them both with the quilt he'd pulled off his own bed, and making sure their stuffed animals were in place. Pippa was snuggled up to an old T-shirt of her mom's, too. The social worker had assured him it was a normal coping mechanism.

After a quick dash into the bathroom, he snuck downstairs and headed for the coffeemaker. A bolt of black zipped past him.

Felina, darting back under the couch by the front window, as had become her practice. At least she was eating and drinking, even if she insisted on doing it when no one was looking. He'd questioned whether it was smart to take the cat because of his mild allergies—Quentin and Kiera's neighbor had been happy to add one more to the three she'd already rescued—but he'd figured one more familiar creature would help the girls. Antihistamine was becoming his best friend, a new normal he could accept if it meant one fewer change for Pippa and Harper. He hadn't anticipated Felina would go into stealth mode, though.

Having five uninterrupted minutes to pack coffee grinds into the portafilter was suddenly a luxury. He was about to press the start button to earn some much-needed caffeine when a knock sounded on the door.

He'd slept in a T-shirt and cotton pants, so he was decent enough to answer.

Daniel Martinez stood on the stoop, a folded piece of paper in one hand and a foil-covered tray in the other. He held them both out.

"For you."

"Uh, thanks." He took the tray, and laid the paper on top of the foil.

Daniel jammed his hands in the pockets of his shorts. In his Otter Dive Shop polo shirt, he looked ready for a shift at his part-time job. "The food is from my mom. She made extra beef Stroganoff last night. She said to reheat it and put it on noodles. She didn't bother sending the noodles, because the rice ones are better fresh, and she assumed your kids would be more familiar with wheat noodles."

Your kids. It was the first time someone had referred to them as such, and it hit him in the gut like he'd been headbutted by one of his sister's goats.

"That's kind of her," he managed to reply, even though his brain was still recovering. "She should really stop cooking for us, though."

"It's her love language."

Clara did seem to have a lot of love to give. What would it be like to be the recipient of it more often? What would it be like if it wasn't platonic?

Not the sort of thing he should get distracted by, especially not in front of the woman's son.

"Is this a note with the cooking instructions, in case I forget?" Lawson asked.

"No, that's Charlotte's number. I told her you were asking about a nanny position, and she said you can call her if you still need someone."

"She's interested?"

"Yeah."

He let out a sigh. A lead, at least. "What a relief."

"For her, too. She's not a fan of working for her brother at the dive shop." The teen's face fell. "Even though we get shifts together sometimes."

Ah, young crushes. Lawson did not miss those days.

"That's probably more about working for her brother than it is not wanting to work with you," Lawson guessed. "And if she's a good fit as a nanny, she'll be spending a lot of time here. I'm sure you could figure out all sorts of reasons to run into her."

"She'd be watching your kids. I wouldn't want to distract her."

Like I was getting distracted by your mom just now? Join the club.

Still, he appreciated the teen's maturity. Maybe losing a parent so young forced Daniel to grow up faster than most, like Lawson and Isla had when their dad had passed away. Come to think of it, Daniel would have been around thirteen, not far off Lawson's age at the time of his own loss.

"As long as Pippa and Harper weren't being ignored, I'm sure you could join in some days." Lawson lifted the tray a few inches. "Thank you for this. And the number. I appreciate it."

After saying goodbye to Daniel, he took the food into the

house and decided to freeze the meal. Then he called Charlotte, who was available to meet later that afternoon.

"I've been promising the girls ice cream from the place on the water—would you be up for joining us?" he asked.

"Sure!" Charlotte said brightly. "The library is open this afternoon, too. Would they like to check it out?"

Hope blossomed in his chest. The fact the young woman knew the library schedule struck him as an excellent sign.

"Great idea," he said. "Why don't we start there, to avoid them handling the books with ice-cream fingers?"

She agreed, and they picked a time.

With that lined up, he felt a bit readier to face the rest of his to-do list. He spent the morning trying to get some yard work done. Pippa and Harper followed him, taking turns with the plastic lawn mower someone had donated to their pile of outdoor toys. Grilled cheese for lunch was, if not a hit, at least tolerated by the girls. Soon enough, it was time to leave. He decided they'd walk to the wharf.

He hadn't calculated for a preschooler's sense of time. Fifteen minutes later, he was stopped on the trail, checking his watch. He was almost to the point of needing to text Charlotte to let her know they were going to be late.

Pippa dragged her feet, lost in some fantasy space. She waved her arms erratically, a clutch of vivid yellow dandelions in each hand as if she were conducting a flower orchestra. She was muttering something incomprehensible.

Harper was sitting in the dirt.

"It's too far," she said. Her pigtails were askew, her face a thundercloud.

"Almost there, peanut," he assured her, holding out a hand. He pointed to the end of the trail, where pastel splashes of paint peeked through thick fir branches. "See the pink building? The library's right across the street. Do you think they'll have a new *Elephant and Piggie* book we could check out?"

Both girls were working on their alphabet, so they didn't

know any words yet, but they loved being read to. Harper loved the silly books with the outgoing pig and her more reserved pachyderm buddy. And Lawson loved reading to both girls, because it was guaranteed to get them smiling.

Unlike trail walking, apparently.

He tried to remember what Quent and Kiera had done whenever he'd joined them for short hikes back home, but nothing came to mind, other than distraction.

"Let's look for rock shapes while we walk. Do you think we could find one with a hole in it? Or one shaped like a heart?"

Harper's brow furrowed. "Or a toe."

"I…" Uh, a toe? Whatever it took, he guessed. "Sure, sweetheart. Let's look for rock toes."

She took his hand and trudged at his side, studying the side of the dirt trail in deep concentration. Pippa danced ahead of them, oblivious to the serious hunt underway.

"I don't see rocks, Unca Sonny," Harper said.

"You're right," he said. The trail had a few pebbles along the edge, but nothing of a remarkable shape. "If we can't find you a toe, we'll look on the beach when we get home."

Now there was a sentence he'd never before said in his life.

Thankfully, the hunt held Harper's attention enough. They emerged from the trail onto the lawn of the small park at the south end of Hideaway Wharf.

Harper frowned, looking around. "The park doesn't have swings. Why?"

"I'm not sure," he said. "But I know the school has them, and it's only a few blocks away. Do you want to go see them after the library and ice cream?"

She shook her head vigorously. "My feet are tired."

Oof, the walk home was going to be a real treat. Even if one of the few rideshares available on the island were available, none of them had two car seats on board.

"*I* want swings," Pippa said. "And monkey bars."

"Let's have fun reading for now," he hedged. "And meeting Charlotte."

To their right, the ocean lapped the rocky shore. To their left, a road branched off into the small residential neighborhood nearest the cluster of businesses adjacent to the ferry dock.

The sun-gilded buildings of the wharf were showing off in the bright summer light. Between the quaint structures, the sprawling cluster of docks hugging the boardwalk and the glistening waves, it was a postcard waiting to happen.

Probably not a meaningful view to four-year-old eyes, though, so he needed to liven things up.

"Can we make a rainbow from all the paint colors?" An easy task, given the vivid variety of paint slapped onto the row of heritage houses facing the water. They'd once been a row of homes, but were now more mixed use, with restaurants and shops on the ground floor and businesses and apartments on the second stories. The Six Sisters pulled in tourists from around the world and kept local cash registers humming during tourist season. He gestured at the island's lone fire truck, parked in front of the emergency services building down the road, a block inland from the park. "That's red. And pink is close to red. See any pink?"

Pippa pointed ahead with one of her dandelion bunches. "There!"

"Good eye," he said, nodding at the middle "sister" and its wrapped-in-cotton-candy hue.

"Orange!" Pippa gestured at a zodiac in the harbor, then at the nearest house, painted a pale daffodil color. "And yellow."

Lawson guided the girls past Hau'oli Brewing, which was part of the old cannery sandwiched between the park and the boardwalk. A brand-new sign hung over the patio area. Crap, he'd been in Vancouver when Matias had hung it.

"I found green," he said, gesturing to part of the logo on the sign. "And I work inside that building, girls."

Guilt crept in. Was Matias managing to get their newest batch of pilsner in cans alone? The front doors were closed, so it was impossible to tell.

"You don't work. You play with us," Harper said.

"I know. And we will, every day. But I will need to come here and do my job, too. We're meeting Charlotte to see if she can be your babysitter and play with you while I can't."

Pippa's lip stuck out.

Harper took her sister's hand. One of the clumps of dandelions fell on the wood planks of the boardwalk. They jutted out over the water and looked over the boats and docks below. "Like day care?"

"Sort of. Except you'll be at my—our—house."

He guided them down the alley, a one-car-wide stretch of asphalt between The Cannery Pub, also owned by Matias, and the first of the brightly painted houses.

Both small faces were screwed up in thought. Should he let them process, or go back to their rainbow game?

Probably process. They needed time to let their feelings settle.

When they reached the sidewalk, he pointed across the street. "We're going there. First, the library. And then ice cream is right next door."

"I'm hungry now," Harper announced.

He pulled a sandwich bag of Cheerios from his backpack. He was not used to having to haul around water bottles and food, crayons and coloring books and small stuffed animals. Thank God for Clara's suggestion to always bring snacks and wet wipes. "Help yourself."

Her brows formed a disgruntled line as she took his offered hand to cross the street. She still had Pippa's hand in her grip on her right. "Mommy always has 'nola bars."

Present tense. Shit. The social worker had warned him how object and time permanence were tricky for grieving preschoolers. Thankfully, he had a counseling appointment set up for both girls on Thursday.

"Okay. We can get some granola bars from the store," he promised.

"Mommy *makes them*."

"Right. Right." Throat tightening, he swallowed. "We could look at recipe books at the library, and the three of us could try making them."

"I want *Mommy's* 'nola bars."

"I know, Harper. I'll see if I can get her recipe."

Kiera's best friend had a key to the house, and while the executor was dealing with the estate, nothing had been packed up yet. Maybe she knew where Kiera had kept her recipes.

He and the girls walked in a short chain of three, passing a consignment store and an empty storefront before reaching the cerulean front of the library.

"Look, blue!" he said. "Quick, someone find purple before we go inside."

Pippa pointed at a wind sock spinning near the front door of Otter Marine Tours. "That's a whole rainbow. And brown and black and white and pink and more blue and more yellow and more purple."

He chuckled at her insistence on naming every color. "Terrific point, Pip. Well done."

He held the door open for them.

The library was small, only staffed and open part-time. He hadn't been in for years, but it looked updated from what he could remember. The shelves and collection were well cared for. A new-release display and periodical shelves filled the front of the long room. At the back, a few seniors sat in a conversation area between the fiction stacks. Off to the side, a vibrant, undersea-theme rug centered a nook. Low shelves lined the walls, full of colorful spines.

In the center of the children's area, a young woman sat cross-legged on top of a smiling orca on the rug. A stack of books sat in front of her. With red hair and pale, freckled skin, she looked enough like both Franci and Sam Walker for him to be certain of her identity. She had on a black T-shirt printed with a line drawing of a man's stern face, plus a stylized *Mr. Darcy Would Never.* At home in the pages of a novel, then.

"You must be Charlotte," he said.

She stood and shook his hand, vigorously enough to make the knot of long hair on top of her head bob. "Nice to meet you."

He barely got out a *likewise* before she was sitting again.

She patted a hand on the rug on either side of her and smiled at the twins. "You must be Harper and Pippa. Nice to meet you, too. I've got a purple sea star for one of you to sit on, and a red octopus for the other."

Both girls sat on the octopus.

"That works, too," Charlotte said. "Want to see the book I found? It's about dogs. Your friend Clara told me you like them."

He blinked in surprise. Had Clara talked to Charlotte at some point yesterday?

His confusion must have been obvious, because she said, "I ran into her at the circulation desk a few minutes ago. I think she's still here." She cocked her head. "Want me to hang with Pippa and Harper for a bit while you go say hi? Or would you rather stick with us while we read?"

"I'm thinking you have reading under control," he said. "That okay, girls?"

They nodded.

Before one of them could change her mind, he scooted out of the nook and peered over the shelves, looking for moonlight-gold hair. He caught a flash over by the new fiction releases, long, pale locks braided up and around her head, almost like a crown. The style, along with the wide neckline of her sweatshirt, exposed the creamy skin of her nape and the fascinating space where collarbone met shoulder. Something about that curve begged for lazy kisses.

Shaking the vision from his mind, he strolled in her direction, trying to appear like he hadn't been imagining the taste of her skin on his tongue.

She saw him coming from a section away. Her face brightened and she hugged the pair of illustrated hardcovers she'd chosen to her chest. "Hi there, you."

"Hey." Why did hearing her voice make his day feel more complete?

It had been a *long* time since he'd experienced this kind of jolt of attraction. Like, since-he-was-with-Violet long.

But it wasn't the time to think about his own heart. He had two little hearts he needed to protect, regardless of how underprepared he felt. More like *because* of how underprepared he felt. Acting on his attraction to Clara would steal focus from his priorities.

He couldn't pursue anything to do with the tug he felt any time he was in her presence. He could, however, focus on being her friend.

"Thank you for preloading Charlotte to help her connect with the girls," he said, leaning a shoulder against one of the sturdy looking wall shelves.

"She seems like a sweetheart. I hope she's a good fit." Her eyes held a measure of mischief. "At least, my son sure likes her."

"I noticed that this morning."

"He wears his heart on his sleeve."

So does his mother.

She seemed more willing to be open and vulnerable than most people he knew.

"Want to join us for ice cream?" he asked, his mouth seeming to function without permission from his brain.

Her mouth curved in disappointment. "My shift at the pub is starting soon. I came here to grab a book I had on hold for the mystery book club I joined, and then I got dragged into the new-release display. I am hard-pressed to resist a flourish of books with uncracked spines."

"SUP club *and* book club. You're running the gamut."

"A trifecta, actually. I'm joining a hiking group on Friday mornings." Her eyes danced. "It's my Year of Yes."

He lifted his brows, waiting for her to elaborate.

"It's my Oyster Island project. I'm going to say yes to things I've never tried before. Or at least in a long time."

"Normally a 'no' kind of woman?"

She shook her head. "Not at all, but... You know how you were asking how single parents ever managed to find time to themselves? It doesn't get better as your kids get into high school. Except now, Daniel's more independent, and I need to break the habit of sloughing off fun opportunities."

"Sounds like a good philosophy." He winced. "I guess I'll be practicing the opposite, now."

For so long, his life had been centered around his own needs. Now, he was going to need to push them to the side.

"Oh, no, make sure you're still doing things for you. Ignoring yourself is a recipe for parental burnout."

He shook his head. "It's not the right time for me to worry about my own fun. I'm already having to leave the twins with someone else while I work."

But as much as he'd accepted having to curtail all the things he used to do in his spare time, he still wished he could come up with a list of things to do with Clara, reasons for her to say "yes" to spending time with *him*.

Chapter Five

Daniel fussed with his hair in the hall mirror. "Do you think Lawson wants me to cut the lawn today?"

Clara laughed to herself. She loved seeing her son volunteering to help with chores, but also, his maneuvering to be outside to catch Charlotte's eye while not appearing to do so on purpose provided endless amusement.

Clara was so relieved Lawson had found a nanny with relative ease. After a couple more getting-to-know-you meetings last week, he'd hired Charlotte, and she'd started this Monday.

Almost immediately after, Daniel's interest in being in the yard had increased. The first hint had been their sparkling-clean car on Tuesday, Charlotte's second day of work. Wednesday, the stone pathway in the front yard had gleamed after a thorough power washing. On Thursday, the edges of the side hedge had emerged, sharp and crisp after a detailed trimming.

"I'm sure he appreciates your help, honey. Though there's no reason to rush out this morning. Lawson works afternoons on Fridays, so Charlotte won't be here yet."

Daniel narrowed his eyes. "You know his schedule?"

"I know everyone's schedule at the pub *and* the brewery," she said.

"I dunno, Mom. He held your hand for way longer than necessary last week. After you fell over like a dork."

"*Dork?*" She held a dramatic hand to her chest. "What happened to your deep guilt over startling me?"

"Time has passed, time has passed."

She sobered. Dating—even flirting—on Oyster Island wasn't like it had been in Portland. How was she supposed to hide potential relationships from Daniel? Their world was so much smaller here. Especially since they shared a *wall* with the man in question. "Were you okay with that? Me holding hands with him?"

He grew more serious, too. "It's okay. But also super weird? And like, sad AF in a way. Not all the time. Just waves of it. Like everything else that reminds me Dad is gone. But really, okay. Does that make sense?"

"That sounds exactly right to me," she murmured.

"Though back to 'weird'…" His lips shifted to a smirk. "Having a dude check my mom out like he does when you aren't looking? Talk about no chill."

Lawson checked her out? A thrill ran through her, not that she'd admit it to Daniel. "No chill," indeed.

"Oh, like it's any different when it's a girl staring at my son?" She shot him a look. "It's your turn in the hot seat, Daniel Eduardo. All your extra work outside—has it led to any actual success?"

"Success?"

"With Charlotte."

Misery streaked what had been a teasing expression. "I don't know."

She rubbed his shoulder and refilled his coffee mug. It took finesse to get info out of him sometimes, and today might not be the day for it. Clara was about to accept that he'd clammed up for the time being, but then he continued.

"We're like, friends for sure. She broke up with someone recently—your boss's little cousin, I think—so she seems kind of hung up on him still."

"People can grieve relationships for a long time," she said.

Charlotte wasn't the only one having a hard time getting over a breakup. It seemed like Lawson still had some unresolved issues from his past with Violet, even though the pair were usually congenial.

Daniel frowned. "Yeah, well, I'm leaving in the middle of September. That's, what, seven more weeks? If she's hung up on her ex, I might not get a chance."

"Man, feelings are the worst sometimes," she said.

He narrowed his dark brown eyes. "Aren't you supposed to be full of advice, Mom?"

She cupped his cheeks. "You, my handsome boy, will have no shortage of attention from a whole lot of people in your life," she said. "There's no rush. If Charlotte's into you, she'll let you know. If she's not ready, you wouldn't have a good time together anyway. But if *you* like *her*, be a friend. Listen. Figure out the things she likes and spend time doing those things together as friends."

"Thanks, Mom." He took his coffee and disappeared back upstairs.

She shook her head at herself. She needed to take her own advice when it came to people she was interested in who happened to live next door.

Argh. No, she didn't need to think about men at all. She had too many fun things planned to worry about the way her pulse skipped when she caught a glimpse of tousled hair and nerdy glasses in the kitchens at work.

Going for a hike with the moms' group was a good start. The trail was challenging but not impossible, the vista at the top of Teapot Hill an excellent one, not to mention the stellar company. The crew of a dozen talked the whole time, and made Clara feel welcome.

Most of the other moms—Archer's wife, Franci, included—had younger kids. Only two had teenagers, and no one had any recent graduates, like Clara.

She didn't feel old, exactly, but was fighting in different trenches than the other women in the group, if not on a different battlefield entirely.

Still, they eagerly invited her to Hideaway Bakery after they finished their return trip, and she was happy to go.

There wasn't much she could eat at the establishment, if anything, but she could get an iced latte or something, so fifteen minutes after accepting the invitation, she brought up the rear of the pack, waiting to order at the counter.

"Franci! You bring that baby up here." Rachel called, waving her hand. "Iris, come see Auntie Rachel."

Franci took Iris out of her all-terrain stroller and scooted to the front of the line. Within seconds, Rachel had a baby in her arms and two tiny fists in her greying blond hair. She was soon joined by her wife, Winnie, who had been on the cash register. An employee took over, but all the cooing over Franci and Archer's daughter slowed the service speed to a molasses-like pace.

Clara studied the menu and the baked goods case.

"Next Friday, we should end off somewhere you have more choices," came a friendly voice.

Clara glanced up from studying the baked goods case to Violet, who stared at Clara with worried blue eyes.

"Trust me—I'm used to it," she replied. For certain social gatherings, she had to come full, or plan to eat at home later. "I always have a stash of emergency snacks in my purse."

"If we went to the pub, you could at least have the fries."

"Don't get me wrong, I appreciate Matias keeping one of the fryers dedicated as gluten free. But if I keep eating the fries at the pub, my blood's going to turn into vegetable oil. I'll be even slower on our next hike. I'm already three shades pinker than you," she said, pressing her palms to her still-warm cheeks. She always turned bright red when she exercised.

Not so Violet, who'd been barely winded by the hike despite her pregnancy.

"Did you and Lawson go running together?" Clara blurted. Oh *God*. Where had *that* come from?

Violet's expression hovered between surprise and uncertainty.

Clara's stomach clenched in embarrassment.

"I am *so* sorry," she continued. "It's none of my business."

"No, I…" Violet lifted a brow, curiosity tingeing her gaze. "We ran together a lot. And I still see him pounding the pavement."

"Yeah, five times a week, it seems." Or seemed, before he lost his ability to do whatever he wanted, whenever he wanted. She should offer to watch the girls for an hour this week so that he could get out and exercise. Charlotte was covering his work shifts, not extra, from what she could tell.

"You're an observant neighbor," Violet mused.

"I promise I wasn't being creepy about it. I always take my coffee on my porch, and he ran right by me many mornings. It was hard not to notice."

"He notices you, too."

If her cheeks had started calming down from her run, they heated right back up.

She wouldn't deny it, though. For one, having a teenager had taught her how adamant protests usually meant a grand-scale emotional cover-up.

Plus, Violet was right. Even before Daniel had pointed it out, Clara had felt Lawson's attention.

Nor did she mind when he directed it her way.

Nothing she'd cop to, though.

"We don't have to talk about this if it makes you uncomfortable," she said instead.

"Six months ago, it would have, but not anymore. And even though Hideaway Wharf is small, it's possible to avoid interacting with someone, or even talking about them. I could have steered clear of him for the rest of my life. But with Matias needing Lawson's expertise at Hau'oli, and with wanting to feel at peace about my pregnancy, I decided I couldn't avoid Lawson any longer. It hurt to talk about our breakup.

We went back to the beginning. All the ugly stuff, why he left and how he hadn't trusted me enough to process how he was feeling about our fertility struggles. He was honest with me about the cause, too. And I had to admit how much I'd allowed his lack of trust and his choices to shape my life in the years after, you know?"

"Mmm, of course," Clara said. She wasn't sure she did know. Fertility struggles? New information, and almost always so painful for the people experiencing them. Her heart ached for whatever they'd gone through. "Though Lawson hasn't gone into much detail. We're just neighbors."

"Oh, yes." Violet blinked. "But if you *were* more than neighbors, I don't think he'd expect you to be his running partner. I'm sure you could find your own shared pastime."

She shot Violet a dry look. Her friends in Portland had set her up with men now and again, but not with such a blithe sense of assumption.

"I'm more looking to find my own thing right now," she insisted. "I haven't had much chance to explore new hobbies since Eddy died, and it's important to me. Ideally, finding something I've never done before."

Though the thought of being close enough to Lawson to have a regular thing together… It intrigued her more than it should.

The line shifted, and Violet sidestepped to stand in front of the till.

"What are you thinking? For your *solo* hobby. Arts? Something on the water? Volunteering?" Violet asked before putting in her order.

"It's hard to decide. I think I'll try everything."

"Oof, don't tell Kellan. He'll have you out foraging every weekend. You'll be up to your knees in mushrooms come September."

Clara laughed. Kellan Murphy, an Irish chef who'd moved to Oyster Island last spring, was now engaged to Sam Walker.

He and Sam were building a successful food-and-diving tour company together, an offshoot of Otter Marine Tours. He also ran a pop-up night at the pub once a month and was gifted in the kitchen.

"Honestly, if it meant I got to eat more of his food, I'd be game to be his assistant," Clara said. "He was the sweetest last month, made sure a few of his dishes were gluten-free." She shook her head. "When I thanked him, he shrugged it off and said they pay more attention to stuff like that back in Ireland. But still, it was a big deal to me."

"He's thoughtful like that. But if you want to do something *not* requiring you to hunch over a forest floor, Mati and I are going sailing tomorrow morning for a few hours. You could join us again."

"That sounds amazing. Let me know what time, and if I need to bring anything," Clara said, then followed suit with her own order.

After waiting for her iced latte, she followed the group outside to the seating area on the side of the boardwalk. The other women had gathered chairs around three round tables, and they were sitting in a misshapen oval, chatting about their weekend plans. Clara let her mind drift for a few seconds. She had her usual Friday, Saturday and Sunday shifts of managing the pub's dining room and kitchen, all from three to eleven during July and August, but her days were wide open.

The weather promised excellent mornings to be outside, if today was anything to go off. The clear sky was a perfect backdrop for the vibrant colors of the boardwalk. The stretch of buildings was ever cheerful, but especially when the sun lit the pastel paint. Cars were loading onto the ferry, and a few people were in the marina, milling around their boats.

At the opposite end of the boardwalk by the grassy stretch of park, a small group of familiar people were having a picnic. Lawson was wearing a navy baseball cap, but she'd recognize his shoulders with her eyes closed. Lopsided pigtails framed the girls' faces. Next to them sat a woman Clara knew from cheese deliveries at work. The owner of Nanny Goats Gruff Farm. Lawson's sister, Isla.

Violet, who'd taken a seat by Clara, seemed to notice the family at the same time.

"It's so nice to see Lawson with Isla. For a while, I was worried they wouldn't mend fences. She was as devastated when he left as Matias and I were. He was working for her at the farm this spring, and practically begged Matias to take him on at the brewery. Partly because he wanted to make up for how badly he screwed Mati over, but also because he hates goats."

She chuckled. "I wonder if he doesn't like animals. He seems to be at a standoff with the twins' cat."

Violet downright laughed. "They have a cat? He is so *not* a cat person. Probably having to mainline antihistamines."

Allergies explained the sneezes she kept hearing through the bedroom wall. She made a face at Violet. "I thought you said it's possible to avoid people in Hideaway Wharf. And yet…" She motioned at Lawson.

"I said, you could avoid *interacting* with people. Avoid seeing them or running into them is much, much harder."

"I suspected," she murmured.

"You really don't seem like you *want* to avoid him, Clara."

"I don't. We're friends."

"I said that about Mati, too. And now look at me." Rubbing a hand over her belly, she grinned.

"Oh, no no no. I am so happy for you and Matias—you're going to be incredible parents—but my pregnancy days are done."

"Totally understandable, but that doesn't mean you can't find *love*."

"Not for me and *him*, though." She flung a hand in Lawson's direction, catching the attention of the rest of the group. Knowing looks passed from one to the next.

Oops. Talk about protesting too hard and making everyone suspicious. She was asking to be the next topic of bakery conversation.

Time to try to fly *under* the radar, not splat right against it.

Which, thanks to Lawson sitting with his family right in her sight line, she managed to fail at spectacularly for the rest of coffee.

Lawson stacked chicken skewers in a Pyrex dish, ready to take them out to the barbecue in the backyard. After two weeks of Charlotte babysitting, they were at least getting into a routine of him getting home from work and making some sort of dinner for the girls. Today, he'd decided to make something fresh, as a person could only handle so many casseroles in a row.

He wasn't sure what Harper and Pippa would think of chicken teriyaki, but at least the skewers would be a novelty. With any luck, it would be a hit, and he'd have one protein dish they'd regularly eat.

The girls were, at least, in love with their new caregiver. And rightly so—Charlotte might still be young, but she had a knack for working with littles. The fridge door was already covered in art they'd created, and their tiny sneakers were perpetually soaked from beach walks. Right now, Charlotte was putting her own shoes on and saying goodbye to the girls at the back entrance to the duplex.

For the second Thursday in a row, the twins were yawning before Charlotte was even out the door. Four weekdays of fun with their very dedicated, creative babysitter tired them out, and they wouldn't see her again until tomorrow afternoon. Friday was the one day a week where their evening routine was thrown off because of Lawson's closing shift in the tasting room.

He could already tell the girls were owly, with matching disgruntled expressions as they carried on a whispered conversation with Charlotte.

"Mind opening the door for me?" he asked her, grabbing the tray of marinated peppers and zucchinis. The girls' fussiness wasn't a reason to always serve them familiar dishes. Their parents had been pretty dedicated to exposing them to produce and flavors, even if they'd ended up eating take-out congee every second day.

Charlotte held the door open, disentangled herself from two pairs of arms and then followed him onto the porch and down to the lawn.

Clutching the trays of food, he was swamped by the comfort of at least one thing going right. "Thank you, Charlotte. Truly."

Her smile brightened. "Happy to help. I'll see you tomorrow."

She turned and headed for her car, and was about to get in when Daniel Martinez jogged into the driveway. The kid had proven to have impeccable timing for the past two weeks. Hands jammed in the pockets of his soccer shorts, he said something for Charlotte's ears only.

If Lawson thought her smile had lit up from being thanked a minute ago, it had nothing on what it morphed into in the presence of Clara's equally enamored son.

If the pair thought they were being subtle about their feelings, they were dead wrong.

Instead of leaving in her car, Charlotte followed Daniel into his side of the duplex.

Amused, Lawson strolled the few feet to the concrete slab where he kept his barbecue, and started dealing with the food. Of anyone, he couldn't point fingers for being less-than-subtle. He'd lost count of the number of times people had mentioned something to do with Clara this past week. Conversations he'd shut down real quick.

He had to watch it. If people were starting to connect the two of them, then he wasn't being chill enough in her presence.

"Unca Sonny?" Harper called from the porch, her sister at her side. "Can we watch *Sesame*?"

"Sure," he said. They knew how to use the voice command on the remote, and it would give him five minutes to monitor the chicken skewers.

He got the food on the grill.

A familiar figure appeared from the same direction Daniel had come.

His pulse jumped.

Clara strolled down the driveway, a cloth grocery bag in her hand and headphones covering her ears.

Pretend to be cool. He raised a hand in greeting.

A slow smile spread across her face. Her cheeks were the same pale pink as the impatiens she'd been babying in the planter boxes hanging off her side of the porch railing.

She slid her headphones from her ears to around her neck. Her gaze traveled from the porch to the lawn and did a quick trip around the yard before settling on him. "Is Charlotte still watching the girls?"

He shook his head and spun the tongs around in his hand. "Harper and Pippa are inside, indulging in a little screen time."

"Ah." She joined him on the cement pad. "Daniel will be sad he jogged home for nothing."

"Oh, it wasn't for nothing. Charlotte's with him in your house." He lifted a brow. "He left you in the dust in hopes of catching a girl?"

"Seems so," she said, laughing. "Who wants to hang out with their mom when they can be with a pretty girl next door, instead?"

"I do," he rushed to say. "I mean, I want to hang out with his mom. With you." *Damn it.* He ran down his face. "Then again, you are the pretty girl next door." *Not better.* "I don't know what I'm saying. That was awkward."

She gripped the handle of her bag with both hands. "Maybe a little, but I still—"

The screen door flew open. "Uncle Sonny, Harper broked the chair. There's *snow.*"

Oh, shit.

Pippa stood in the doorway. Her expression was in tattle mode, not in my-sister-is-hurt mode.

Even so, Lawson tossed the tongs on the side table and jogged toward the house.

"Snow?"

"The chair snowed."

Uh, what?

Wails burst from the great room on the other side of the kitchen. He sped up.

Every inch of the room between the fireplace and the couch was…white.

A howling Harper stood in the middle of a field of miniscule Styrofoam balls, the remains of a beanbag chair behind her.

Ah. Snow.

"See?" Pippa accused. "She jumped on it and *broked it.*"

He got to his knees and wrapped the crying preschooler in a hug. "Hey, sweetheart. Those are pretty big tears for an oops. Were you jumping on the chair?"

"From the *couch*," Pippa said.

"Pippa did, too!" Harper screeched.

"Shh, shh, shh. We'll figure it out."

"Knock, knock." Clara's voice came from the kitchen. "Everyone okay? Need a hand?"

"Come on in. The girls are okay," he called back. "But the beanbag chair…"

"Oh, shhh-oot," she said from somewhere behind him. "It died a valiant death."

"Mommy and Daddy died," Pippa said.

The statement sucked the air out of the room.

He could feel them all teeter, like the pause before losing one's balance.

Harper buried her face in his neck and sobbed harder.

Pippa's eyes widened and her face crumbled. "Did Mommy and Daddy have snow inside, too?"

Clara inhaled loudly. "Oh, honey, no. I used the wrong word."

Wringing her hands, she connected with his gaze and mouthed, *I'm so sorry.*

He opened his other arm to make room for Pippa, but she went over to Clara instead, wrapping her arms around their neighbor's knees.

Clara knelt and swallowed the girl in an embrace. She whispered something in Pippa's ear, too quiet for Lawson to hear it.

No pile of Styrofoam beads mattered compared to his nieces.

A knock sounded on the back door. "Mom? Are you in here? Lawson? Something's smoking on the grill."

His heart sank.

Two girls crying, a destroyed living room *and* burned dinner? He was the top candidate for Uncle of the Year tonight.

But then he caught a hazel-green flash of sympathy and was able to breathe a little deeper.

What was the magic in Clara's eyes that grounded him so fast?

"One thing at a time," she murmured, then raised her voice to ask her son to check the food on the grill.

One thing at a time.

The girls, then dinner, then the mess.

"This feels like a big ask, because I'm sure you have your own dinner to worry about, but would you, uh, be willing to stay and give me a hand?" he asked.

"Of course."

He breathed a sigh of relief. With her here, he could conquer a real mountain, let alone the veritable ski hill of Styrofoam filling in his living room.

Chapter Six

Three hours later, Clara stood in the middle of Lawson's living room, surveying the finally clean floor. She wanted to feel victorious, but really, was there any winning with Styrofoam? The material had seemed to replicate itself the longer they worked at piling it.

Lawson hovered in the archway between his living room and kitchen. "Can I get you anything?"

Clara heard the unspoken "Before I sit down, forever" loud and clear. She was with him on the sentiment.

"I'm okay," she said.

What an evening. After calming the girls and setting them back in front of *Sesame Street*, she'd made some GF noodles from her own pantry and reheated the Stroganoff from the freezer while he tossed his burned barbecue dinner and cleaned the grill. It wasn't a question of whether or not she'd help him and spend the evening with them. It felt right, so she did it, and he appreciated the pair of hands.

While he got Pippa and Harper into bed, she'd started in on shoveling staticky beads into large paper yard-waste bags. She'd barely made a dent.

The process sped up a bit once he joined her, but it was still ten by the time they were done.

She sat on his couch, a little sweaty from the exertion, and a lot wanting to ease the mix of tension, frustration and uncertainty in his gaze.

"Are you sure you don't need a drink?" He stretched out an arm and palmed the edge of the archway. Did he realize how often he showed off his arms? Or maybe she was extra tuned in to noticing them. "Water? Diet Coke? And I have a bunch of different beers. Some of the most recent Hauʻoli pilsner."

Her smile edged on regretful. "Thanks, but I'm not thirsty. Also, there's gluten in most beer."

His face fell. "Of course, there is. I knew that. Sorry."

"I'm not bothered. For one, it's been years—I'm used to it now. I've either found or created equally yummy recipes. And with certain foods making me sick, I've built up an aversion of sorts to some of them. It's not like a food intolerance where a person gets an upset stomach for a half hour and then recovers. If I get glutened, it can be days or weeks until I feel better."

He trudged over and sat on the other end of the short couch. "Yikes. Beer is a big part of my life, but it wouldn't be worth illness."

"It isn't."

"I didn't realize *gluten* could be used as a verb," he said lightly.

"Oh, yeah…" She chuckled. "It's a celiac community thing. Not a medical term, but gets the point across."

"Well, if there's anything I should be doing to make sure I don't put you in danger, let me know. Or shoot me a link or a title of a good book or something. It's not your job to teach me."

"I'm used to being a teacher." It had been part of her identity for so long. And yet, was it time to start letting go of it? Whenever she pictured going back to teaching after this year off, she couldn't. She let out a long breath. "I should get out of your hair."

She couldn't quite will herself to stand, though.

"There are some good gluten-free beers available," he mused. "I know a few brewers who specialize in them."

"I haven't run into one I like, yet," she said.

His mouth flattened as if he were problem solving, then relaxed as his gaze settled on the remains of the beanbag chair.

"That cat has it out for me," he lamented.

He stared at the shredded hole in the cover like it offended his very soul.

While cleaning, they'd tried to puzzle out what had caused the catastrophic stuffing failure. The best they could tell, the cat had used the backside of the beanbag chair as a scratching post, leaving enough holes in the fabric for it to explode when jumped on.

The carcass was draped over the coffee table. Three yard-waste bags sat by the fireplace, taped shut to prevent the filler from spilling out.

"I know we cleaned, but I think I'm going to be finding tiny white bits around for the rest of my life," he said.

She nodded. A few of them were still stuck in his hair.

"Stay still." She scooted closer, her knees bumping his thigh. She pinched a bead between her nails and dropped it on the coffee table, then another. She went in for a third one. Her fingers brushed his hair.

His eyes fluttered closed.

She paused.

Her *hand* paused.

It was just…soft. Too easy to pluck the last ball from the sun-kissed wave over his left ear and then slide her fingertips into the thick strands.

She shouldn't.

She shouldn't be touching him at all, let alone be running her palm down the five-o'clock shadow on his cheek.

The rasp of stubble, so different from the ridiculous softness of his hair. Her fingers tingled from the contrast.

His gaze, too. Gray and serious and curious, stealing all reason from her brain.

Let go, for God's sake.

She knew he didn't want this. Couldn't tell herself *she* didn't want it, though. She wanted to get *lost* in Lawson's eyes.

His cheek warmed her palm.

And Lawson…

He leaned forward.

Oh.

Did he want it?

Maybe he was unsure or torn.

Eyes glinting, he shifted another inch, another, another, until his lips were on hers.

His *taste*. A little sweet, savory.

A kind of familiar unfamiliarity, twigging curiosity. A million different possibilities branched, different ways to explore, secrets to discover.

He slid his own hands on either side of her face, and kissed her like she was bringing him back to life.

Wow. He was *not* unsure.

Tender fingers traced her jaw, his kiss consuming, blazing through her.

She kissed him back, sliding her fingers back into his hair.

Letting out a low sound from deep in his throat, he backed off a fraction.

"All sorts of unexpected happenings tonight," he said, voice ragged.

"Yeah," she whispered.

His gaze traced her face, warmth fading into resignation with every second. "Damn, you're beautiful."

He said it like it was the saddest fact in the world. The emotion pulling at the corners of his mouth tore at the words, rending them a facade of what they might have been.

She withdrew, easing her hands away. The hint of cloves and mint clinging to him still teased her nose.

"Why are you frowning?" she asked.

He rubbed his fingers over his lips. "This seems like the

kind of situation where I should be falling over backward to apologize."

"You're sorry you kissed me?"

"I wish I could lie and say yes, but you deserve the truth, always."

"I'm confused."

"I don't think you know everything about me. And once you do..." He shrugged, regret scrunching those eyes and that jaw she wanted to memorize, millimeter by millimeter. "I think *you'll* feel this was a mistake."

"Try me," she said.

"Do you know how hot you are? Like, freaking magnetic. You go through the world, knowing what to do in every situation. Even if it's just earning one of those little-girl laughs from Pippa or Harper." His mouth tilted. "Your heart is so big, Clara. Like an unending well of compassion. And I don't want to—"

Groaning, he dragged his palms down his face and flopped back against the couch.

Her throat was tight from his openness. "That's all... I mean, *wow*. But it's not connected to what I do or don't know about you."

"Mmm, I'm stalling."

It felt like one of those moments where a character in a movie breaks the fourth wall for a laugh midscene. She couldn't hold in her own, and it came out more like a giggle. "And being honest about it."

"I will always be honest with you. Even if it means being hellaciously awkward."

"Okay..."

"Matias welcoming me back into the brewery still feels like a miracle. I'm never going to expect him to invite me on as a partner again, and I'm glad he got the investment money elsewhere, but even to work for him and contribute to the creative side—it's more than I hoped for when I moved back to the island."

She assumed he wasn't nearly done, so she waited, scooting sideways against the back of the couch with her knees curled in front of her.

"Me working for Hauʻoli meant Violet needed to forgive me, too," he added.

"Hasn't she?" It seemed like it, from the outside. Violet and Lawson were cordial whenever Clara saw them together.

"She has, and God, it took a heavy serving of grace on her part." He pressed his lips between his teeth, and his throat bobbed. "Everyone thought I left because I got headhunted by Mill Plain Brewing. Their willingness to buy into the rumor was sobering, to say the least. Most of the people I loved believed I'd walked out the day before my wedding for the sake of an impressive job offer."

She winced.

"Exactly," he said. "Didn't say much about my character. But I went along with the assumptions. Pretended working for Mill Plain was worth more to me than the brewery I'd been planning with Matias, or the vows I intended to exchange with Violet."

Oof. Hard to excuse walking out on a fiancée and a business partner in one fell swoop. But the way he'd worded it, and his tone, made her listen closer. She took his hand between both of hers and stroked her thumbs along the work-roughened spots on his palms.

His gaze darted to hers, eyes wide and silvery gray.

Another squeeze. *I'm listening.*

"I didn't leave because of the job. I'd already turned it down. Had to beg Mill Plain to reconsider, to let me rescind my refusal, once I'd left Violet and Matias and no longer had a job or a home here."

He was circling the meat of the story, but she wasn't going to rush him.

The warmth of his hand melded into hers. Her thumb rested on the inside of his wrist, and his pulse fluttered against her skin, getting faster by the minute.

She stroked a circle against the sensitive spot. "I'm not here to judge you, you know."

"I know. Of anyone…" He sighed. "Violet and I struggled with fertility, both with her getting pregnant and staying pregnant. We had some wonderful times together, enough to think we wanted to try for forever, but it was all under an umbrella of loss and disappointment. Years of it. I hadn't processed how traumatic her miscarriages were—for both of us—until much later."

Her heart pitched. She wanted to gather him up and soothe the hurt from his face. But also, what was he not saying? Stilling the small touch, she said, "Did you leave because you weren't able to have kids together?"

Obviously, that was enough to destroy some relationships. And she hadn't been there, she didn't know what the day-to-day was like. Terrible disappointment could wear down a couple's love until it was worn and fragile, easily shattered. But she wanted to believe he didn't think biological means were the only way to make a family. He'd accepted the twins so wholeheartedly…

"Yes, and no?" His tone veered toward pleading.

Tightening her grip on his hand, she silently urged him on. His palm was sweaty, and the skin creased at the corners of his eyes. It looked like he'd rather close them, block out having to make eye contact.

He didn't, though. He turned his head enough to look at her straight on. "It wasn't about us not being able to have kids *together*. I'm not sure I can have kids with *anyone*."

"And that was a deal-breaker for Violet? That doesn't sound right."

"Because it isn't right. I'm sure she would have understood. Except—" He muttered a curse under his breath. "I'd had fertility testing without telling her. It was something I wanted to face alone, for some reason. We'd talked about both getting testing done, but we put it off because of the wedding... Except I didn't put it off, and my results were delayed. My doctor sent them to me two days before my wedding day. I discovered I have a chromosomal disorder. Doesn't impact my health at all, but it makes the chance of miscarriage much higher than average."

"Oh, Lawson." Something in her chest threatened to break.

"I walked out. Went on the ferry to run a wedding errand the day before the ceremony, and just kept going."

Her brain glitched. His choices had been...not good. But also, he must have been hurting, so very much. She didn't know what to say.

He saved her from having to think of an appropriate response. "I regretted it almost immediately. I knew I'd done the wrong thing. But I also knew I'd broken something irreversibly. I couldn't excuse it. Couldn't fix deserting Violet. So I...stayed gone."

He pulled his hand away. Linking his fingers together, he leaned forward, resting his elbows on his knees and hanging his head.

"That's, well—"

"Please don't make excuses for what I did. Hell, I didn't even come back for my stuff. Paid a moving company to retrieve it."

"I *won't* make excuses. You made a massive error in judgment." She laid her hand on his back. His T-shirt was thin, and his skin so warm. "It helps to understand the reason, though. And when you're grieving, or in shock from unexpected news, it's hard to have a level perspective."

"Kind of you to think that."

"I *know* it. I've been there. Not exactly where you were, but I've had my entire foundation demolished before. As I adjusted to life without Eddy, I was overwhelmed twenty-four seven.

Yelled a lot, until I decided to work through it with my counselor. I didn't always make rational decisions or react with a level head. Ask Daniel." She chuckled. "Or ask him about *his* irrational choices."

"Is it fair to compare a teenager's decision-making abilities to those of a grown-ass man?"

"No, but let me tell you, from having gone through what I did, and also from showing up to work every day and teaching teenagers who deserve far more credit for being incredible people than society is usually willing to give them—no one should be judged solely on their lowest moment."

"I hurt people, and I don't want to hurt anyone else."

Who hasn't?

"And I'm sad for all you went through. I'm sad you made that decision, both for how it affected Violet and Matias, but also for how it affected you. It left you alone, Lawson, and no one should have to face a loss like yours alone."

Still staring at the floor, he nodded. "Being alone sucked. I had Quentin and Kiera in Vancouver, but I still knew what I'd lost. What I had thrown away."

"Why did you come back?"

"Healed enough to know I couldn't live the rest of my life without trying to make amends. Went to a lot of therapy. Realized coming back and having the real, painful conversations would be better than cycling imaginary apologies and reactions over and over in my head."

"And then you stayed."

"It's home. The island… I missed being here. Even if I fit in differently than before I left."

"Selfishly, I'm glad you're here. Otherwise, I wouldn't get to smell your coffee every morning."

He sighed. "I'm not good for you, Clara."

"That's a big assumption."

"I'm still learning how to make up for what I did in the

past, let alone get involved with someone in the present. And now, with the twins…"

"In terms of *them,* I'm with you. They're your focus. And I don't want to steal your attention from them."

"You don't, really. Look at tonight—you're the kind of friend a person never quite feels like they deserve."

Friend. The correct word, for sure.

But part of her wanted something bigger, splashier. She was cautious about being in a new relationship, but not opposed to it. She never thought she'd spend the rest of her life alone. Finding a man as worthy of sharing her life as her late husband was no small task, though. Maybe Lawson could have fit that bill, were it not for the changes wrought on his life from the guardianship.

Were it not…

Reality meant setting some boundaries.

"Friends don't usually kiss like that," she said.

He blew out a breath. "Which is why we shouldn't do it again."

"Agreed." It hurt to say.

It hurt even more to see the spark of yearning in his gray eyes.

"I'm still not sorry, though," he said.

"I'm still not telling you that you should be."

She'd hold the memory tight, even though they wouldn't be making any more of them.

The following Monday, Lawson sat at one of the tables on the brewery's patio, surrounded by emails he'd printed out, and notes on recipes, new ingredients and rough diagrams. He had his tablet and phone, too, though as usual was having more success brainstorming with paper.

The early morning breeze necessitated Lawson weigh his notes down with rocks, but the weather was too beautiful to set up shop inside the brewery. His shift started at ten, which gave him a couple of hours to work on his personal project. Eventually, his brainstorms might be useful for Hauʻoli, but for now, they were still too new to float in front of Matias.

After his conversation with Clara last week, where she'd so patiently talked about her celiac disease, he'd suggested Matias order a wider variety of gluten-free beer and to up their cider and alcoholic kombucha stock, both for Clara and for other people who needed or wanted the product.

But for Clara, buying someone else's creation didn't feel like enough.

He wanted her to drink something *he'd* made. Something she'd end up loving, not shrugging off like she had when she'd mentioned not being a big fan of the ones she'd tried. Maybe he'd make one and she'd know for sure malty flavors weren't for her, but he needed to try.

And if she did end up disliking a GF beer of his making, then maybe he could *also* branch into kombucha or cider—

Getting ahead of yourself, Thorne.

Clara sure had a way of making him get carried away.

He'd emailed four fellow brewers over the weekend, two in Canada and two in California, about any resources they'd recommend for GF brewing. Though they were understandably hesitant to share any proprietary knowledge, they'd all been generous with the basics, enough for him to see the glimmers of a way forward. A few major stumbling blocks scattered the path, cross contamination being the major concern, but he preferred to think about what he *could* do, rather than get caught up in potential problems right away.

Recipe, supplies, facility… This was all in his wheelhouse.

An hour later, the stacks of paper were even higher. He needed to clean up soon, but something about research and development was so damn rewarding. Especially doing it on a beautiful summer morning on the harbor, getting to wave at friends and neighbors as they went about their days.

For years, he'd assumed he'd permanently severed his connection to Hideaway Wharf and all its eclectic islanders. He'd never take the little moments for granted again. In the last hour, he'd spotted Sam and Kellan saying their morning fare-wells at the bottom of the staircase up to their apartment, been the recipient of a smile from Violet as she embarked on what looked like a super slow morning jog and had ducked over to Hideaway Bakery when the cinnamon-bun scent drifting in the wind had gotten too tempting to resist. Only crumbs, a smear of Rachel's secret-recipe frosting and a paper bag re-mained of his second breakfast.

A perfect morning.

Looking up for a second to release the kink in his neck, he spotted something more irresistible than one of Rachel and Winnie's pastries, trudging toward him along the wood planks of the boardwalk.

A long, blond braid. Soulful hazel eyes. A brightly striped cardigan adding an extra layer of softness to her lush frame.

No question—he had a staring problem.

Clara seemed lost in her thoughts, staring at the harbor but far off in the middle distance. Her arms were crossed, and the closer she got to the patio, the tighter her mouth seemed.

Damn, was she okay?

Hard to tell if she'd welcome a hello, though…

Maybe not. She deserved her peace and quiet.

Refocusing on his work, he forced himself not to stare like an infatuated weirdo, but he was incapable of processing his notes after seeing her unhappy expression.

After a minute, she caught his attention again.

She was only a few yards from the patio fence. Français plodded next to her on his leash. And it looked like *she* was fighting the urge to watch *him*.

He had to hold in a foolish grin.

"Hey, Clara. Good morning."

"Hey," she replied, almost too softly to hear.

"What's wrong?" he asked.

She paused to lean on the fence closest to his table. Her dog sacked out on the ground with a huff.

"Nothing," she said, gaze darting to the side.

"You sure?" He didn't want to be pushy, but she'd been a hell of a sounding board for him, so returning the favor was just fair. "I mean, you don't have to share, but—"

"I miss my son, and he isn't even gone, yet."

He nodded. "Ah. Early empty-nest pangs?"

She nodded back. "My parents and a few older colleagues I have back home keep telling me I should enjoy the freedom, and how it's a gift I get to take this time to figure out who I am aside from being a mom and teacher, but I worry."

"From my extremely small sample size—I mean, weeks of parenting compared to years—it seems like worrying is part of the game."

She let out a dry laugh. "It is. His whole diving gambit is terrifying for me at times, and the thought of dropping him off at college—" she pinched the bridge of her nose "—it's physically painful. But as much as I'm concerned for him, I am for me, too. I've literally never lived alone. I went from my parents' house to a dorm with a roommate for a year, to living with Eddy, and then Eddy *and* Daniel, and now only Daniel. Coming home to an empty house…"

She sniffled and clenched the leash handle in both hands.

His heart ached for her. Rifling through his pocket for one of his ever-present Kleenexes—thanks but no thanks for the dander, Felina—he handed it to her.

She took it and dabbed the corners of her eyes.

"Uh, I hear you," he said. "Loneliness has a way of making a heart raw. And as much as Hideaway Wharf is full of people who love to fold new arrivals into their circles, I can see why the thought of an empty house would be hard for you."

"Thanks." Her damp gaze dropped to the ground. She looped the leash around one of the fence posts, then pressed the heels of her hands to her eyes. After a minute, she sniffed and pasted on a smile. "This is why I promised myself I'd say yes to things. So I *don't* get lonely."

"So, if I offered to go get you a coffee from Matias's office, you'd say yes to coming and sharing my very messy table with me?"

"We share coffee together almost every morning, Lawson."

Truth. More often than not, they sat on their respective porches and watched the water at the same time. Sometimes in silence, sometimes chatting through the screen of faux greenery. And he didn't want to give her the impression he was asking for any reason other than friendship.

Her company was irresistible, though.

"We don't usually have this particular view of the water, though," he pointed out.

Her snort-laugh was so damn cute.

"Okay. Somehow, it's impossible to say no to you."

Holy hell. His brain liked the implications way too much.

She studied the fence around the patio. Because of liquor licensing, they kept the gate padlocked. She glanced down at her tied-up dog. "He isn't going anywhere. I'll go around to the side entrance."

He stood. "I can give you a boost."

"I don't know, Lawson, I—"

Reaching over the fence and putting his hands on her waist, he said, "I've gotcha, if you trust me. You're all of five feet tall. Tiny. Hold on tight."

Bad idea. Bad, bad idea. Her waist was so soft, warm, *touchable*… He waited, eyebrow raised, in case she wanted to say no.

She didn't. Biting her lip, she gripped both his shoulders. "I'm short, but I'm in no way *tiny*."

He lifted her over with ease, earning a squeal and ten fingertips digging into his lats. He set her on the planking less than a foot from his front. "Says who?"

"Says the size on the tag of my leggings."

"Clothing sizes are a scam. You're lighter than most of our sacks of malt."

She laughed again, more genuine than the first two he'd coaxed from her. She also wasn't backing up or releasing her grip on his shoulders. And for some reason, his fingers refused to let go of the beautiful curve of her waist.

Her hands slid down to his biceps, and she stared up at him, lips parted.

"Kiss the Girl" from *The Little Mermaid* popped into his head.

Only because he'd been playing Disney soundtracks with the twins during dinners, *not* because kissing Clara again would be smart—

Goddamn it. He'd told himself he wasn't going to do this. They were friends. *Friends.*

Backing up, he let go and splayed his hands at his sides, trying to release the sensation of his palms on Clara's body. "Coffee. I promised you coffee."

"I—*right.* Coffee. Three creams and—"

"Two sugars. I'm on it," he said, already halfway to the door into the brewery.

Thank God for the few minutes it took him to prepare her drink. By the time he returned to the picnic table, his pulse was almost back to normal.

He passed her the mug, and she took it in both hands, blowing on the top and making little ripples in the pale tan brew.

"It's amazing you can taste any coffee at all, given it's mostly cream and sugar," he teased.

"You're missing out, Mr. Splash of Milk," she tossed back, her pretty mouth twitching with a smirk.

Them being familiar with how they each took their coffee didn't mean anything, right?

I'm overthinking this.

She tapped a finger on one of his stacks of paper. "Whatcha working on?"

He scanned all the visible text to make sure she wouldn't know what he was doing. Until he had a concrete plan, he didn't want to share it.

"Playing with some new recipes," he said.

"You're not set on your fall menu? I thought Matias said it was finalized. Winter, too."

"Mmm, but spring isn't."

He hoped, anyway. He and Mati hadn't discussed yet whether Lawson's term with Hau'oli had a definitive end. Once they'd worked the kinks out, Mati might not need Lawson anymore.

Shoving away his rising fear, he focused on the woman sipping coffee across from him.

Sharing the exceedingly normal activity was a good reminder. Spending time with Clara could just be about the usual give-and-take between friends. Doing things together now and then, too.

Surely, that was harmless.

Especially if they had two tiny chaperones, around whom he had no intention of flirting with their neighbor.

"Are you working Saturday morning?" he asked.

"No." She sipped her coffee. "Need something?"

"Not 'need,' but I'm taking the girls to my sister's farm to meet the holy terrors. Do you want to come?"

She raised an eyebrow. "Holy terrors?"

"Uh, yeah. Have you met goats before? There's a reason why I begged Matias for a job."

He was not made for having to watch his back while filling troughs and sweeping dung out of the barn. And their *eyes*... Shudder. However, the girls getting time with their aunt was important. And if he happened to bring a friend along, well, it felt like a *more the merrier* situation.

The corner of her mouth twitched. "Can't say I've been around goats much, but they seem pretty harmless."

"You say that now. Do you know how many pairs of pants I lost to those jerks while I was working for Isla in the spring?"

She snorted. "They are called 'Nanny Goats Gruff,' I hear."

"And they live up to the 'gruff.' You'll see."

"Perfect. I'll haul out my rubber boots."

"You'll need those. And full-body armor," he said.

Her uncontrolled laugh seeped all the way into his soul.

How could a sound, a smile do that? Talk about full-body armor—he'd built something similar around his heart after Violet. Hell, he'd probably had it in place since his dad died, and never truly let Violet in.

But something about Clara… If he wasn't careful, she was going to knock those shields down, one by one.

Clara used her Thursday off to take the ferry off-island. She checked off a list of errands as long as her forearm, mostly in Bellingham. With her car full of things difficult or impossible to get on Oyster Island, she arrived back in Hideaway Wharf right as Daniel's dive tour was wrapping up. From her view as she waited at the back of the boat to disembark, she caught glimpses of her son hosing equipment on the dock and then heading into the shop.

Given his shift was ending in minutes, instead of driving home, she pulled into one of the diagonal parking spots out front of Otter Marine Tours. All the perishables she'd bought at Trader Joe's and Costco were in a cooler on ice, so wouldn't go bad if she waited fifteen minutes to give her son a ride home.

Plus, it might give her a chance to have a quick visit with Archer. Between him and Franci being busy with a toddler and his job having essentially opposite hours to Clara's, she hadn't seen as much of him as she'd have liked to in past weeks.

A rack of cable-locked stand-up paddleboards lined one side of the door. Through the front window, she could see her friend's dark head near the glass display case and the mounted tablet they used as a point-of-sale terminal. She pushed through the door.

The bell chimed, and Archer lifted his head. He grinned. "Hey, stranger."

"I could call you the same."

"Here, have a seat. Danny's in the shower," Archer said, pushing a rolling stool in her direction.

She took it and sat, leaning her forearms on the low half of the counter Sam had built for the times when, like now, Archer used his wheelchair.

Her friend sat behind the counter. His short, damp hair curled like it did when it got wet and he didn't style it right away. He had on his usual post-dive sweatpants and T-shirt, the short sleeves of which showed off the tattoos he'd been collecting through his years in the Coast Guard and after the accident.

Once upon a time, getting inked had been something he and Eddy had done together. And after Eddy was gone, Archer had asked her if she wanted to get one with him, in memory of Eddy. She'd been too nervous of the needle to go through with her own, but she'd gone to the tattoo parlor with Archer and watched him have an intricate design of a clock inked onto his chest, the arms of the timepiece forever pointing at the time her husband died.

His gaze followed hers to the black lines on his forearm, an otter peeking out from behind a bull kelp bulb.

"You know, if I *was* going to get a tattoo, it might be an otter. God, they're adorable."

"Yeah, I like this little guy." He traced a finger along the animal's whiskers. "A heads-up—Danny's been talking about wanting one. Wasn't sure how you'd feel about it. But I think it's something he associates with Eddy."

She winced. "I'm not going to bar him from doing something he really wants to his body—I can't, at this point, given he's eighteen—but he's young to be choosing what ink he'll have for the rest of his life. Or at the very least, something expensive to remove."

"The place across the street is clean and reliable. I could go with him," Archer offered. "Lend some perspective of having gotten a few when I was younger myself."

"I'd appreciate that. Wanting them to live their life, but also reducing regrets, is an age-old balance, and he might listen to you more given you have experience."

He guffawed. "We all have regrets, Clarabelle."

"Yeah. And worries about developing regrets."

"Sounds like it's been on your mind," he said.

"I'm hoping I don't regret moving here for the year. Maybe I should have planned to be in Portland, closer to Daniel when school starts. He seems…nervous."

Archer ran a hand through his hair and exhaled with a loud *phhhh.*

She blinked at him. "Something I should know?"

"I doubt it's anything he hasn't told you. But he's certainly more nervous about school than I'd expected him to be, considering how much he's talked it up for the past couple of years."

"Yeah, diving seems to have superseded any of that," she said.

"I feel I should apologize."

She waved off the sentiment. "I'm the one who signed him up for his introductory dive course."

"Fair." He sighed. "I *am* sorry Eddy's not here to see it. I miss him, and I wish he were here leading Danny on his dives."

She scooted her stool closer and leaned in for a hug. "Thank you for teaching my son. You're an incredible mentor."

He grunted and held her tighter. "We're family. I love him. And for as long as he wants to pursue diving, I'm here for him. But, like you, I think he'll excel at school, too. He's so damn smart."

She exhaled. Some of her worry drained away. Getting

Archer's perspective on things always helped when she was seeking assurance she wasn't messing up parenting royally.

She gave him one last squeeze and then scooted the stool back a few inches. "Enough about my kid—how's yours?"

They chatted about Iris's latest escapades for a minute, until Daniel barreled out of the staff-only door behind the cash register.

"Mom! Guess what! We saw orcas. The whole pod. Like, *forty* of them. It was wild."

"What? We've been wanting to see them since we got here, and you managed to without me?"

Not exactly surprising, given he was out on the water ten times as much as she was.

"There's always a spot on the *Queen* for you, Clarabelle," Archer said, twirling a pen in his fingers.

"Ugh, I know, but I can't exactly tag along every day in hopes of seeing something cool."

"I took a ton of video," Daniel said, pulling his phone out of his shorts and showing her a series of social media posts he'd shared. "I have never seen anything so wild. They are the best apex predator."

"You'll have so much to talk about during your enrichment class," she said.

Daniel had registered for a two-week enrichment program in advance of the fall semester, focusing on marine science. He'd gotten in due to his stellar grades and had been thrilled about the opportunity. Not so much recently.

His whale-related excitement faded. "Uh, right. I guess."

She shared a look with Archer, whose eyes widened.

"You not looking forward to your class, Dan?" he asked.

Daniel shrugged. "I guess. It means leaving the island two weeks early, though."

"Yeah," Archer cajoled. "Exciting, right? You'll have a huge head start."

Daniel's mouth flattened further.

Nerves fluttered in Clara's chest. She needed to change the subject. "The whales, uh, didn't come near the boat, did they? And you weren't in the water?"

Her words squeaked, and Daniel's expression shifted to disbelief. "No. And Mom, they don't eat people. Jesus."

"I know," she said defensively. "I saw a pair once before when I was out fishing with your dad. And I think they're amazing, and would kill to see them again, but I also have a healthy respect for them. They might decide you were a seal and needed to be punted in the air thirty feet. I've seen those YouTube videos. Not to mention the orcas in Spain who go after sailboat keels."

"Well, the ones here ignore us," her son assured her. "We cut the engine, of course, and watched them go by. It took, what, fifteen minutes?"

He glanced at Archer, who lifted a shoulder and confirmed, "Around there."

"You didn't tell me today was such a banner day," Clara said to her friend.

He shrugged again. "More fun for Danny to get to relay the news. I see them a few times a season. And not that it ever gets old, but there's something about the first time."

There was.

Like, say, first kisses. The one she'd shared a week ago with Lawson had blown her mind. Having his mouth on hers was ten times more incredible than witnessing a whale pod doing their thing.

And given they'd agreed not to repeat the moment of pleasure, it was probably as rare, too.

Chapter Seven

Without question, Lawson's sister's farm was a joy-filled operation. The cartoon logo of a grumpy goat on the sign at the base of the driveway was only the first indication of how Isla Thorne approached life with a smile on her face. The farm itself teemed with hints at its owner's free-spirited nature.

Clara stood in the driveway between the ramshackle farmhouse and the shiny cheese-making facility, soaking in the Saturday sunshine on her face and mostly bare shoulders. Lawson had run off a minute ago, calling out an apology over his shoulder, holding a small hand with each of his, having to deal with twin bathroom emergencies. Not having been to the goat farm before, Clara didn't mind the minute to herself. A big part of her home ec curriculum had focused on local producers, so getting to see food production in action always piqued her interest.

The corrugated metal siding of the barn was immaculate. The eclectic paint on the house, not so much. It wasn't in disrepair. It just didn't make much sense. The cobbled-together collection of colors and shapes suggested it had undergone multiple rounds of renovation, likely by different owners. She'd assessed similar projects at school, when each group member had a different idea for how their sugar cookies should be decorated, and the batch ended up in three different, unrelated shapes, and covered with eight colors of icing. The window frames on the top half of the house looked like they could be on a baked good, with frilly white edges stark against olive green paint.

A screen door banged shut, and Clara glanced toward the noise. Not Lawson, but Isla. Aside from weekly cheese deliveries, she'd seen the woman in passing more often since the twins moved in last month. They'd exchanged waves the couple of times Isla had been coming or going from Lawson's side of the duplex.

The other woman wore a white tank and yellow denim overalls. Gum boots the color of army fatigues covered her from knee to toe. A wide straw hat shaded her friendly smile.

"Clara, hey," she said, reaching Clara and sticking out her hand. "Welcome. It's nice to meet you away from the pub. Lawson can't shut up about you."

"Uh, *oh.*" *Wow, way to be articulate.* Taking the offered handshake, Clara scrambled for a proper reply. "Well, uh, hopefully it's all good things. I'd rather not devolve into a neighbor-versus-neighbor feud and end up having to search for a new place to rent."

Isla's eyes danced. "I doubt you have to worry there."

"Never know," she joked. "He might decide he hates what I've done with the raspberry patch and evict me."

Isla shook her head. "You probably have a home for life if you want it. My brother is nothing but reliable these days."

She lifted her brows. "He'd be glad to hear you say that."

"Oh?"

Hmm. Should she share something he might have said in confidence? Then again, he included Isla as one of the people who he'd hurt the most. "I think he worries people expect him to run off again."

Isla nodded, but didn't look concerned. "If three months of shoveling goat dung while avoiding getting horns in the rear didn't make him bolt, nothing will."

The twins burst from the same side door Isla had used, then bounced across the gravel drive.

"Isla, Isla!" Pippa crowed. "A goat is on your truck! I saw it from the bathroom window!"

Isla sighed and cocked her head in the direction of the front of the house. "I bet it's Cashew. He loves to escape. Should have named him Houdini." She strode away from the two of them. "Lawson knows his way around. I'll catch up once I've caught my tiny marauder."

A few seconds later, Lawson made his way out of the house. He slid his sunglasses from the top of his head to his face. The corners of his mouth were turned down.

"Girls, how come I found water splashed all the way up the mirror?" he asked with a hint of sternness to his tone.

The twins pointed at each other.

"So, both of you, then."

Two bottom lips quivered.

His frown softened. "I know Auntie Isla is family, but let's still be mindful guests in her house, okay?"

Matching angelic nods.

"Did you tell her about Cashew?" he asked.

"She went to find him," Pippa said.

"He loves to ec-athpe," Harper explained.

"Escape?" Lawson confirmed.

"Yeah, ec-athpe. Auntie Isla went that way." She pointed to where her aunt had disappeared.

He glanced at Clara, his mouth twisted to the side.

She wasn't sure if he wanted confirmation of the story, or maybe he was wondering at what point children stopped mispronouncing words, but she could assure him all was well on both accounts.

"Your sister wasn't worried about Cashew, and said you know your way around. I think she's assuming we'll get started without her," Clara said.

"All right, then. To the goats." His smile was overbright as he pointed toward a gate.

God, she'd worn a similar smile over the years, putting

on a happy face for the sake of doing something that Daniel wanted to do but wasn't up her alley.

The girls skipped ahead. He hung back until Clara got to his side.

"You're doing a good job, you know," she assured him.

He opened the gate to a small, empty pasture. The grassy space connected to the long barn. Across the stretch of green, another fence traversed the property. Dozens of hairy, horned heads poked through the cross boards.

She swore she caught Lawson shuddering on the way across the field.

"Uncle Sonny, can we go through the fence?" Pippa asked, yearning on her small face.

"No, love. We're going to pet them through the fence today."

Harper stuck her lip out.

Pippa carefully stroked the animals' ears. "Can we feed them?"

"They like the leaves, if you hold out one of the little branches for them," he explained. A variety of tree branches were scattered along the fence line.

The girls followed directions, and giggled as the animals flocked to the branches, trying to get in on the offerings. More laughs. The girls could not have been more rapt.

Their uncle was not.

"Your nose-wrinkle is showing," Clara said.

He glanced at his nieces, and then looked at Clara and feigned a gag.

"They are not to be trusted," he said under his breath. "Their pupils alone... I cannot."

"Aw, they don't deserve a bad rap," she said, unable to hold in her amusement.

"You say that now, until you wake up with one standing on the end of your bed. When I first returned to the island, I rented a room at a B and B for a while, until Isla took pity on me and put me up. Put me to work, too, which was fair, don't get me wrong. But tiny hooves on my comforter were not part of the deal."

"Your sister lets them in the house?"

"No, but Cashew can teleport, I swear."

"Come, now."

He glowered. "We figure he squeezed in through the cat door."

She snorted. "How small is he?"

He pointed toward the gate they'd come through, where Isla was carrying a black-coated goat under her arm like a football. It looked pleased as punch.

"Lawson. He can't be more than two feet tall." Clara's lips twitched. "He's adorable."

"My *bed*, Clara."

"And he got in through the cat door? Even small as he is, it would have taken effort. He must have been desperate to snuggle."

"Cashew *loves* Lawson," Isla said.

Evident by the way the goat fixed his gaze on Lawson and wiggled to get free.

"Aw, he wants to snuggle with you *now*," Clara said.

"I'd humor him, but if I put him down in this field, he'll escape again." Isla smiled as the girls spun to greet the smallest goat, reaching up to give him scritches behind his ears. "He has a wandering spirit. He never goes far, though. He knows where his dinner dish is."

Lawson snorted. "He *prefers* eating things that aren't his dinner. Mainly, my clothes."

"Oh, he did that *one time*," Isla said. "He's just curious."

"Mmm, yes, a curious, miniature Satan."

Cashew nosed one of Pippa's braids and she squeaked and jumped back.

"Hey," Lawson soothed, "he won't hurt you."

"He does like hair." Isla whispered the reminder.

"Maybe put your braids over your shoulders. Here." Holding his hands out, he took the animal from his surprised-looking sister. He sat down on the dusty ground, an infatuated goat filling his lap. Cashew wanted nothing to do with escaping when he was in Lawson's arms.

Clara couldn't blame the animal.

"Here, love," he said to Pippa. "He'll be easier to pet down here."

Oh. Oh my.

Goats were a lot of things, but they weren't romantic. However, watching Lawson be sweet with his nieces, holding an animal he outright disliked for the sake of making the girls happy, made Clara's heart do unacceptable things.

Shaking her head, she tried to clear away her very un-friend-like thoughts. She focused on Isla instead, who was watching her brother and his nieces with amusement.

"Can we take a peek at your cheese operation at some point?" Clara asked. "I love seeing food in progress. Every term, I'd try to get my students to a cheese-making facility for a field trip, but we usually went to one with dairy cows, not goats."

"There are some similarities and differences, for sure," Isla said before launching into a more detailed spiel than Clara had expected to get.

After the girls were done petting the goats, Isla led them all through a tour of the process, keeping it engaging for the girls at their level, but also for Clara and her moderate familiarity.

Eventually, the girls started fading, and their aunt shuffled them toward the tiny tasting shop with the promise of snacks.

"You're sure you don't want to go check out the storage room you asked about?" Isla asked her brother as she rounded the glass-front refrigerated case to stand at the small serving counter.

"Not today," he emphasized.

"I got it all cleaned out for you to get set up tomorrow."

"Which I appreciate a ton, but I'll look at it then."

Clara couldn't quite read what he was trying to silently communicate to his sister, but the way his gaze flicked to her made her feel like she was getting in the way of something important.

"Don't let me stop you if you have business to attend to," she said. "I can watch the girls for you for a few minutes."

"No, no," he said. "I just don't want to get sucked into business while we're supposed to be here having fun."

All right, then. Not *her* business, apparently. She pasted on a smile. "Cheese is always fun."

"I have so many flavors for you to try. Different ones from the few I send to the pub," Isla said, clapping her hands as if to say "let's go." "I play around with my cheese as much as Lawson does with his beer."

Lawson shot his sister another look Clara didn't quite understand.

"Yum. I can eat it off spoons," Clara said. "Unless you have gluten-free crackers? If not, I think I have some in my bag."

She rarely had to worry about eating cheese, so she did so with great abandon. The vessels, however, took more thought.

"If you don't have any on hand, Isla," Lawson interjected from over by the display of goat soap, fending of two pairs of hands from touching everything, "I have some in my trunk."

Clara's jaw dropped. She stared at him.

He blinked nervously. "Should I not have?"

"Uh, gosh, no. All good," she said. "It's sweet you thought of it."

"What are friends for, right?" he said.

"Right," Clara said.

Isla rolled her eyes.

Uh-oh. Were Clara's feelings that obvious?

"Save your box for when you have Clara over to your place," Isla said. "I've started using rice crackers for all my tastings because the flavor doesn't overpower the cheese and most people can eat them. Feel free to check the ingredients, of course, but I think they're safe for celiacs."

She proceeded to run them through a generous tasting of her entire cheese menu.

"I can't decide my favorite," Clara lamented, after trying at least ten. "You're so creative with the soft ones. They're all so tangy, but delicate, too. The rosemary-and-cracked-pepper one is unreal. But the hard one…and the brie-style, it was almost lemony… Argh, I can't choose."

"I like *orange* cheese," Harper announced, not that any of the adults had missed the first five times she'd made her preference known.

Neither girl had been willing to try the offered samples, and Lawson seemed to have decided not to die on the hill of eating adventurous food today. They were happy enough chomping on crackers, a jar of locally made jam and some dried apricots Isla had behind the counter.

"I could make this one orange," Isla said, pointing to a few small cubes of the hard cheese similar to Parmesan. "But I like to show off the color of the milk my goats make. When cheese is orange, it means the maker has dyed it with something called annatto."

Harper nodded solemnly, as if she had a frame of reference for anything Isla had just said.

Who knew, maybe she was interested. Clara had been watching people, including other teachers, underestimate children and teenagers for her entire career.

"You've been too generous," she said to Isla, rubbing her stomach. "It was almost enough to count as lunch."

"My brother bringing a woman by the farm is a special occasion," she said.

"Today's trip was for the girls, not for me," Clara corrected.

"Mmm-hmm," Isla said, clearly disagreeing.

Ugh, Clara really needed to correct whatever misconceptions Lawson's sister had. But how could she, without drawing attention to the situation in a worse way? She should deflect.

"Do you ever hire help?" she asked. "I can't think of much better an existence than being surrounded by cheese all day."

Lawson looked up sharply from where he was dejamming Pippa's and Harper's hands with a wet wipe.

"But the goats," he muttered. "You can't be serious."

"About cheese? I'm *always* serious. And the goats are cute."

"I know, right?" Isla gushed. "It's why I do this. I mean, I love the animals. But the cheese. And if you're serious, we can talk about what you'd be interested in doing. I have two summer employees, but they'll both leave at the end of the season."

"You're working for the pub," Lawson said. "You want a second job?"

"Mati only hired me until the end of August."

"I don't see him going back to the pub. The brewery's going to keep him busy."

"A conversation he and I need to have," Clara said.

The corners of his eyes went sad. "I guess so."

How much did he regret being an employee instead of one of the decision-makers?

"Doesn't mean he can't have a similar conversation with you, too. If you want to stay on with him."

"I can't ask him to give me more than he already has, Clara," he said.

"But Lawson, you have so much to—"

He lifted his eyebrows and glanced meaningfully toward the twins.

She wasn't going to let him deflect entirely, but she got he didn't want to talk about it in front of Harper and Pippa. Maybe even not in front of his sister, either. Later, then.

A month ago, she wouldn't have dreamed of pushing. Now, after all the time they'd spent together, after watching him adjust to earthshaking news, she knew this man.

His place was here. His people were here.

She had to help him believe that truth.

"You headed out soon?" Matias walked past where Lawson was fussing with a gauge on one of the brewhouses.

"Yeah, the girls' counseling appointment is at three," he replied.

"Cool, cool," Matias said. "Oh, with the brewing equipment you mentioned the other day—if you have something you want to test out without doing a full batch, you can use my old setup in the side room."

"Actually, I have a favor to ask. I do want to experiment, and I can clean up your old equipment, given it's glass and stainless steel, but I can't brew this one anywhere in the vicinity of our current projects. Cross contamination."

Matias drew back. "Huh?"

"I want to work on something gluten-free. And given grain dust can stay in the air for twenty-four hours, brewing it here wouldn't be safe."

Understanding dawned on Matias's face. "Ah, *that's* what this is about."

"It won't get in the way of my work for you," Lawson insisted.

"Never thought it would. So, where do you want to set up?"

"My sister has space," he said. "Would it be okay to take your equipment there?"

"Yeah, it's too small for us to use here. It's all yours."

"Thanks. I have new tubing ordered, along with some millet and buckwheat malts and dry yeasts," Lawson said, backing away from the brewhouse and pushing up his glasses. Getting a brewing setup for his test run had almost felt too easy, but then again, not everything in life needed to be a big struggle. Sometimes, a friend just helped out another friend. "Oh, and…don't mention it to Clara, okay? I want it to be a surprise. In case it's an utter bust."

Matias grinned. "Yeah, you got it. My lips are sealed."

"It's not a big deal. I just want to try to make something for her."

"Pretty expensive not-a-big-deal, given the specialized ingredients you're going to need."

"You're not wrong." He raked a hand through his hair. "Really, though, my interest is piqued. And it's hard to let go of an idea once I have one."

"I'm not giving you enough to do," Matias said, the corners of his mouth falling.

"No, no. You are. I'm loving Hau'oli. But you know how it is with some ideas. They're like earworms. Won't get out of your head."

"Especially when they have to do with a woman."

"Christ, don't say it like that. She's my neighbor. My *tenant*. She's helped me out a lot. I want to do something nice for her."

He passed Matias the clipboard with updated temperature readings.

His friend took it. Something knowing dawned in his expression. "If you need more help with the girls, let Violet and me know. I want to support you."

Sometimes, believing he deserved the support was hard. After everything he'd done to Matias and Violet, their willingness to let him back into their lives was a gift.

"Once the girls have had more time to adjust, I'll take you up on the offer. I'm trying to keep things predictable right now in terms of childcare—Charlotte's doing a terrific job—but in another month or two, they might be ready. Just...let me know if I'm not pulling my weight here enough."

"Dude. Don't worry about it. It's a huge transition," Matias said. "Do you want a hand with the gluten-free project? If it's something feasible, maybe we should consider it for Hau'oli."

He shook his head. "I'm still playing around with it."

And it was something special. Not for the whole world yet, only for Clara.

Chapter Eight

Clara had always enjoyed Monday nights—the tangible evidence she'd conquered the hardest day of the week. During the school year, reaching seven o'clock on any given Monday was a victory. She'd overcome the Sunday Scaries and the first-day-of-the-week sleepies and the underlying teenage bitterness about the weekend being over that she got from both her son and all her students.

Not so on Oyster Island. With working evening shifts most of the week, Sunday Scaries were no longer her reality. For one, in two weeks, when Labor Day rolled around, she wouldn't be returning to the classroom. And it had been months since she'd had to pry her son out of bed. Daniel didn't resent getting up for work, not when it meant he'd be logging diving hours, or at least making a paycheck on the days he was scheduled to work the Otter Marine Tours cash register or as one of their deckhands.

Monday night was simpler here. A cup of herbal tea and Français snoring in her lap as they shared her favorite chair on the porch, watching the color in the sky fade into a dim blue. Today, she was sipping the warm, lavender-and-chamomile blend she'd bought from Isla's shop, while enjoying the ache in her muscles she'd earned from taking on a new hike with Violet and Franci.

It gave her a few easy moments to make a mental list of the packing Daniel needed to start considering. God, he got

a frown on his face every time she brought it up. Though tonight, his smile had returned when Charlotte emerged from
Lawson's half of the duplex, the pair disappearing with Clara's
car.

He'd been a bit vague about where they were off to, but in
six weeks, she wouldn't know what he was doing on a regular
basis. She owed him the freedom, so long as he was responsible with the vehicle.

Whenever he was with Charlotte, or anything diving related, he was at his happiest.

The rest of the time? Not so much. No matter how much
encouragement she gave him, any mention of college seemed
to set him off. She didn't know how to make it better. They'd
decided on him attending a science program at the university
in Eugene over a year ago, and his school-designated bank
account from his grandparents reflected the commitment.

Her breath hitched at the back of her throat, caught by a
tight pinch.

Okay, fine. Monday night on Oyster Island *wasn't* simple,
not when it involved mentally preparing to ship her son off
to college.

Then again, the island wasn't to blame in that regard. She'd
have had to say goodbye no matter where they were.

*But had I stayed in Portland, I wouldn't be a state away
from his school.*

She shook her head at the worry. Daniel had begged to come
here for the summer, wanting to work with Archer. This had
been his choice as much as hers, no matter how badly she'd
needed a change of scenery.

And what a change of scenery it was, compared to the years
she and Daniel had spent in the suburbs since leaving Eddy's
last Coast Guard assignment. A bit isolated, sure, but the quality of people was top notch. Nor was it possible to get prettier
than the vista beyond the tree line. Waves slapped the shore.
The rhythmic *whoosh* soothed better than any white noise

machine in the world. Somewhere in the distance, a seagull called, then the more frenetic cry of an eagle.

The shriek of an almost-four-year-old girl followed.

Then a wail.

She winced. *Uh-oh.* Someone next door wasn't happy.

A crescendo of angst, as one sister joined in with the other's upset.

Speaking of leaving windows open—one must've been cracked on Lawson's side, as the volume was as if the girls were standing on either side of Clara, voicing their angst to the wind.

The part of her trained to launch into action at a child's cry urged her to dash next door and make sure everything was okay.

Not every crisis was hers to manage, though. Like her own experience with Daniel leaving, the only way forward was through for Lawson as he adjusted to being a parent.

Still, her heart hurt as the crying fit went on for what had to be five minutes, then ten, then fifteen… ·

Leaving her tea on the side table next to her Adirondack chair, she stood, and then put Français back in the house. Maybe she could knock on their door with a question of some kind, so it didn't seem like she was trying to interfere—

"Clara? Are you outside?" Lawson rushed into view, screeching to a halt on the cement walk next to her porch steps. "Oh, you are. Thank God."

"What's wrong?"

"Hair emergency. And with yours being so long, I thought you might have some wisdom. YouTube is failing me on this one."

"How can I help?"

"Well, with scissors, unless you are a miracle worker."

She followed him upstairs to the main bathroom, where a tearstained Pippa sat on the closed toilet, hugging her stuffed rabbit. A round brush protruded from a knot of frizzled hair, stuck to the side of her head right around her ear.

The second she locked eyes on Clara, the wails started up again. Harper, sitting on the floor at Pippa's feet, followed close behind.

"Oh, honey," Clara soothed.

Round brushes were the devil.

"I didn't want pigtails! Harper got braids. It's no fair." Pippa yanked at the brush.

She cringed. "Oh, no, no Pippa—let's not get it stuck more."

"When I googled it, a few pages suggested conditioner," Lawson said, standing behind her, rubbing the back of his neck. "But it didn't seem to do much."

"Let's relocate to the kitchen and try coconut oil. If you don't have any, I'll get mine."

Ten minutes later, Harper, Pippa and Lawson were sitting close to each other at the kitchen table, playing Memory with a deck of small cards printed with ocean animals in Indigenous art styles from up and down the west coast. With both girls distracted, Clara stood behind Pippa and coaxed pieces of hair out from the tangle. Keeping the twins occupied with the game seemed to be the best method for reducing Pippa's rising and falling panic.

Clara paused to allow her to take her turn. A tiny hand reached out and flipped over two cards: one otter, one orca.

"Otters are so silly in the water," Clara said. "But also fierce."

Pippa's shoulders slumped. "My cards don't match."

"Maybe next turn," Lawson said.

He flipped a card. A sea urchin. Clara had been watching, and the other one was in the far corner from where she stood. Lawson had to have mentally tracked it, too. But he reached for a card in the middle instead.

"I know where it is!" Harper crowed, reaching for the grid.

"In a sec, love." He flipped his second card. "Oh, an otter," he said pointedly. "Huh. Go ahead, Harper."

Harper chose the sea urchins and grinned.

Pippa went right for the two otters. "I did it!"

Clara glanced at Lawson, who lifted his eyebrows a fraction, a hint of *Victory is mine.*

She melted.

With Lawson and his girls in her heart, was she destined to spend the rest of her life as a puddle?

Lawson and his girls.

In her *heart.*

God, the layers there.

Stomach flipping, she teased out another strand of hair.

First, the girls. His priority, rightly. They needed so much love right now, and Clara was happy to give them some, no matter what her relationship with Lawson.

But he was there, too. With every moment Clara saw him love Pippa and Harper, she felt her grip on her control slip a bit. She had it in her grasp right now, clutching for dear life to keep him at an emotional arm's length.

If she let go, he'd fall right into place.

Or, rather, *she'd* fall. For him.

She didn't want to. He'd been clear he wanted to keep things friendly. But how much longer could she hold on?

The safest thing would be to walk away, but she was too far in with the girls to step back, now.

Another chunk of hair came free, with a little *ouch* from Pippa.

"Good job, sweetie," Clara said soothingly. "Almost done."

"No scissors," Pippa said.

"I'll do my best."

With the girls, with Lawson…

And with me. My whole focus was supposed to be figuring out what the rest of my life is going to look like.

Did getting caught up in Lawson's life mean she was losing perspective on her own needs?

Time to stop worrying. Having a healthy friend circle was going to be necessary this winter. And she had love to give—no harm in spreading it around. She wasn't getting off track, even though this wasn't what she'd expected.

Hell, part of saying *yes* this year was to welcome the unexpected.

A few more flips of the cards, and Memory was finished, with Harper and Pippa tying for matches.

Lawson looked satisfied, as if he couldn't have masterminded a better outcome.

Her own insides were surging in victory, too—only a bit of hair was tangled around the brush still.

"How much longer?" Pippa's plaintive question.

"So close. You're doing great."

"*You're* doing great," Lawson said, making eye contact with Clara.

Another surge in her belly. Nothing to do with hair.

Oof.

"One…" A tug and a twist. "Two…" A little combing out with the pick. "Three and…free!"

The brush was out. She handed it to Lawson.

"For the garbage," she teased, then took the girls' no-ouch brush and went to work on a few of the remaining knots.

"Stooooop," Pippa begged.

"A few more knots, sweetie. Though we could cut them out. They wouldn't show."

"Might be best," Lawson said.

A half hour later, she was back in her Adirondack chair with her dog curled up on his porch cushion, the vision of Lawson reading to the girls on the living room couch post–hair trauma refusing to leave her brain.

The sun was down, the birds quiet.

The screen door on the other side of the faux barrier

squeaked open and then snicked shut. Maybe he was going to sit, have his own quiet.

Footsteps on his stairs proved her wrong.

He appeared, handsome face twisted in a sheepish grin. "No panic this time. Just a big thank-you."

"It was a two-person job," she assured him.

"Yeah, that's the problem." He fidgeted with the handset of the monitor connected to the base in the girls' room. "There's only one of me."

She nodded. "That feeling can be Sisyphean."

He opened his mouth to say something, but covered it with his crooked elbow and sneezed.

"Allergy meds wearing off?" she asked.

He made a face. "Felina, one. Me, zero."

Français snorted, as if agreeing.

"I mean, it could be worse. She could be a goat."

Lawson mock shuddered.

"You didn't need to come over to say thank-you again," she said. "I figured you'd be soaking up your well-earned peace and quiet."

He rubbed the back of his neck. "I have another favor to ask, as much as I hate to impose on you again."

"Whether or not you're imposing depends on what it is." She patted the arm of the chair next to hers.

He climbed up the stairs and then sat. His feet were bare, and they tapped a nervous rhythm. He spun the monitor on the arm.

"It's just me, Lawson," she said quietly.

"There's no 'just' when it comes to you, Clara. Sometimes I suspect you're a miracle."

"That's putting a lot on a very fallible human, you know."

"Ah." He dropped his head back against the wood slats of the chair. "Good point."

"And I do know how to say no to favors. So far, I've wanted to help."

"Yeah, well… Can I braid your hair?"

She blinked and coughed. "Sorry?"

He groaned. "That came out weird."

"Okay…"

"I need to learn how to braid hair faster, so I can do more than one hairstyle in a day. Also, they keep asking for fancier types, like crowns and Dutch, and I'm clueless. I've watched videos. I can't do it without trying it. And they're too impatient to sit while I practice."

There was that melting again.

"You can use me as a guinea pig, Lawson."

A long sigh left him. "Thank you."

"All good." She could handle having his hands in her hair for a while. "When?"

"On a day where I don't feel like I've been hit by a truck," he said.

She nodded.

His hand was on the arm of the chair.

She reached over and covered it with hers.

He trapped her pinkie in the crook of his thumb and stroked.

Her breath caught. Just a thumb and her littlest finger, but it was lightning.

"Why do these things keep happening?" he murmured. "Like, I'll take food out to the barbecue, or they're in the bathroom for two minutes and I'll think 'They're going pee—what could go wrong?' and then *wham*. Disaster."

She tightened her hold on his hand. "It's parenting. It's what kids do. They try stuff. Usually, their first few ideas aren't good ones. And then they learn."

"I appreciate that's true. I also feel like I'm a fricking failure."

"Show me a parent who doesn't feel they are screwing up sometimes, and I'll give you a million dollars."

"A slight overpayment of your rent."

She laughed, then sobered. "By the time they're Daniel's

age, they're ready to go off and make all these decisions without their parent hovering over them. So don't worry—we eventually fade from relevance."

He let out a low whistle. "Deep stuff, Clara."

"Holding Daniel in my arms as a baby, I knew." Her throat filled. "A decade ago, watching *Inside Out* and bawling—I knew one day, I would be Bing Bong, fading behind him as he shot higher and farther with a trail of imagination and hope fueling his journey."

"You won't fade, Clara." He readjusted their hands to envelop hers with his larger, rougher one. "I'm miles past being eighteen and I still talk to my mom regularly."

"And did you call her regularly when you were in college?"

"I did when I needed to. And Daniel will know you're here for him when he needs you."

Had she somehow swallowed Français's tennis ball? Felt like it. She coughed, her gaze landing on the edge of the lawn. "Weeds are starting to poke up on the edge of the concrete. Want me to yank them?"

"Hey. Clara." He squeezed her hand. "Look at me."

Mustering the emotional capacity to connect with his gray eyes was beyond her at the moment. She could choke out the truth, though. "I don't want to lose him."

"We're both going through it, aren't we?"

"Yes."

"Do you know how comforting it is to hear I'm not alone in my struggles? I know the age difference between the girls and Daniel means it looks different on the outside, but on the inside, the feelings are the same. And cut yourself a break. You aren't falling short. If this time *didn't* feel like a big transition, *that* would be a concern."

He turned partway in his chair and reached his free hand to cup her cheek. Not forcing her to look at him—he wasn't pushing—but just enough pressure for her to know he was there. A supportive hug disguised as a small touch.

Concern flickered in those quicksilver irises.

"There she is," he said. "Some days, looking at you...fixes something. It's kind of undefinable. But it clicks into place, you know?"

His hand was warm, a tether to something that *didn't* feel difficult, unlike everything else. She got what he was trying to say—it was hard to explain—but when she was around him, things were *right*.

"I think I do know," she said.

A swirl of wind came off the water, tossing strands of his hair this way and that.

She brushed it off his forehead.

"I also look at you, and wonder why the hell I'm not kissing you," he said.

"An important question." She leaned closer. "But I think we already know the answer."

"Yeah. I really can't handle commitment right now."

"I know. And if I'm trying to figure myself out, getting tangled in a relationship isn't a good idea, either."

"So, no kissing then."

"*Or*, we *keep it* to kissing."

He chuckled. "I have a feeling if I kissed you enough, I'd want more."

"I already want more, in that way. But I meant no commitment. No expectations."

"I had not expected a friends-with-benefits suggestion from you, Clara Martinez."

She hadn't expected it, either. She'd honestly thought her next relationship would be something with more commitment involved. But Lawson had a good reason why he couldn't do that. So for now, she'd take him as he was, what he *could* do.

"I guess I'm full of surprises."

"Yes, yes you are."

His amazement, in that low tone...oh *God,* it turned her on. She climbed in his lap, straddling his denim-covered thighs.

His hands settled on either side of her hips, holding her in place.

Mmm, she could get used to this. "Good thing my landlord bought chairs that fit two people."

"He has his moments of brilliance." His lips trailed from her mouth to her neck, then her collarbone.

Savoring the rush, she let her head fall back. The nips along her neck were soft, careful, but with purpose, the clear need to taste and savor but also to pleasure.

She let out a gasp.

Teasing fingers crept under the hem of her untucked T-shirt, rasping against the sensitive skin above the waistband of her denim cutoffs. One brush of his thumbs, and she was melting like icing on a fresh-from-the-oven cupcake.

She shifted forward, giving in to the need for pressure between her thighs.

Now he was the one gasping, the uncontrolled breath hissing across the skin of her neck.

His hands slid up an inch. Not quite high enough to brush the undersides of her breasts, but close enough she could imagine how good it would feel. And she wasn't wearing a bra. Oh, God, he was going to notice the missing garment in about three seconds, given how quickly her nipples were pebbling from the promise of his touch.

She'd missed doing this with someone who was more than a casual date. Strong hands on her body, tempting lips pressed to her own. All made more intense by being able to read the gleam in his gray eyes.

More than *want* or *need*.

Closer to *delight*.

And having that effect on him brought a heady satisfaction.

He took one of his hands out from under the thin cotton of her shirt and speared it into her hair, claiming a hard kiss.

Her own hands were on his pecs. She let him take charge, falling under his control.

Squirming in his lap, not swallowing her needy moan. Making it clear she loved every stroke of his tongue on hers, the slow creep of his hand upward along her ribcage. The barest tease of his thumb on the curve of her breast.

He groaned. "You're not wearing a—oh, *shit*."

The world lurched. She was suddenly standing, chest pressed to Lawson's.

Somehow, he'd lifted her off him and at the same time, gotten to his feet.

Her head spun. "What's—"

"Mom?" Daniel waited at the bottom of the stairs. His cheeks were crimson. "Uh, hey, Lawson."

"Hey, man, sorry, your mom and I were just—"

"Not my business," Daniel said. His hands were raised, as if in surrender, as he sped past them without making eye contact. Français darted after him, dog tags jingling, squeaking through the door right before the screen swung shut.

"You have lipstick on your face, too, you know!" she called, embarrassment searing the back of her neck.

Lawson muttered a curse.

Clara took a deep breath. "He probably didn't see where your hand was."

"Let's hope not." Lacing his fingers together, he braced them behind his head. "Hopefully, he'll be able to look me in the eye again at some point."

She sighed and backed up to lean against the railing. The space gave her a full view of Lawson. God, he was edible. The amount of time she'd gotten to explore his shoulders and chest had been pitiful, compared to the hours the task deserved. But who knew if she'd get the chance now? Her son catching them might have made things impossible.

"It's embarrassing, but I suspect he'll live."

"Says someone who hasn't walked in on their mom making out with a new man. It's, to say the least, weird. And when it happened to me, I was twenty-six, not Daniel's age."

Lawson said it lightly, but he was also right. Her relationship with Lawson was uncharted territory, for both Daniel and herself. "I hear you. And if Daniel's upset, I'm not going to minimize his feelings, or tell him to get over it. He deserves the time to process."

"What, exactly, do you want to tell him?"

"Ugh, I don't know. No teenage boy wants to hear his mom has a friends-with-bennies arrangement. But implying we're more serious wouldn't be right, either."

He sat, not in the chair where he'd been, but on the inside arms of both of them, which were close enough together and heavy enough to be a seat. It brought him almost at eye level with her. Almost at kissing level, were she to scoot forward between his knees and finish what they'd started…

"My mom gave me some good advice when she was Vancouver with me. I was struggling to connect with the girls. Harper and Pippa were asking big questions about death, ones I'll probably never have the answers for. And Mom reminded me not to overexplain. Give little bits of information at a time, and they'll walk away satisfied with far less than my initial instinct told me to give. And I've never raised an eighteen-year-old boy, but I've been one. In this situation, less is more might be the best policy."

"Less is more," she echoed.

He stood. "Not, however, in terms of you and me, and finding time together."

She lifted a brow in question.

"I still like our original plan."

"I do, too."

He captured her chin with a hand and leaned down to kiss her. "It'll happen."

Their lips touched, only a hint of what they'd shared before.

Then he was walking down the stairs, taking her sanity with him. Once on the concrete pad, he turned and walked backward for a few steps. His tilted smile made her belly all fuzzy and wanty.

"Good luck," he said. "Text me later, if you want."

She might just do that, after she climbed Mount Awkward with her son.

She went into the house, but he was nowhere to be seen in the kitchen or living room.

Climbing the stairs, she called, "Daniel?"

Down to his shorts and towel in hand, he darted from his bedroom across the hall to the bathroom that was essentially his. "I'm going to take a shower."

"Should we talk?" she called as the door shut. "Do we need to?"

"I don't need to know anything, Mom."

"Are you sure? I figure I owe you a bit of context."

The door opened.

He was clutching his towel in both hands, knuckles bleached white and his cheeks still fire-engine red, splotches against his summer-brown skin. His complexion had always been somewhere between Clara's pale and Eddy's medium brown, but with all his diving and time on the beach with Charlotte, he was getting closer to his dad's rich shade every day.

Hell, he was looking more like Eddy by the minute.

What would her husband think, were their situations reversed? If Clara was the one who was gone, and Eddy the one who'd been walked in on? What would he do to smooth things over?

Laughter, no doubt. Love and humor had been his usual game plan.

Heart aching for what they'd lost, she tried for a light smile.

"As minimal as you can, Mom. *Please*."

"Well, it's not going to be like you and Charlotte, schmooping around all cute and blushing together."

He jammed a hand into his hair. "Yeah, uh, please don't."

"We are…seeing each other. Low-key. Not really in public, because—"

"I get it, Mom. Hooking up with the neighbor. Sweet. All good."

"You don't sound 'good.'"

"Jeez, what do you want me to say?"

"Nothing specific. I just want to make sure you feel supported while we're going through new steps—ones that might bring up tough feelings."

His hand dragged from the top of his head to cover his face. "I wasn't even thinking about Dad, okay? It was more about erasing the sight of a dude with his hand up my mom's shirt."

She cringed. "I'm so sorry."

"No worries, Mom. Honestly, I'm happy, you know? I don't like the idea of you being lonely once I'm at school."

"Thanks, honey."

His face scrunched. "I *don't* need to witness any not-loneliness, though."

"Understandable. And sorry if I made assumptions about how you were feeling."

"No. You weren't entirely wrong. Like I said before, sometimes seeing you with Lawson reminds me that Dad is gone, and it hurts. But so does diving and seeing Archer's tattoos and every time I open a bag of Cheetos. And those feelings all eventually pass. And this will too. And I'm just going to pretend Lawson had his hands in his pockets."

He backed into the bathroom and shut the door.

"I didn't know about the Cheetos. For me, it's daisies on the side of the road," she called through the barrier. "Back when I was in school and money was tight, your dad would pull over on his way home from work and pick me bouquets of them."

"I remember that." She could barely hear his words. The shower turned on. "He was the best."

"He was. And the best thing he ever did was raise you."

* * *

After a work week of long looks while passing each other in the no-man's-land hallway between the pub and the brewery, Lawson was itchy for an actual conversation with Clara. It never materialized, though. Work had them at cross purposes. Clara had been running around all week, after one of the kitchen employees had quit abruptly, leaving the pub down a set of hands.

Friday afternoon, as Lawson was in the middle of moving Matias's smaller brewing equipment to his sister's truck, he finally caught Clara alone in the hallway.

Between his time off and her happy-hour-to-close shifts this weekend, they'd be ships passing in the night again, so he jumped on what might be his sole chance to catch her while neither of them had a kid—or two—nearby. Grabbing her hand, he pulled her into Matias's office.

Before he could second-guess the impulse, he shut and locked the door.

"Lawson, I'm almost on shift," she blustered.

And yet, her hand was still in his.

"Key word—almost," he said, backing up and guiding her with him, until his calves hit the edge of the worn couch. "And I'm almost off shift. And tomorrow, while you're off, I'm going to be at my sister's working on a little project while she entertains Harper and Pippa with the four-legged gremlins. The earliest we'll cross paths will be Sunday. So give me five minutes."

"To do what?"

He sat, tugging her with him.

She landed in his lap with a noise of protest, adorably graceless. After a second, she ringed her arms around his neck.

Victory. For the first time in days, he was able to get air all the way into his lungs.

"You've been a hard woman to get hold of," he said.

"I've essentially been working two jobs." Her fingers

landed on his temple, a tiny kiss of pressure. They slid down to his unshaven jaw.

He cringed. Rough-around-the-edges was not his best look. "Sorry. The girls have been up at the ass crack of dawn the past few days and I've been putting off shaving."

"I like it."

He buried his face against her neck and nuzzled.

"Yeah, definitely like it." She delved her hand into his hair.

Happiness smacked him in the face. Man, she was perfect.

"I shouldn't like it this much at work, though," she lamented.

"Like I said, five minutes."

"Four and a half, now."

"Better maximize my time, then," he said.

He kissed her.

Pressing his mouth to hers was like entering another stratosphere. Everything supercharged. Somehow distilled down to the breath catching in her throat.

That little moan, too—

Yeah.

Earning the needy noises she made for him made up for every minute he'd spent lying in tangled sheets this week, thinking about her on the other side of the bedroom wall.

He'd considered texting her something suggestive. Decided against it—for the first few times they explored each other, he wanted to be able to see her face.

Damn, he loved her face. The glint of gold in her hazel eyes. The hint of freckles, more pronounced from the time she'd spent in the summer sun. And when her mouth was against his and he got to taste her... Perfection. Three times now he'd been lucky enough to feel her lips on his, and he could tell it was a bare scratch on the surface of what it could be.

They had the ability to combust.

Hopefully, they also had the ability to keep it about pleasure, and to keep their feelings out of it.

"You're going to make a mess of me," she said.

It tipped between a statement and a complaint, but then, how upset could she be when she mumbled it against his cheek, her hands disheveling him by the second?

I'm already a mess for you.

Except following the glimmers of temptation to let himself feel more for her would be irresponsible at best. Devastating at worst.

Nothing soul deep. Just surface. Hands, mouths, teases.

Around two more minutes of it, if he was going to stick to his promise.

"How much of a mess can I really accomplish in such a short time?" He skimmed his hands down her sides. If they weren't at work, he could go exploring like he'd done the other day, see if, like then, she'd gone without a bra.

She snorted and shifted in his lap, probably enough to notice his body's flash reaction to her closeness.

"Well, aside from that," he joked, then captured her earlobe for a second, soaking in how delicious her shampoo smelled. She hadn't been at the pub long enough for the scent of fries and gravy to cover up the cherries and vanilla teasing his nose.

"We're making things harder for ourselves. I'm going to have to work my shift while pretending I'm not thinking about you the whole night."

He stilled. "You think about me, Clare-bear?"

"*Pshhh*, I won't if you keep calling me that."

"I'll think of something more creative."

One last fleeting kiss, and then she was off his lap and halfway to the door. "Less dreaming up nicknames, more thinking of places to do this that aren't our boss's office."

She disappeared out the door, leaving him short of breath on the couch.

From the kissing.

Also, though…*boss.*

The word *chafed* sometimes.

This wasn't his office.

It could have been.

All the *could have been*s.

What would his life look like had he not walked out? Had he not created so much freaking drama and pain for him and Violet, for Matias's and his plans for a brewery...

A few months ago, during one of the conversations with Violet where they'd worked toward a new normal, they'd agreed their relationship had been headed for an end, regardless of whether he'd stayed on the island. Probably wouldn't have ended before they got married, of course, making for an even more complicated breakup.

Changing any of it might have meant Matias and Violet wouldn't have found happiness together. The fact they were expecting a child who would be very, very loved...

Lawson shouldn't have left the way he had, but acknowledging how some good things had followed his shitty decisions was getting easier.

And one of the best parts right now was getting to kiss Clara Martinez.

He planned to do it again. Often, even.

Who was he kidding? It would be hard to ever get enough of her.

Chapter Nine

Clara was finishing up with Wednesday evening SUP club, putting her deflated board in the hatch of her vehicle, stacked next to Violet's. She'd given the other woman a ride from town.

"I'm excited I managed *not* to fall in this week," she said to her passenger, who stood beside the car, wringing out her towel. "It bodes well for autumn and winter."

"Yeah, we'll hit a point in late September when the air temperature drops and sliding into the water, even in a wet suit, is a shock," Violet said, rubbing her belly. "Though I have to recommend sitting and paddling. I haven't fallen in for over a month."

Clara snorted. "Like you ever fall in. I'm not sure I'll ever be as steady as you are. You're a natural. Your balance is amazing, even while pregnant. Though I get why you want to be careful by sitting."

"I cut my teeth balancing on logs with Archer in the water out front of our house when we were kids. Our older sister always rolled her eyes at us and went back to reading her book in a lawn chair, but Archer and I used to roll anything into the water and try to stand on it. We one hundred percent proved two people can fit on a floating door. The end of *Titanic* was a scam."

"Sounds like fun." She couldn't help but picture two UV-suited girls playing on the beach, a view she'd enjoyed from her porch last Sunday. "I wonder how long Lawson will stay in the duplex, and if Harper and Pippa will get to grow up on the water."

"Hey, Clara?" Rosa Suarez, principal of Oyster Island's small elementary-through-high school, called as she closed the tailgate of her small pickup truck. She'd parked across from Clara in the gravel lot that provided access to the boat launch at Buckle Spit. "I've been meaning to talk to you."

Clara turned and smiled. "Oh? Just a sec."

She unlocked her car with the fob. Violet went to sit in the passenger seat.

"I know you're working full-time at the pub right now," Rosa said, wandering to Clara's side of the parking lot. "Will you continue in September?"

"Not sure. Matias and I need to figure my hours out soon." Hadn't seemed like something they needed to hurry on, especially since she'd been filling in some important blanks in the kitchen. She had to admit she'd missed cooking in a working kitchen, even if making meals at The Cannery was nothing like doing classroom demos.

"Any chance you have a Washington teaching certificate?"

"Not currently, but I had one eons ago. Eddy was stationed in Port Angeles for a few years, right after I finished my master's degree."

"You'd be eligible for a substitute license, then. Any chance you want to apply? We're always desperate for good substitute teachers. And the first day of school is tomorrow in our district."

Clara paused. Her first reaction was to say yes. She was used to it when it came to teaching. But it wasn't the *yes* she'd committed to this year. She rolled the possibility of showing up at the small island school. Packing her lunch in the morning. Seating plans. Lesson plans. Assessment. Taking home the stress and the worry, and having less of herself left over for the rest of her life.

She didn't regret the time and effort she'd put into her career. The impact of teaching was immeasurable.

Importance didn't require forever, though.

And yet...

"Desperate, huh?" she asked.

"Always."

Guilt rose in her belly.

She let the feeling pass before allowing it to settle.

I'm desperate, too. For new horizons.

She was here to take a break from teaching, even on an on-call basis.

Rosa tilted her head. "Clara?"

"Sorry, sorry," she said. "It should be a simple question, I know. I never like hearing a school is short staffed, but where I'm at right now, I don't think I'm the right answer to your problem."

"Ah. That's a shame." Rosa smiled kindly. "I understand, though."

"Thank you. It's hard to say no when it's something so important."

However, *noes* were as important as *yeses* sometimes.

When she got in the driver's seat, Violet was waiting with a curious look on her face.

"She wanted to hire me on as a substitute teacher," Clara said.

"Oh." Violet frowned. "You don't want to stay on at the pub?"

"I don't know if Matias wants me to," she said quietly. Talking to her boss's fiancée about it first was a bit odd.

Violet made a huffing noise. "Oh, he does, all right. So long as *you* want to. But no way will he be able to keep up with the brewery's growth *and* manage the pub *and* be a dad to this little one *and* a partner to me."

Clara's mouth twitched. "That's a lot of *and*s. He's a busy man."

"He is. You're the only one keeping him sane right now. Well, you and Lawson," Violet said, her tone turning cautious. "Would you rather have a teaching job?"

"I—" Guilt rose, along with her answer. "No, I wouldn't."

"You don't sound happy about it."

"Well, when you're a teacher, you get constant messages about how it's your vocation, and the most important thing you'll ever do, and to do it out of the goodness of your heart and don't complain about being overworked and underpaid…" She sucked in a breath and started the car. "Sorry, that's way more detail than you asked for."

Violet shook her head. "Not at all. I get why you'd feel that way."

"Thank you. The guilt over feeling done about it all is pervasive."

"How done do you feel?"

"Enough to know I'm not going back."

"Back to Portland, or back to your school?"

"Definitely not back to my school. Portland… I'll have to see come next spring. I signed a year-long lease with Lawson."

"Something tells me he wouldn't hold you to it if you were miserable."

"I'm not, though," Clara said. "The opposite, really."

Violet rubbed Clara's shoulder. "You're welcome here, you know. For as long as you want to stay."

She hoped Violet was right. It was hard to imagine ever wanting to leave.

The next morning, Clara was at the pub early, prepping all the mise en place the kitchen staff would need for lunch and dinner services.

Matias was there, too, piling fruit into the industrial blender to make a smoothie for Violet, who was out for an easy run before she caught the ferry for a day of midwifery appointments on a few of the other islands in the San Juans.

"With being in her third trimester, the home appointments must be getting tougher on her," Clara mused, straining capers from a jar.

"It's hard to get her to admit it, but yeah."

Discomfort whirled in her stomach. "Feels like it's something I should have asked her about yesterday. We drove home together, but were mainly talking about my work situation."

"Complaining about your boss, Clara?" he teased.

She snorted, then gave him a rundown of her conversation with Rosa Suarez.

He regarded her cautiously. "If you'd rather take a job at the school, let me know."

"Oh, no. I have no interest. In fact, we should talk about what the fall might look like. Lawson's sister was threatening to poach me."

"You're a valuable employee. The pub is ticking along like a Swiss clock with you in charge. And with how word spreads on the island, you're a hot commodity," he said.

Might as well be direct about it. "But we're flipping the calendar to September next week. We should decide on an end date for my 'summer job' here."

He poured the bright purple drink into a large mason jar, then screwed on a plastic drinking lid. "Violet mentioned talking to you about it. Mainly from the angle of our current sanity and future marriage. The more help, the better, in her view. And I get where she's coming from. We're both nervous."

"Don't you cut the pub's hours in the fall, though? There won't be as much for me to manage with shorter hours."

"Sure. But with the baby coming, I'm going to be at home more often. The Cannery isn't as busy from October through April, and the brewery will have minimal tasting hours, but we are going to be upping production. I'll be stretched thin between Hau'oli and home. I could rest easy if I knew the pub was taken care of."

She looked at him, not bothering to hide her confusion. "The brewery will be stressing you out? What about Lawson?"

He fidgeted. "Lawson's going to get bored not being at the helm."

"What's giving you that idea?"

Matias made a face. "He's already started to work on his own projects. I know why he's doing it, but it doesn't seem like a good sign."

"I doubt he has room to be bored right now, with how busy Harper and Pippa are keeping him." She sighed. "But if you're worried he's unhappy working for you, then *talk to him*."

"He and I talked recently."

"And what did he say?"

"That he's happy."

"So why are you worried?"

"He's said he's happy before."

Her heart sank. "Mati. It's...understandable you'd have doubts. But don't you think his situation is different enough now?"

"Maybe. Though, it's easier to stress about work than about how I'm going to be a dad in a couple months."

"Also understandable."

"Having a partner who's an expert in birth and babies is intimidating," he said.

"I bet she doesn't feel like an expert in her *own* birth. I'm technically an expert in dealing with teenagers, and yet I've never felt like I know what I'm doing with parenting."

"Aw, Daniel's a terrific kid. Sam and Archer can't say enough about him. Apparently, he reminds Archer of your husband, especially underwater."

"Yeah, Archer's mentioned that before. And your high opinion warms my soul, truly, but it's been a whole lot of trial and error on my part."

He nodded.

Violet arrived, damp running shoes squeaking on the flooring. Her ponytail was a sodden clump, stuck to the back of her neck. "Uggggh, it's gross out."

Matias wrapped her in a hug.

"I'm sweaty."

"I don't care."

"Aw, young love," Clara teased.

"Aren't you my age?" Matias asked.

"Irrelevant."

Violet poked him in the chest. "Did you finalize things for fall?"

"We were going to, but got off track."

Violet turned to Clara. "What does he need to offer you? Gold? Silver? His firstborn child?"

They all cracked up.

"Honestly, if you don't need a full-time manager during the fall and winter, I'd be happy with keeping some management tasks and taking on even more of the early-morning kitchen prep that doesn't involve tasting. It's meditative. And I have some ideas for some gluten-free recipes."

"You and Lawson both," Matias said.

Clara glanced at him. "Huh?"

Matias froze, his throat bobbing. "Yeah, we can create a workable schedule for you, if you want to keep doing any cooking you can safely do. And try whatever you like. Just let me know what to order. We could start having a rotating 'Clara's Creation' on the menu."

"I like that," she said.

Violet took a long slurp of her smoothie. "Take whatever ownership you need. We owe you."

"Maybe Lawson needs that, too, Mati," she said softly. "Not literal ownership over the brewery, but the sense he's more than an employee."

Violet and Matias shared a look.

Ugh, they had so much history, and who was she to interfere?

"Sorry. Ignore me," Clara said. "I shouldn't stick my nose in where it doesn't belong."

"Can't claim to be an Oyster Island resident, otherwise," Violet said.

She laughed.

If only it were so simple.

Lawson had been watching the brewery get busier the further they got into August. The tasting room had been full of tourists for weeks, exceeding his and Matias's estimates for seats filled and kegs sold. But with the threatening weather today, things were a bit slower despite the impending long weekend rush, enough he decided to leave his Thursday shift an hour early. He had enough time to walk home and get his car, do the grocery shopping and hit up the hardware store before Charlotte's eight hours were up.

Before someone could delay him, he snuck out the brewery's harborside door. Staying under the short overhang, he eyed the sky. The slate gray clouds were heavy with rain, and a few splotches marked the wood of the boardwalk and the russet-stained tops of the picnic tables. If he hurried, he might make it home before the skies opened up.

He strode along the boardwalk.

"Lawson! Wait up!"

God, that voice. The memory of it kept him awake at night. He glanced toward the streak of bare arms and blond hair barreling his way.

Why was Clara out in this weather in a tank top? If it started to pour, she'd be soaked. Then again, in his sweatshirt, he wasn't much better off. A hell of a day not to bring a raincoat or umbrella.

"Headed home?"

"Yeah," she said.

"Me, too. When I walked to work this morning, it was bright sunshine."

Once she caught up to him, he started walking again. She matched his strides.

"Perils of coastal life," she joked. "I was in a daze when I left the house, I guess. Didn't notice the sky until I got out of the car."

Their steps started to crunch as they hit the gravel trail along the park's foreshore.

"Left it for Daniel at the dive shop?" he guessed.

"Yeah. I took pity on him. It'll be dumping down when he finishes his dive tour." She glanced up at the sky. The flat light turned her hazel eyes a tart-candy green. "Talk about threatening clouds."

"Breezy, too," he said, stripping out of his hoodie and passing it over.

"Here I was, thinking it was still summer." She took the garment, but only hugged it to her chest. "Won't you get cold?"

"Let me be chivalrous," he said. A few drops pattered his shoulders, marking his T-shirt but not soaking through.

Her gaze was full of heat, defying the damp chill in the air. She held up the sweatshirt a little. "You're sure?"

"Very."

She pulled it over her head. It hung to midthigh on her, almost covering her running shorts. Ankle-socked feet in lavender foam Birkenstocks rounded out the look. Damn, she was adorable. Doubly so in his sweatshirt.

They entered the archway to the trail. The foliage burst green and lush from the branches of honeysuckle and huckleberry bushes, all under the canopy of the taller maples and firs overhead. The water was barely visible through the leaves. As soon as they turned a slight corner, there was only trail at their front and back.

Privacy. Just the shuffle of rubber soles on dirt, the occasional drip of rain through the leaves and the even sound of Clara's breathing. Their steps slowed, no longer rushed like they'd been when they'd crossed through the park.

"Mind if I throw Daniel a going-away thing next Thursday? I know it's late notice—he's been lukewarm about the idea—but it seems wrong not to do something."

"That is one lovesick kid, and he's not even gone."

"I know," she murmured. "I hope he'll be okay."

"He'll adjust. And if you want to have a party, go for it. Let me know how I can help."

"Thanks." Scooting closer to him, she brushed her hand against his, then laced their fingers together.

She peeked up at him, her cheeks flushed pink.

He lifted their joined hands to his mouth and kissed her thumb knuckle.

A few hundred yards into the treed trail, she glanced up at him. "You're quiet."

He tightened his grip on her hand. "We haven't managed to be this alone in a while. And I don't feel like I need to fill the silence with you. Unless you want to make small talk."

"Small talk? No."

"I'm not sure I have something more significant in me today, Clara."

They got to the end of the path, where it split into a trail to the beach or a connection to the gravel edge of the road a few blocks from their duplex. He went to take the road, but she halted, pulling him to a jerking stop.

"Are you okay?" she asked.

"I will be." If only the trail was miles long instead of hundreds of yards. Walking it with her made him feel like he was able to take a breath for the first time in a week.

"Silence is fine." Compassion softening her gaze, she wiped the hair plastered across her forehead to the side. She tilted her head toward the ocean-access path. "Come on. Let's listen to the water instead."

He shouldn't take the longer route. It was indulgent. The grocery shopping wasn't going to do itself.

Hang on.

Grocery shopping?

He was passing up time with Clara, who he'd been desperate to get alone for weeks, for an *errand*? He was out of his mind.

"I'll take the girls grocery shopping with me," he blurted.

She eyed him, brows narrowed. "What?"

"I was planning on running errands for the next hour. But I'd rather walk on the beach with you. It might invite chaos to have Harper and Pippa with me at the store, but…time with you is worth paying in pandemonium."

Her smile spread, slow and easy.

Something leaped, deep in his chest. The need he'd been suppressing for weeks, maybe. The desperation to be with *someone*, but in particular with this woman, who lit his world like a firework-show finale.

He followed her to the beach. The tide was out halfway, and unspoken, they stuck to the stretch of smaller rocks near the property lines, instead of walking farther down to where larger, slicker stones scattered the shore.

"Careful in those shoes," he said.

"You might have grown up on these rocks, but I've had practice walking them, too."

"I'd hate to see you slip, Clarey."

"Uh, can we talk about how there is no way to turn my name into a nickname that doesn't sound silly?"

"Sure. I'll stop trying to find one." But something about her begged to be called something unique. A little signal he cared for her, and that he held a special place for her, too.

A minute or two down the beach, and a raindrop smacked his forehead. Then three. Then ten.

Then a deluge.

Pigeon-gray rocks were painted dark in seconds. The air was still, the water pale and colorless like the sky, lapping against the shore. The rain sparked and danced across its surface.

The shoulders of his T-shirt soaked through.

Clara stopped walking, looked up at the clouds, and laughed, holding her free arm over her forehead. Rivulets of rain streaked over her cheeks. "This is bananas."

His shirt was already sticking to his chest. At least she had the thick layer of his sweatshirt. He pulled the hood up for her.

"It's all soaked at this point," she said.

Those luminous eyes stared through his soul. Like a portal to worlds he'd only dreamed of.

He couldn't keep fooling himself. He wasn't made for the kind of love she deserved.

Nor did he have the will to walk away.

"You look cute in a hoodie," he said with a rasp that threatened to give away all his secrets.

It wasn't about *a* hoodie. It was seeing her in *his*.

Her teeth tugged the inside of her lip. "It's like you're keeping me warm."

"Do you want me to keep you warm, Clara?"

"Yes. And my house is empty right now, unlike yours, unless Charlotte has the girls elsewhere today."

He didn't need to be told twice. He took her hand and they hurried along the beach.

About ten properties were sandwiched between the trail and his own yard, and he couldn't get past them fast enough. Modest houses blended into the evergreens surrounding them.

"You know, once upon a time, I pictured buying and tearing down one of these character homes, and building a cedar-and-glass monstrosity for Violet and me to share."

Her lifted eyebrow betrayed her puzzlement. "She doesn't seem like the monstrosity type. Nor do you, for that matter."

"One of the many ways I was clueless," he said. She needed the reminder of why their plan to keep their feelings out of this was so freaking necessary.

"Are you happy in the duplex?" she asked.

Mainly because of my cute tenant.

"It's easy to make it comfortable for Harper and Pippa. Priority number one."

"So between those champagne, new-house dreams and now, you've puzzled out a few things."

"Don't give me that much credit, Clara."

"I can give you all the credit I want. You deserve some."

His left foot skidded on a rock. Only his grip on her hand kept him from face-planting onto the beach. Why did she see things about him that weren't there?

Up ahead, the boulder on the edge of his property loomed. He wanted to slow down, savor this space of time where no one was asking anything of either of them and they could just *be*.

He also wanted to get her out of the rain. Her fingers were chilled, even in his tight grip. She'd pulled her other hand inside the sleeve of the sweatshirt. And her feet had to be freezing. Her socks looked soaked through, her sandals providing no protection.

As soon as they got to the waist-high rock the twins had deemed their "castle" to conquer, he peered through the sparse trees along the edge of the property. Movement flashed in the kitchen window on his side of the duplex.

His heart sank. "The girls are going to see me the second we step onto the lawn. No such thing as privacy once that happens."

She pressed her lips together, her gaze darting around the yard. A smile spread, softening her mouth into a tempting curve.

Tantalized, he leaned in.

Before he could steal a taste, she stepped back, eyes glinting with mischief.

"I'll go run interference. Once I'm in the house and the door is closed, head for my porch." She backed up a few steps with him in tow.

"Aye, aye," he murmured, putting his hands on her waist to turn her in the direction she'd set.

Damn, she was easy to touch. Curves for days, irresistible even through the cotton of his sweatshirt.

Maybe it was worth darting across the lawn with her, risking being spotted.

She forged an erratic trail past the thick band of logs and driftwood, over the small ridge of boulders protecting the property on days when winter-high king tides tossed angry waves against the shore.

He followed. Christ, he would follow her wherever she went.

"Stay here, behind the trees," she ordered. She kissed him. Heat built, enough that he wouldn't have been surprised to see steam rising off his wet clothes.

"Two minutes," she said, then darted up the small, stacked-log steps to the lawn. As she jogged, she stripped out of his sweatshirt. She was on his porch and knocking on the door in a flash. Two small figures answered and pulled her in.

She turned her head and winked at him before disappearing into his kitchen and closing the back door.

That was his signal. He dashed across the lawn, shoes squelching through the grass, then tiptoed up to her porch and waited, leaning a shoulder against the siding by the door.

A minute later, she strolled up the porch stairs, finger pressed to her plush lips in a silent *shh*.

She scooted next to him, hands fumbling with her keys.

The lack of his hoodie exposed so much more of her skin. He nuzzled his lips against her neck and slid a hand along her now-bare shoulder.

A desperate squeak sounded at the back of her throat. Her keys hit the doormat with a metallic clatter.

"Shh," he teased.

"Lawson," she said, his name a bare whisper. She snatched her keys off the ground and tried the lock again. "We'll get caught."

Stilling her shaking hand with his, he guided the key into the lock and turned.

Two seconds later, the door was locked behind them, and he had her between him and the door and his lips on hers.

"We're finally—" he skimmed his hands under her hips and lifted "—alone *inside*. You distracted them with my sweatshirt?"

Her fingers clung to his shoulders, and she hooked her ankles around his waist. "I told them I found it draped over one of your lawn chairs. It's hanging in the tub in the girls' bathroom."

"Do I get to peel off your tank top, since I missed taking my hoodie off you?"

"I'll be mad if you don't, Lawson."

He grinned. No other thing to do. Hell, he'd been waiting a long time for this. The very heat of her pressed against the fly of his jeans, cloaked by the thin layer of her shorts and whatever underwear she had on underneath.

He wanted to trace his fingers under her shorts to discover what fabric lay beneath more than he wanted his next breath.

Wanted to make every layer *vanish*.

He didn't trust himself to carry her all the way up the stairs like this, but he could make it to the kitchen island.

With a few short strides, he had her perched on the edge of the granite surface. He ran his hands up and down her arms.

"I think we've well established the 'friends' part of our relationship." She nipped the corner of his mouth. "But I'm so curious about the 'benefits.'"

"Benefit number one." He slid his hands under her tank, exposing inches of stomach, then a sliver more, and oh *man*, a peek of pale flesh through navy blue lace.

Her shirt hit the floor with a wet slap.

"One that you need, too," she said, tone hitching. "You're more drenched than I am."

Her fingers snuck along the waist of his jeans, then eased off the wet cotton of his T-shirt and dropped it on the counter.

Appreciation flashed in her gaze as it drifted along his chest.

He bent his head, kissing her collarbone.

The cleft at her throat.

The shadowed valley between her breasts, right above the tiny bow on the strip of fabric joining the cups.

Her head fell back and her back arched, inviting his mouth to drift, to travel. He licked a hot stripe through her bra, the lace soft against his tongue. *Goddamn.* Her nipple beaded under the material.

She whimpered, driving her hips forward against his. Her fingers fumbled with his belt buckle.

"Hey," he said. "Wait."

She frowned. "No? I thought—"

"You thought right. But unless we want to end up like Violet and Matias, we need a condom. I don't have one in my wallet."

"Good. I think we're old enough to know latex degrades," she said. "I have some in my room."

He backed up a step and helped her slide off the counter.

Eyes bright, she took his hand and led him up the stairs, to the room at the end of the hall.

He knew which one was hers, but he'd never seen it with her furniture or decor in place. She'd asked to paint, but he hadn't asked what color she'd chosen.

He paused in the doorway for a second, taking in the whimsy of Clara's choices. Pink the same shade as Pippa's ballet slippers on the walls. A plush scattering of chocolate-colored velvet throw pillows. The same white wood blinds he'd installed in all the windows of both sides of the duplex, but with beige raw silk swags draped over a silver curtain rod. The silky looking comforter was striped in the same pink and pale brown, like Neapolitan ice cream.

Her mouth tilted as if she was uncertain of his reaction. "I need a bright, airy space to sleep."

"It's delicate. I don't want to make a mess of your bed with my wet jeans."

"Then take them off." She went back to his belt buckle, her hands steadier than they'd been downstairs.

Damn, he'd have to up his game, get her all shaky and out of breath again.

He kissed her, a leisurely pass across her mouth. A tiny lick to the seam of her lips, and she opened for him. The taste of her flooded his senses.

When his jeans dropped to his knees, he stepped out of them awkwardly, not wanting to take his mouth off hers to undress with more finesse. He eased her back against the bed, then peeled the comforter back. It only took a second to deal with her shorts and his socks.

The sight of her creamy skin against sheets a shade or two darker, more of that sweet vanilla, made his mouth water. Her body was *lush*, soft and pliable under his hands.

And her hair... It was still damp, but little curls escaped the braid, teased by the weather and his fingers.

He was a lucky man. No way was he leaving this room without tasting more of her, so long as she was willing.

"What do you like, Clara?"

"I like you in my bed. I like your mouth on mine. Your tongue on my nipples. I bet it's good in other places, too. If... if you're into that."

"Baby, any man who isn't into getting you off with his mouth isn't worth your time."

She made a raw, needy sound. It made him as hard as the damn bedpost.

He smirked at her as he lowered his way down her body. "I take it that's a yes?"

"Yes, *please*."

"Mmm, let's see if I can make you forget your manners."

He might not be worthy of her heart, but he had dwindling minutes left to bring her pleasure, and he'd use every second making her writhe and melt.

Chapter Ten

The soft colors of her room blurred. Heat blazed along Clara's skin. Gripping handfuls of her sheets, she arched her hips toward the promise of being shattered and reshaped.

Lawson knew *exactly* what to do with his tongue.

His fingers, too.

His masterful employment of both was fuzzing out the edges of her existence. And his hair, so soft between her fingers as she toyed with the strands. The silky sensation tethered her to reality.

A swirl of his tongue coaxed a bottomless ache in her belly. He stroked a finger around her wetness. The hint of a rasp on his fingertip…

She gasped.

"Clara, honey, those noises are going to be the death of me."

The desperation in his tone matched hers. His intent must, too—this was going to end with her in pieces.

She bit her lip. "If you want me to stop…"

Two fingers thrust into her, as if he had all the time in the world.

The neediness in the sound at the back of her throat verged on embarrassing. She bit her lip and tried not to grind against his face.

Her body was moving of its own accord, though.

"Does anything—" another languid rasp of fingers against

her inner walls "—I'm doing here make you think I want you to respond *less*?"

She gave him a blissed-out grin. "Just checking."

"I want you wild." He withdrew his fingers, then pressed a kiss against the empty, wanting craving he left behind.

His tongue thrust in, making tiny circles.

Small. Yet utterly *ruinous*.

The world glitched, a hitch in time, a shift so deep it rippled the fabric of her existence.

Something infinite weighed down her limbs. She gasped and fell into the spiral of white.

Seconds of erratic heartbeats, *her* heartbeat, out of control, setting the rhythm for the buzzing in her ears and the waves of pleasure ebbing in her veins.

"What was that?" she rasped.

Lawson lifted his head and rested his weight on an elbow, then dipped a kiss to her thigh. Tousled hair fell across his forehead, framing an expression so smug she would have flicked him on the nose, were she capable of movement.

"Well, Clara, when a boy likes a girl, sometimes he decides to give her a kiss somewhere very cheeky and—"

"You know what I meant," she grumbled.

Her heart squeezed. What he was clearly wanting from this—pleasure, some fun—fell far short of the intensity still singing along her limbs.

Wild was tempting.

But did she know how to let go like that without feeling more?

Because she'd just let go. Reached toward the indescribable.

And she'd let something out that couldn't get boxed up.

She aimed for a sexy smile, but it wobbled.

The sliver of arrogance slipped from his gaze and he shifted up the bed.

"Are you okay?" he asked.

"What's there not to be okay about?" she said.

"Any number of things. If you've changed your mind—"

"I haven't." She pressed her lips to his. He tasted like her, like her pleasure. "My world shook for a few seconds."

"You sure know how to build a man's ego."

"Mmm, yes, that's why I dragged you up here," she said dryly. "To give you a confidence boost."

He stilled.

A hint of vulnerability flashed behind the cocky light in his eyes.

Oh.

Oh.

Did he need assurance?

Threading her hands into both sides of his hair, she pulled him in close. "I'm really glad you're here, Lawson. I love how you make me feel. And I want to feel it together. The world shaking you gave me."

He smiled into the kiss.

She reveled in the weight of his body, the thickness of his erection against her thigh. She did love how he made her feel, and even more, the evidence of him wanting this, too. His hands were everywhere, tender and possessive.

"Condom?" he murmured.

"Nightstand." She reached a shaky hand to the side, but he beat her to it, then sheathed himself.

"Not that I *want* to rush…" His kissed his way along her neck, her collarbone. Another breath, and his mouth brushed one of her nipples, hard against the dampness of his tongue.

A wordless plea choked her.

"We can't take forever, though," she said.

"This time."

He settled between her thighs, the thick head of him sliding along her slick flesh.

The yawning stretch built, like taffy pulling and folding between them. Tempting and sweet.

"You're so sure we're going to do this again another day?"

she said, sliding her fingers from his hair to the taut muscles of his shoulders. If he slipped the tip of his arousal up another inch, she'd be gone—

"Only getting to taste you once would be one of life's biggest disappointments, Clara."

He gazed at her, an eyebrow lifting in a silent, golden question as he nudged inside her.

She nodded. "Please."

He groaned, swearing as he thrust forward, his forearms resting on the pillow on either side of her head. The soft hair on his chest grazed her breasts.

"Never mind. I don't want you to stop with the manners."

"What, they work for you?"

"Too much."

She mouthed a path from his mouth to the soft skin by his ear.

"I'll remember that when I'm feeling ungovernable," she whispered.

He finally moved, withdrawing with ease, sliding forward like he'd been put on this earth to tease her until she lost the tether on her existence.

"As if…" A hand shifted, settling over her breast. His thumb dragged a heavenly half circle around the tight bud, a thread tugging low.

"What?" she said, struggling to form the word.

"You're a constant threat to my sanity."

No complaint rang in his tone.

Just awe. And care.

His gaze was too much. She let her eyes fall closed.

Their bodies, hands and instinct, and reaching for the gestalt of it all, the sum being so, so much greater than what it should be, what she wanted it to be—

"*Clara.*"

His back muscles grew rigid under her fingers.

"I'm close, too." Reaching a hand between them, she touched herself, closing the last bit of distance—

"Come again, baby," he begged. "Please."

She came.

He followed with a groan that probably carried through the wall.

But her ears weren't working again, and the world was fuzzy and wispy, so who knew if she was hearing anything right?

Tender, tiny kisses trailed along her cheek.

"Thanks for inviting me over," he mumbled.

There was no "I wish I could stay."

No "I think we should be more."

She'd agreed to limits. Didn't mean she didn't want to see him all the time, just the same.

"How about you practice on my hair after dinner?" she asked.

"Yeah, I'd love that."

There wouldn't be another chance to be close like this tonight, but at least it was something.

"I don't think it goes there, Uncle Sonny," Pippa said solemnly.

Silky ribbons of hair draped between the pointer and middle fingers of each of his hands, but even he could see they were not crossed in the right direction.

Plus, he had the most observant audience on earth for his hairstyling lesson.

The girls were sitting at the table, each munching on a bowl of strawberries Clara had picked from the everbearing plants in her raised, net-covered garden bed.

No, technically my garden.

Well, ours. He sighed. *It's totally hers.*

She was the one who'd cleaned it up and made it thrive.

But she wouldn't be able to take it with her when she went back home to Portland before next summer.

"You sound stuck," Clara said gently. "I wish I could see what you're doing."

Yeah, I'm stuck, all right. On what to do about you.

"I must be doing it backward."

Not that he minded struggling a little. Any time with his hands in Clara's hair was well spent. And as much as he wanted to get better at braiding for the sake of making the girls happy, his pride didn't need the boost of being a natural.

"Here." She held up her phone for him and played the video again. She had it slowed down to half speed, and he tried to keep up with the movements that should have made the inside-out looking Dutch braid.

Key words: should have.

He groaned.

"It's a French braid," Pippa announced.

"Alright, you," Clara chided. "If you're going to give your uncle a hard time, you need to be the one in the chair."

His heart sank. Clara watching him would likely help, but he hated the loss of the ribbons of pale blond against his fingers.

Pippa stuck her lip out. "I want to watch."

"I will do it!" Harper sprang to her feet, smiling sweetly at her sister.

Clara stood and let his niece take the seat, looking like Felina if she'd deign to come out from under the couch to catch a canary.

"As if this exact activity isn't a battle on every other day," he whispered to his exceedingly patient teacher.

She snorted and stood in front of him.

Damn, she smelled like heaven. The warmth of her back against his front reminded him of every second they'd spent in her bed a couple of hours ago.

Annnnd enough of that, Thorne.

"All right, hair in three chunks," he narrated as he picked up equal-sized pieces off the top of Harper's small head.

"Yes, and then under and to the middle."

He followed the direction.

Clara nodded. "I assumed that's where you'd gone wrong. The *other* under, champ."

Holding her hands over his, she fixed his mistake.

And then, because it felt too good to have an excuse to have her hands over his, he let her guide him through the whole braid.

Grab hair, under, middle. Grab hair, under, middle.

He affixed the elastic to the end and admired his progress. "A little cockeyed, but not too shabby. You are a great teacher."

"I had an eager student," she said in a tight voice. Her shoulders went more rigid with every word.

Hmm. Bending to her ear, he whispered, "Can I try yours again, now?"

"I should probably—"

"I want one!" Pippa announced.

Clara scooted away from him. "That's my cue to head home."

He barely kept himself from reaching out a hand to her. "But—"

"It's time for the girls' bedtime anyway, right? They'll need your full attention."

"Yes. They do," he said.

Thank God she was there to remind him.

After the brilliant time they'd had this afternoon, and seeing her easily manage the girls, he was liable to start dreaming of ways to try to parent *and* be with Clara.

"You're going to put the goats off their milking," Isla announced, coming up from behind Lawson and startling the crap out of him.

"What the hell?" He gave himself a shake to regain his equilibrium. Without steady hands, he'd risk spills when he transferred his experimental wort from the kettle into the fermenter. Hopefully, the yeast would do its magic like he predicted, and would transform into something beautiful. Working with sorghum, buckwheat and millet wasn't his norm, but he had a hunch the nutty-smelling wort was going to turn into something interesting, if not downright delicious. And if this recipe didn't work, he had two more he planned to try, filling Matias's three smaller fermenters over the next week or so. He was going to play with the grain ratio, and also with adding molasses and cacao nibs.

His life was overflowing with beauty, from the two little girls playing with Play-Doh on a kid-size table in the corner of the room, to the growing sense of closeness with his sister, to the fraction of a day he'd spent with Clara yesterday.

"You're humming," Isla said.

"Since when is your barn a hum-free zone?" he griped, waiting for his pulse to drop back below cardiac-event levels.

She hitched a hip on the stainless-steel table he'd appropriated and crossed her arms. "Oh, no. Hum away. Especially when it's the *Sesame Street* theme. I'm always here for Muppets."

"That wasn't what—"

Okay, fine, it was. He couldn't get it out of his head.

Couldn't get *Clara* out of his head, either. He could still feel her curves under his hands, her breath against his ear, her words...

God, her *words*.

The woman wove a spell he couldn't counter.

One short hour in her bed, followed by an hour with his hands in her silky hair, and he couldn't tell up from down.

"Can I have your spent grains?" his sister asked, jarring him from reliving one of the best hours of his life.

"Huh?"

She pointed at the plastic tub where he'd discarded his

spent millet and buckwheat. "Can I have it? I could feed it to my chickens."

He blinked, surprised he hadn't thought to offer her any of the by-product from Hau'oli before. Farmers often fed left-over brewer's grains to livestock and chickens. "Sure. Help yourself."

"Are you going to make me be the first tester for your beer, given you're making it in my barn?"

He paused. "It truly is a test situation."

"You don't think it will work?"

"I do. I trust my research, the advice I got, my recipe... It's rare for something to be perfect on the first try, though. I mean, how many times have you tweaked your cheese recipes?"

"Never," she said impishly. "I always get them right on the first go."

"Right, of course." He raked a hand through his hair. "It's crucial I get this one right."

"Because you're all of a sudden super passionate about serving the needs of the gluten-sensitive community." Her voice was as dry as the hop pellets he'd added during the boil.

He ignored her, focusing instead on what Clara's face might look like if he got this right. Her smile had the power to shift the tides.

"Look at you, grinning like a fool. That is not your beer-making smile, Lawson. That's your I-kissed-a-girl-and-I-liked-it face."

He rolled his eyes and began pouring the wort into the fermenter using the spigot on the bottom of the kettle. Man, playing around with recipes on a smaller scale was fun.

Isla lifted her water bottle to her lips, then froze. She leaned in. "You had sex."

He blinked. "And that's news?"

"Yes," she said between clenched teeth. "Trust me, over the years it took me to decide neither sex nor romance are for me, I've spent a lot of time thinking about how intimacy can change and complicate a relationship. So when you're banging your *friend*, yeah, it's news."

Lifting an eyebrow, he continued to monitor the flow of rich, brown liquid. Ever since his sister had come out as asexual and aromantic, he let her take the lead whenever sex and connection entered a conversation. He wanted to respect any boundary he might not be aware of. "How much do you want to know?"

"I don't need the details, but I do like the idea of you being happy."

"And I'm not sure happiness would be the result. I doubt it would be, in fact. If I start dating someone, especially Clara, it will disrupt what I have going on with the girls, Isla."

"Or maybe having a girlfriend will mean your own well is fuller, and you'll have more to give Harper and Pippa."

He clenched his hands. "Clara's not an emotional prop."

"Of course not. But she has her own burdens. Just…share your lives. You already are in some ways."

"The last time I…"

She waited, then corrected, "You didn't. Not with Violet. You didn't share."

"Yeah, no kidding," he murmured, then remembered there were four little ears in range. Harper's tiny hawk gaze latched on him like she was taking notes for a courtroom transcript.

"So make different choices this time."

He sighed. "It won't last forever. With Daniel attending college in Eugene, I'm sure she'll move back to Portland after her leave is up."

Would she even be interested in something short-term? Somewhere between expecting forever and messing around as friends? Because the first seemed impossible, but the second already didn't feel like enough.

Could I ever be enough for her?

"I thought she wasn't going back to teaching," Isla said. "I wasn't kidding when she and I were talking about her taking on some tasks around here."

"She's poking her fingers in a half dozen pies," he said. "Trying things out, I think. But she's not moving here forever."

His sister scrunched her face, clearly unconvinced.

"Let's say I 'make different choices...'"

How, when he didn't trust himself not to walk away again? She stilled. "You can, you know."

His throat was full. "But with Violet..."

She glanced at the girls and came closer. "Tell me this. Are you going to do to them what you did to Violet?"

"Of course not," he spat out. "I love them. They're mine. And I'm theirs."

"So maybe you'd be able to love someone else, too," Isla said.

"You think it's so easy as juggling everything going on?"

She snorted. "Of course it's not easy. And choosing to live alone, and to focus on loving family and friends and kids and pets—that's fine. It works for me. But Law... All signs point to you preferring to be part of a pair."

"*Argh*. Clara's impossible not to want."

Maybe she'd be up for something a bit more...involved. Short-term, of course. But being open about what seemed like their real connection. Stuffing his heart into a box all the time wasn't going to work.

The stubborn organ clamored for immediate answers, but this conversation required more thought. Clara didn't need to be distracted by this while she was juggling all the packing and party-planning tasks involved in Daniel's departure.

After she got back from taking her son to college in a couple of weeks, he'd broach the subject. Hopefully, she'd be willing not only to hear him out, but to wade a little deeper together.

Chapter Eleven

Food to be barbecued? Check.

Tables set out? Check.

Ogling of landlord's shoulders while he hangs string lights from the eaves to the gazebo and around the fanciful wood structure? Check.

That last one wasn't technically on her list.

The amount of time she'd spent doing it suggested otherwise, but...

Focus. Focus on Daniel.

She'd have months to herself soon. For now, she'd keep her eyes and hands *off* Lawson.

Tonight was the chance to remind Daniel he still had a home base, even if it wasn't the same one they'd shared while he was in high school. Their life on Oyster Island wouldn't be forever, but for while they were here, it was good. Sometimes she wondered if Daniel loved it even more than she did.

He was leaning his whole self into the *bitter* of the *bittersweet goodbye.* She'd thought he might end up in tears this morning as he headed off for his last shift at Otter Marine Tours. Hopefully, she'd get the chance to check in with him before the party got underway. Might not be possible, though, given he was getting a ride home with Sam and Kellan, who were on the guest list.

Lawson climbed down from his stepladder and put his

hands on his hips, then stared at his finished project with a critical eye.

She busied herself with arranging the cornhole set, pretending she hadn't been taking advantage of his perfect glutes being at eye level while he descended.

"Are the lights high enough, do you think?" he asked.

Weatherproof strings swooped across the space where she'd set up the tables. When she'd checked with Lawson to make sure he was okay with a party in the backyard, he'd offered to put up more lighting. She'd suggested ordering bulbs similar to the vintage-looking ones Matias had in the tasting areas at the brewery.

"I think it looks perfect. We'll have to wait for the sun to go down to see what kind of illumination magic is in play, but my guess is the amber-tinted bulbs were the right choice," she said. "It'll make our cozy backyard a bit fanciful. The girls will love it."

He stared at her like she'd said something off base.

Had she? She'd given a compliment, affirmed they'd chosen the right option, called the backyard cozy and fanciful—

Oh. Not the *backyard. Our backyard.*

She winced. "*Your* space, I mean. Not ours."

He glanced around, from where the girls were having a tea party in their plastic playhouse to the flowers she'd been babying in planters all summer to the produce bursting in her fruit-and-veggie plot. "No? You don't see your imprint on it?"

"Doesn't make it mine. Or mean we have something shared."

Pressing his lips together, he gave her a long look. "What do I need to do to make you feel like it's yours, too?"

"You don't need to do anything. It's my reset year. I'm like a transient orca, swimming by for a season of my life," she teased, thinking about the pod of impressive animals that dipped and dove into coves around the island in late spring and summer. She was still super jealous Daniel had seen them last month. Maybe she'd manage to spot the pod before it moved on to warmer waters in a few weeks.

He blew out a breath, making his lips puff. "Right. Fair."

It didn't quite seem like he believed what he was saying. "Did I say something wrong?"

"No, not at all. If anyone understands needing to reset, it's me. Not that your reasons for doing so are anything close to what mine are, of course. You…you don't need to prove anything to anyone."

"Hey." She stepped close, ringed her arms around his torso and hugged. A real one, seamless, her cheek to his chest and her head under his chin and her palms flat, one over a shoulder blade and one by his waist.

He paused for a second, as if catching up, then returned the embrace.

"What's this for?"

She kept holding on. "I'm not going to tell you how to wrangle your demons. You have to take it on the best way for you. But in terms of me? You don't have to prove a thing."

"You weren't here before, Clara." One of his hands cupped her head and the other banded her shoulders, holding her to him like the hug was giving him life. *"Then."*

"Which means I get to decide you matter to me based on who you are now."

"I'm still the same person."

"Yes, and no. Parts of us stay consistent throughout our lives. But sometimes life-altering things happen. And we can sure as hell learn how to make better decisions over time. So you aren't the exact same as you were. If you were, Lawson, you wouldn't be on Oyster Island. You'd still be in Vancouver, working for Mill Plain and hiding from the people who matter most."

He pressed his lips to the top of her head.

As much as she hoped the hug was comforting him, it was doing the same for her, warming a few of the icy spaces that were expanding and cracking inside her as she got closer to Daniel's departure date.

"At least I can support you today. I know this is a huge time for you and Daniel," he said, giving her another kiss and then releasing her. He stepped backward and shoved his hands in the pockets of his shorts. His face wasn't blank, but it was guarded.

Time for distance, then.

"What's next?" he asked.

She scanned the yard. Chairs were in place, tables and games, too. "I'll wait until everyone starts to arrive to bring the food out, so for now, we're done."

A hint of mischief glinted through his measured expression. "Up for a game of cornhole while we wait?"

"You don't know what you just opened yourself up to. I am going to wipe the lawn with you," she boasted. "But sure."

She proceeded to hand him his ass for two-thirds of a game, until Pippa and Harper clamored over and asked to join in. Lawson and Clara each teamed up with a twin and coached them through some spectacularly cockeyed throws, until Daniel, Sam and Kellan arrived.

"Welcome!" she called out before turning to the girls. "I'm going to need to cut the game short, okay?"

They nodded, lower lips puffing out in matching pouts.

"I'm going to shower, Mom," Daniel said over his shoulder, darting into the house. "I'll be quick."

Daniel's boss and his chef fiancé each toted a giant tray of delicious-looking food. Through the plastic wrap, she caught sight of clustered mason jars and ramekins—one tray weighed down with glossy dips, and strips and sticks of veggies, the other a dessert board with what looked like various types of chocolate and caramel sauces, and marshmallows. Also, though, pretzels, wafers and cookies. Damn. She'd have to avoid that one. They'd asked if they could bring something, and they knew she was celiac. She'd figured Kellan might do the math.

However, it was Daniel's party, not hers, and Kellan wasn't obligated to serve everything for her. She'd live. She had her own platter of GF cookies. Between the burgers with her own buns, and the french fries she planned to cook in batches, there was plenty to eat.

The pair put their offerings down on one of the large tables. Kellan started fussing with the layers of plastic wrap. He caught Clara peering at the dessert platter.

"All safe for you to eat, love. I played with a variety of flours and starches and I'm rather chuffed with the results. Of course, you'll be the best judge."

"*Oh.* I'd assumed they weren't gluten free," she said. "I'm used to people not knowing what works and what doesn't. I don't usually ask people to bring anything, quite frankly. Easier for avoiding cross contamination. You doing all this is amazing."

He looked at her, eyebrows raised. "It's your house. I'm not about to bring something that'd make you ill, like."

"Thank you so much." She gave him a huge hug and scanned the tray again. "Did you make the marshmallows by hand? We'll have to compare recipes. I used to have my classes make them during the holiday season."

They chatted about kitchen tricks and tips. Kellan gave her a hand ferrying out some of the food from her own kitchen, and took on setting up the deep fryer for when she started crisping the batches of fries.

"Wait. *Wait*," Kellan enthused. "You have to come foraging for chanterelles with me. I've been making a map of all the places I think will be rife with them as soon as we get a bit of rain. I have a whole plan for a wild mushroom gravy to serve on a special poutine on my next pub night."

She smiled. Foraging was an easy *yes,* especially if it meant a Kellan-special poutine on the last Friday of the month.

"Name the date and time," she said.

"Oh, it's on. I've been wanting another minion—I mean, assistant—all season, given how solidly Forest and Brine has been booked this summer."

"I live to be a minion. Banana!" Laughing, she scooted inside the house. She was about to call for her son when voices carried from the living room to the back of the house.

"How can I be sure?" Charlotte's voice sounded wet and pleading. "You'll be back when, Veterans Day? Or Thanksgiving?"

Daniel's girlfriend must have come in through the front door. Her chest tightened for her son. Growing up, learning how choices and sacrifices had to be made, was always hard. Not that she thought his relationship was doomed. She and Eduardo had certainly been young. They'd spent numerous stretches of time away from each other because of Eddy's Coast Guard service.

"Thanksgiving. It's too far for only a three-day weekend." Daniel sounded equally raw. "You think I'm happy to be leaving? I *love* you. Being away from you is going to *suck*."

"Nic broke up with me because he didn't want to do long distance. What if you get there and decide the same?"

"I won't," her son vowed. "You know I don't want to leave. I'd rather be here, together. Finish up my required dives and start working for Sam full-time. But I promised my mom I'd go. And Archer always talks about how proud my dad would be that I'm going."

Clara flinched, both at his unhappiness and at her own eavesdropping. She let the back door slam shut. "Daniel, honey, are you in here? Your friends arrived."

He swore just loud enough for her to hear, then said something in a low voice.

Clara passed through the kitchen and stuck her head into the living room. Her son was in shorts and flip flops. He hadn't put on a shirt yet. He held Charlotte to his chest, much like how Lawson had been embracing Clara not that many minutes ago.

"Everything okay?" she asked.

"Yeah, Mom."

A lie.

Charlotte scrambled back, wiping her eyes. "Sorry."

"For hugging?" She waved a hand. "Goodbyes are hard. I get it. Daniel's dad and I—we had years where we were apart for months at a time, especially when Daniel was small and his dad was lower rank. I won't minimize the difficulty. But we did manage. And you two will, too."

Charlotte's mouth wobbled.

Daniel's eyes narrowed. "Were you listening, Mom?"

"Bit hard not to hear, Daniel. But I didn't catch much."

Just enough for doubt to settle in her heart.

He grabbed his T-shirt off the arm of the couch and pulled it over his head. "We'll be out in a second."

"You bet. I'll go show your friends where the soda cooler is."

She held in a sigh as she retrieved a few last condiments from the fridge and headed outside, her chest aching as she ferried her load to the food table.

If her son had any intention of not being a committed boyfriend, he wouldn't string Charlotte along. But college had the potential of being such a wonderful experience—he'd been talking about going to Oregon State for years. However, she didn't want him to feel like he was leaving half of his heart behind on Oyster Island.

She glanced at Sam and Lawson, who'd been joined by Archer and Franci.

Maybe more than half his heart, given how passionate he is about diving.

God, it was one of those nights where she ached for Eduardo. He would know what to say to Daniel. And he would have agreed college was the right path for their son, even though it meant some sacrifices. She knew that to the bottom of her heart. After Daniel had been born and she and Eddy had made sure they had food on the table and a safe roof over their heads and clothes on their bodies, the very next priority had been for Clara to finish her education. Eduardo had been her loudest cheerleader and the first person in her corner.

He also would have loved to be standing on this lawn, shooting the breeze with his best friend. He would have been endlessly amused by how hard Archer had fallen for Franci. Probably would have gotten all moony over Archer and Franci's baby, too. Clara could almost hear his voice, jokingly harassing her about having a second child after everyone went home, even though they'd always known one kid was the right choice for their family.

"Hey. That's a long face," Lawson said, coming up to her.

She'd been so lost in her own world, she hadn't even noticed him drift away from the other group.

"Being maudlin," she admitted.

"About Daniel?"

"Eddy, actually. I'm having one of those nights where I wonder what life would be like if he were here." What was the point in hiding it? If he couldn't handle knowing she'd always love her late husband, he wasn't worth her time.

Lawson nodded thoughtfully.

"I bet he was a hell of a guy," he said. "Might not have thought much of me, though."

She snorted. "It's impossible to do the math on that. Don't bother."

He shot her a relieved smile.

"I don't have to guess at how he would have felt about me moving on, though. He and I discussed it. A few times."

His eyebrows rose. "After the accident?"

"No," she said quietly. "Things were so chaotic after the explosion. I didn't talk to him in the following hours. Doctors told me he was showing signs of the bends about an hour after surfacing, and soon after, he had his heart attack. Never… never regained consciousness."

A lump formed in her throat. She didn't always cry when talking about it, but her emotions were close to the surface tonight.

Lawson held out his hand, and she took it. "Losing him had come up before, then?"

"Yeah. Part and parcel with being in the armed forces. And let me tell you, he was very clear that if he died, I should sleep my way out of my grief."

Lawson's spit take of his beer sprayed out at least a yard. He let go of her hand to wipe his chin, then gaped at her.

She chuckled. "He was kidding. Sort of. But I've never felt like I can't move on because I'll be doing him wrong in any way. I know a lot of people do feel that way—it came up in my grief group a number of times—but I was thirty-four when he passed. I knew I'd want company at some point."

"And for whatever reason, you picked me," he said lightly.

"One hundred percent because of the way you twisted your tongue," she deadpanned.

"My foolproof strategy."

"May also be my wild enjoyment of your company." On that, she was completely sincere.

He rubbed the back of his neck. "You're going to make me blush."

"I hope so." She aimed for teasing again. "Get you back for how quickly the tongue thing made *me* blush."

He leaned in. "You more than blushed, baby. You begged."

With a wink, he walked away.

Her jaw dropped.

She certainly turned pink.

Nearly begged again.

Smarten up. Still not the thing to focus on in the middle of a party.

She got busy at the grill, feeding everyone, enjoying the

company. Daniel perked up, goofing around his friends. The party was of those perfect gatherings where the crowd mimicked the setting sun, growing brighter as it sank toward the horizon. Then, people slowly drifted away as the light faded, until the only glow was from the string lights overhead, the rising quarter moon and the sated stragglers clinging to their good time. A core of people remained, relaxed and full of good food, chilling in the circle of chairs. A few of Daniel's friends, including Charlotte, were lounging on the wooden benches ringing the inside of the gazebo, but Daniel himself sat next to Lawson in one of the Adirondacks they'd brought down from the porches. The two were deep in conversation. Clara was catching snippets of it. Lawson seemed to be talking up his own college experience. Daniel was drinking it in.

"I'll be down your way at the end of October," Lawson told Daniel.

Really? For what? Clara put down the tray she'd been about to clear from the depleted food table and made her way over to the pair. She hitched a thigh onto the outside arm of Lawson's chair.

Looking up at her with a grin, he put his arm around her and settled his hand on her hip.

"What's this about being in Oregon next month?" she asked, making sure she sounded curious, not concerned.

"Oktoberfest in Salem," he said, lifting his beer. "Friend of mine is on the organizing committee and a space opened up. Matias and I weren't sure about accepting the invitation—he can't leave the island then, with Violet being due right after Halloween. But I talked it over with Isla. We figure the girls are ready for me to be gone for a weekend. And Hau'oli is certainly ready to get some attention."

She nodded. "Sounds like a good opportunity."

"I hope so. I'm eager to do this for Matias." He glanced at Daniel. "You know, if you ever needed chemistry-related job experience, once you're twenty-one, a brewery would be a good place to get some. Or if you run into any issues with your introductory science courses, you could text me. Sam or Archer would be the experts on marine biology, but I have the chem and physics and math covered."

Daniel nodded. "Thanks, Lawson."

Her heart squeezed happily, both at seeing her son receptive to positive messages about school and at Lawson taking on a mentoring role of sorts. From Archer, who'd left with Franci and Iris a couple of hours ago, to Sam and Kellan and Matias, her son had no shortage of positive male role models on Oyster Island.

She and Daniel had found the summer adventure they'd both been hoping for. But even more than that, they'd found something a whole lot like family.

"It's...not huge," Daniel said, sitting on the edge of his freshly made bed and glancing across the three feet of space to the desk, built-in shelf and tiny closet on the other side of the room.

"Perils of lucking out and getting a single." Clara started pulling books out of the bag they'd put on the desk. They'd gone to the bookstore earlier and loaded up on his first semester's pile of assigned reading, plus the extra materials he'd need for the enrichment course he'd start on Monday.

"Leave it, Mom. I'll decide where I want books and posters and crap to go later."

"At least let me get your bathroom caddy organized."

"I'm not ten on my way to summer camp. I'll remember to wash myself, I promise."

"Wear your shower shoes," she mumbled.

He lifted an eyebrow.

Not hard to interpret *that*. One eyebrow and multiple meanings.

Thanks, Captain Obvious.

You're hovering.

I want to be alone.

"I was on the swim team for like, a decade. I know how to deal with a shared bathroom."

Despite the room being cramped, he looked small, hunched forward with his elbows on his knees.

He hadn't even needed to "borrow" milk crates from behind some unsuspecting grocery store. Isla had passed along four for him to use. By next week, he'd have them unpacked and would be using them to jack his bed up to create some space underneath it where he could stash sneakers and his ball hockey gear. No doubt some dirty laundry, too, like any self-respecting eighteen-year-old boy.

"I'm going to call Charlotte," he said. "She wanted me to check in when I got in my room."

"A dozen texts didn't do it?"

"No." He shifted, shoulders stiff. "You, uh, can take off."

"You don't want to come for one last free dinner? Aunt June assumed you'd be game for sushi. We'll drive you back after."

"It's far."

"Not really. An hour away from Aunt June and a little under two hours from your grandparents. If you need a home-cooked meal, they'll come get you."

Clara was going to stay the night with her childhood friend, who lived in Salem. She planned to head back to Oyster Island tomorrow after having breakfast with her parents in Portland.

He shook his head. "I'll go to the caf. That's what you want, right? For me to start fitting in?"

"Daniel Eduardo Martinez. Sad and nervous is one thing. Snotty is another. Of course, I want you to start fitting in. I'm sure the group of guys in the common lounge will be up for a new arrival. Hell, they're probably nervous and a little sad, too. But if you do want to come for sushi on my tab, you're welcome to."

"I'll be fine, Mom."

His gaze brimmed with nerves.

"Sorry," she said. "I shouldn't have middle-named you. You will be okay, but it's normal to feel uncertain right now."

He shrugged. "Make you a deal. I promise to go hang in the common lounge after you go, and I'll put my whole self into being social. *You* can promise not to text me ten times tonight, asking for updates."

Ouch.

She probably would have, though.

"That seems fair. How about two texts? And if you're busy, you can reply with *K* and I'll know you're having a good time."

"Or just a time."

"If 'just a time' is the best you can do today, honey, then yeah. 'A time.' Whatever you manage, I'm proud of you."

"Uh-huh."

"And if you need to text or call *more* than twice, that's okay, too."

He sighed, then stood and gave her a long hug.

She let him shoo her out the door. Before he'd even closed it, she heard, "Hey, Char..."

Then a click.

She tried not to look too out of place as she walked down the hallway.

Tried not to laugh as she overheard "The new guy's mom is hot" from the common lounge.

Hopefully it didn't haunt Daniel too much.

She appreciated the absurdity of it, though. It helped hold off the snowball of tears in her throat, gathering thickness with every step toward the door to the stairwell. A hot mom, a guy could live through. A bawling one might lead to some repercussions.

Even though her eyes were stinging, she jammed the keys into the ignition the minute she got in the driver's seat. She'd parked Isla's truck in the loading zone, so she moved it, relocating to a parking lot next to a different campus building.

She let the lump dissolve.

Fine, she ugly cried until she'd emptied all the tissues from her purse.

If Lawson were here, he'd probably convince her to slide over and sit in his lap so he could hold her until she cried herself dry.

She paused.

When was the last time she'd done something Daniel related, and she hadn't thought of Eddy, first?

Huh.

She pulled her phone out and found her text thread with Lawson.

Well, he's in.

He replied a second later. There's extra Kleenex in the glove compartment.

She leaned over and opened the latch. The door flopped open. Eight travel-size packages of tissues were stacked on top of each other. Underneath, two four-packs of Reese's Peanut Butter Cups peeked out.

She smiled and snatched one of them, then opened it. She took a selfie, miming taking a huge bite.

He sent a picture back. His hair was disheveled, his glasses a bit crooked. One of the brewhouses loomed in the background.

You're hot, she replied.

Simple, accurate. God, he made her heart race.

Back atcha, came his response.

Oh, I know. I overheard one of Daniel's floormates saying I'm a hot mom.

Okay there, Mrs. Robinson

I shudder to think.

When will you be home? he asked.

Her heart skipped.

Four months ago, Portland was home.

Having moved from one Coast Guard posting to the next a few times, she was used to home being more about people than a location.

And when she drove away from the college, as soon as she got the will to turn the truck back on, she'd be leaving part of *home* behind.

Over dinner with June, and then late into the night on June's couch, she lamented how odd it was going to be *not* seeing Daniel every day. Ran through it the next morning with her parents, too, having stopped in Portland for a quick brunch.

She didn't manage to get a breath all the way to the bottom of her lungs until she was standing next to the truck on the ferry, inhaling the mid-September sea air.

Daniel would be okay.

She would, too. Especially if she managed to see Lawson tonight.

Your porch, tonight, 11:00?

Unlike Clara, who'd changed her schedule this week to move Daniel, Lawson was working his usual Friday shift at the brewery. Charlotte would be minding the girls, her last regular nannying day since she'd start back at her online college program next week.

Clara's stomach dropped. She'd been so consumed with Daniel starting school; she hadn't spent much time thinking about how Harper and Pippa would be starting their combo preschool–day care on Monday. She bet she wasn't the only parent who needed some encouragement this weekend.

His reply came after a minute. It's a date. I'll bring the wine, you bring the snacks

Cheese and crackers, she replied, then added, something easy.

I just want to see you.

A simple declaration, but the impact of it rippled down to her toes. She wasn't sure what exactly he was offering, or what exactly she wanted to give, either, but she could return his honesty.

I want to see you, too.

A little while later, Clara was off the ferry and parking Isla's truck in her own driveway, having agreed to return the vehicle tomorrow.

She had a few hours until Lawson got off. She'd be able to rattle around in her house, getting used to how the space felt with no one but her to fill it. Make some popcorn for dinner like a responsible adult. Wallow her way down to the buttery crumbs at the bottom of her biggest mixing bowl.

She rounded the corner of the duplex. An abrupt "Shh!" sounded over her footsteps.

A dozen or so heads peeked over the top of her porch railing. The red curls were obviously Franci, and she spotted Winnie's favorite knit beanie, Violet's messy bun and Rosa's pixie cut.

Oh, my goodness. How many women from her SUP club and hiking group were hiding behind the wooden slats?

She snorted. *Hiding* was a stretch.

She cleared her throat.

They all popped up with a big "Surprise!"

"I'd say so. What's this all about?"

"Filling your house!" Franci held up a bottle of sparkling wine and a bottle of nonalcoholic cider.

"Salt and sugar," Violet said, arms full of a jumbo-size bag of Chicago Mix popcorn. At that size, she must have picked it up from Costco in Bellingham.

Winnie and Rachel had a stack of sink-shaped Rubbermaid tubs and a variety of bath products between them.

"A spa," Rachel explained. "And Matias is going to deliver dinner from the pub in an hour. We can set up inside or out-side—whatever you're ready for."

With her feelings still brimming right at the back of her throat, it didn't take much to make her eyes sting for, oh, the fifteenth time today.

"Thank you for thinking of me. This is so fun," she choked out, burying her face in her hands.

Rachel passed her armful of nested tubs to Rosa and jogged down the short flight of stairs to give Clara a hug. "We're going to distract you, I promise. It *will* be fun. But we're all good with tears, too."

The women followed through on Rachel's promise in spades. They mopped her up, fed her, kept her glass and her belly full. Even better was the laughter, warming her from her core to her skin. They formed a circle in the backyard. The heat of the day dissipated a bit, but it was pleasant enough to be outside in shorts and a T-shirt. That would change, soon. Fall on Oyster Island promised to be stunning.

At 10:30 p.m., with a happy glow on and still wearing a face mask and foam toe separators for her freshly blue nails, she was getting more and more aware of the time, but also didn't want the fun to end. Lawson would understand, wouldn't he? She texted him to make sure.

I have impromptu company. Not sure we'll be done when you get home.

Ahhh. That explains Charlotte's noise complaint.

Oh, damn, seriously?

No. He'd tacked on a winking emoji to the end.

Before she could reply, he added, Should I stay up?

She sent back a kissing emoji.

God, it looked silly. What was she, fifteen?

He didn't leave her to worry for too long.

I mean, I didn't want to assume, but...

Assume away.

A throat cleared beside her.

She jolted and looked up from her phone.

"That's some smile, Clara," Rachel said.

"Oh, sorry." She flipped the device over and put it on the wide, flat arm of her chair. "Rearranging some plans I made."

"Must be convenient, having him right next door," the older woman commented with a twinkle in her eye.

"Oh, we're not..." *We're not what?*

They were something. Still private, though. Unsure of how to answer, she let her nonanswer stand.

"Of course not," Rachel agreed. "To think, when he first came back to the island, I thought he wanted to get Violet back."

"Violet was already gotten," the woman in question said, clearly having overheard the mention of her name. "She is willing to vouch for him, though."

"Oh, I don't need references," Clara joked.

"Yeah, you're already gone for him," Violet said. "It can't hurt that he's making—"

"*Vi. Tsst.*" Isla cut their friend off with her sharp tone, and slashed her hand across her throat.

Clara blinked. She knew they were hiding something, but she didn't want to be spoiled if he had a surprise for her. It would be more fun if it stayed a surprise until he was ready to reveal it.

Violet bounded out of her chair with more energy than Clara would have expected from a seven-months-pregnant person. "Let's go check out the bioluminescence! It's rare we get it this many weeks into September, so we should take advantage. With the tide and the protection of the bay, it should be glowing super bright here."

"A swim, you mean?" Clara said. "I might have enough towels."

"Towels, schmowels," Franci said. Of course she was low-key about it—with all her diving, she was used to drip-drying.

And honestly, why not?

"I'm happy to get some, but if not—" Clara stripped out of her shirt, down to her bra "—let's go swimming!"

The dash across the lawn, with women tossing various garments on the grass, would be one for the history annals of the island.

Down to her underwear on top and bottom, Clara kept her flip-flops on as she led the way across the tide-shortened beach to the water.

She squealed. The water slapped at her ankles. Warmer than she'd expected, but still a shock.

"Give it a second," said Franci, leading the charge through the calm waves.

Clara wasn't backing down now. But it was hard to even care about the temperature of the water. Holy crap. Each small wave slapping the shore was sort of...lit from within.

Sparkles, like the tiniest fairy lights, striped the water nearest the shore.

"I know, right? And the best part is when you do this." Franci beckoned to the crowd, just barely lit up by the far-off glow of the strands of bulbs over the lawn. "Watch your step!"

They splashed in as a pack, until they were twenty feet out from shore and up to their waists or their breasts, depending on their heights. Clara was the shortest by far.

"Damn, I wish I was taller," she lamented.

"Cold on the nipples, isn't it?" said Wren, the nurse who worked at Violet's midwifery clinic. She was only an inch or two taller than Clara, and was holding her shoulder-length box braids on top of her head with a hand.

"Worth it, though," Violet crowed. "Look down and churn the water up a bit."

Clara followed instructions, then gasped.

An eerie, blue-green light rimmed the edges of her limbs. Faint, but unmissable. All the parts of her underwater... gleamed? Not quite like glitter, but like she'd dipped herself in the thinnest layer of glow-stick liquid. Anywhere she dragged her hand, a galaxy sparkled in its wake.

"That's some wild science right there," she said.

"My word, it's like I'm an alien life-form!" Wren exclaimed. "I can't believe I haven't done this before."

"I can't, either," Clara agreed. Kind of surprising, given how much of her life she'd lived by the water.

But now, she had. Another new, brilliant thing.

Laughing, she spread out her arms and fell backward. The water chilled, caressed. She exhaled, letting the mixed feelings from the last few days turn into light-gilded, turquoise bubbles.

Chapter Twelve

The minute Lawson got out of his car, splashing caught his attention. Was there some sort of animal on the beach? Hoots followed the sounds of water being disturbed. The laughing, high-pitched kind of hoots, not the nocturnal bird variety.

He glanced around the yard. The overhead yard lights were on. Wineglasses and soda cans perched on the arms of the porch furniture and filled the cupholders of folding camp chairs. Not to mention the trail of clothing scattered across the lawn, from the gazebo down to the beach access.

Right. Clara's "company." Quite a large group, it seemed. Her group of friends was doing an outstanding job of cheering her up, by the sounds of things. Which was great, except he'd been looking forward to sharing a nightcap on her porch.

Shaking his head—since when had time with her become something he counted on?—he trudged to his side of the duplex and went to unlock the door.

"Lawson!"

Ah, yes, his sister. A wave of women in bathing suits, all shapes and sizes, cascaded onto the lawn. They darted in a pack, high-kneeing it across the grass in a cascade of levity, gathering up their clothes on the way.

Rachel led the cavalcade, waving at him, mouth wide with a smile. "Hi, honey!"

Oh, *wait*. They weren't in bathing suits. They were in their underwear.

He groaned.

He lifted a hand at the bakery owner, who really, was as covered as if she was in a bikini.

Isla, though? Not so much. *For crying out loud.* He fixed his gaze to the ceiling of his porch overhang. Maybe one day, in a year or a decade or when he was ninety-four, he'd manage to erase the sight of her *not* in her underwear.

"Towels are inside," Clara called. "Linen closet is under the stairs on the main floor."

He couldn't tell where in the pack she was, not while examining his soffits.

Footsteps trampled up her side of the porch. When the door closed, he assumed he was safe to lower his gaze.

And he was. But he wasn't alone.

A curvy figure stood right in front of him. Water dripped from the long braid draped over her shoulder. A soft smile teased her lips. Her white underwear and lacy bra flirted with transparency.

He swallowed. "I'm a weak man, beautiful, and I'm trying not to scope my fill, but…"

But shadows… Nipples, faint circles through her bra. A triangle at the apex of her thighs.

"I came here so you *would* look, Lawson."

With a wink, she stood on her toes and kissed him, just the corner of his mouth.

Before he could reach for her, she darted away, down the stairs and behind the barrier between their porches.

"Clara, where are you going?"

"I have guests, silly!"

Her door closed again.

Guests. Damn.

He went inside and got the lowdown of the night from Charlotte before sending her on her way.

He was closing the door to the girls' room, having retucked two blankets and ensured all stuffies and blankies and articles of Kiera's clothing were in the exact right spots in case either twin woke up, when his phone vibrated in the back pocket of his jeans.

My guests are gone.

Oh. Well, then. Already?

The swim was the capper of the evening, not a sign the party was getting started.

Going to bed, then? He almost tacked on an invitation to join him in his room. *Almost.* But he wasn't quite ready for sleepovers yet. It would no doubt end with a tiny knock interrupting at his bedroom door and an ultraawkward explanation to follow.

Her reply came quickly. No. I'm out on the lawn.

Still in that pretty bra and panties? He couldn't resist asking.

You'll have to see.

He groaned, then typed, Let me take a quick shower. I smell like a brewery.

Be real quick.

Should I be reading into that?

Depends on how fast you are.

He took the shortest shower possible, threw on thin shorts and a Nanny Goats Gruff hoodie, grabbed the monitor and headed for the backyard.

She lounged in a chair, a glass of something clear and sparkling in her hand.

"I poured you one," she said, pointing to another glass on the side table in between what was becoming their regular spot. "It's just from my SodaStream."

"Uh, thanks." He meant it, given his throat was all of a sudden beyond parched. He drank his fill of Clara's lush form, not bothering to be subtle.

A thigh-length, thin cotton robe covered her body. The palest pink, and he bet it was like a cloud to the touch. It parted over one of her crossed thighs.

"Quite the sight I came home to," he said, trying to tease but sounding strangled. "I'm tempted to call you all the dirty dozen."

"Oh, I assure you, we were all very clean after our swim," she said. "We were glowing, Lawson. Bioluminescence."

Her awestruck tone nestled right between his heart and his good sense.

She was glowing, all right. From the inside out. And he was alight for her.

"Swimming in bioluminescence was one of my favorite parts of the summer, growing up here as a kid. Last time I saw it was out kayaking one night with Violet. Years ago, though, obviously. I wonder what the girls would think. Then again, they'd have to stay up past their bedtime, which might not be a great idea on the weekend before their first day of day care."

"Maybe not. Or they might think it's actual magic. I mean, no pressure—you know them best. But we could ask Archer if he's getting any over in his cove. Taking the girls would be safer if we could stand on a dock and dip something in the water, like a paddle."

He sat, thrown by her casually tossing out how he knew the girls best. He supposed it was true, even though impostor syndrome loved to tell him he still didn't know a thing about

parenting. Leaning forward, he put his elbows on his knees
and hauled in an insufficient breath.

"If you hate the idea, it's not a big deal," she said. "There
will be other summers, so long as you're planning to stay on
the island with them."

His heart rate ratcheted further.

"Lawson? Are you okay?"

"Uh, I guess. I got reminded of how I'm their most important human, now, and had one of those moments of feeling
grossly unqualified for the job."

"Oh, no, no, no," she said, voice light and teasing. "Only
one of us is allowed to feel angsty about parenting in this
yard at a time."

"You're right." He chuckled. "We need to take turns. Tonight's your night. I'll put a pin in my self-doubt until tomorrow."

"No, at *least* until Wednesday. I left my son at *college*. That
has to be worth a half a week of uninterrupted dramatics."

"Aw, Clara..." She had to be hurting, no matter how much
fun she'd had with her friends.

With her legs crossed, one of her feet bobbed right by his
knee. Her toe skimmed the skin right over his knee, along the
hem of his shorts.

Since when could the brush of a foot light part of his leg
on fire? He swallowed.

Gaze flicking to his throat, she took a sip of her water, the
picture of innocence. "The last time we sat in these chairs, I
had designs on you. But then we got interrupted."

Another slow tease of her toe.

His breath caught.

"We won't tonight," he said. "Get interrupted."

"Shh, you're daring the monitor to light up like a football
stadium. That happened to Eddy and me all the time."

She winced.

"It's okay," he said. "Talk about him all you want. It doesn't make me uncomfortable."

"I figured it killed the mood."

He shook his head. "It's a key part of you. Whenever he crosses your mind and you want to bring him up, I'd love to hear your stories. They're part of what makes you who you are. And I feel lucky to be getting to know all of you."

Her lips parted.

"Only when you want to," he reiterated.

That toe went back to driving him mad. "To be honest, I wasn't thinking we'd be doing much talking at all tonight. You probably need to get to bed. But before you leave..."

He took her foot in his hands and rubbed her instep with his thumbs.

The moan she let out went straight to his groin.

He shot her a quick, knowing look. "I'm lucky to be the one to coax that noise out of you, too."

She bit her lip. A cross between a whimper and a laugh sounded at the back of her throat.

Thumbing the curve of her jaw, he said, "Mocking my joy, Clara?"

"More like turned on by it. But also...you sound pretty proud of yourself."

"More like honored," he said. "I love earning your reactions."

Her cheeks pinkened.

His heart lurched.

As much as he knew she was processing a big change already tonight, he couldn't keep the words in anymore. "I don't know if I can keep my feelings out of this."

Well, now he'd done it. Verbal can opener, meet can of worms.

"What do you mean?" she asked.

That I'm screwed. That I'm risking hurting you.

How could he trust his feelings, based on how he'd acted

in the past? If he let himself love Clara, and then hurt her like he had Violet...

But he couldn't minimize how he felt. Not anymore. His heart was begging to get closer to her. Before he'd returned home, he'd promised his therapist he'd open up, even in small ways. Having identified *not* talking, hiding, was at fault for a lot of what went wrong with Violet, he'd be better doing the opposite with Clara.

Even if his heart was in his throat when he did it.

"Nothing complicated. I'm just into you. A lot. And I can't seem to compartmentalize." He shook his head. "Scratch that. Even if I could, I wouldn't want to."

"Okay," she said, voice slow with caution. "But what does it mean in practice?"

"I'm not sure. I'm not ready to make any promises. It's too hard with the girls. But I also want to let myself feel, Clara. I don't want to ignore or avoid how good things are when I'm with you."

"Okay..." She tugged her lip between her teeth, and he barely managed to resist leaning in and having a taste himself. "So we live in the moment, then?"

"Yeah, but more than messing around. I like the idea of telling you I care about you."

"Monogamous living in the moment, then," she said lightly.

He tightened his grip on his glass. "I can't imagine looking at another woman right now."

Maybe not ever.

"I'm okay with getting closer, but with not making promises yet," she said.

"Yeah?"

She climbed into his lap. Her robe split in the front, exposing creamy, lush thighs and a flash of miniscule turquoise shorts.

Was she *trying* to kill him?

"We meet again," she said, winking. Her hands were so, so

gentle on his chest, fingertips tracing delicate swirls through his hoodie. "I'm assuming 'more than messing around' guarantees we *will* mess around."

"At every opportunity."

"Well. Lawson's hands, meet 'opportunity.'"

Didn't have to ask him twice.

He skimmed a trail up those soft thighs, tucking his thumbs under the lacy edge of her shorts. Temptation in a few scraps of fabric. He nuzzled into the crook of her neck. She smelled of vanilla and a hint of the ocean. Her cheeks were flushed, her eyes bright. This woman had ideas, *plans*, and he was desperate to know every one of them.

He captured her lips in a long kiss.

Kissing her. Holy God.

Life-giving. With her fingers threaded in his hair, her hips restless, she held all of him in her thrall.

"I wish I could sneak you into my room," he said. "But Pippa comes and finds me there too often."

"We can be creative."

Creative apparently involved making out like teenagers for far longer than either of them should have been awake.

He lost track of time. Her body was a damn paradise, and having her squirming in his lap with his hand between her thighs was a freaking gift.

Tasting her lips and neck, coaxing her to rock against him, he traced circles over every inch of her panties until the fabric was soaked.

They were in their backyard, but the hedges were high on both sides, and the light was dim, and...screw it.

He slid his fingers under the wet material and thrust two fingers deep into her vagina.

She bit her lip, barely suppressing a strangled moan.

"How quiet can you come? Can you be good, Clara?"

She squeaked something close to a *yes*.

"Yeah, that's right. You're always good for me."

"Lawson," she whispered, grinding onto his palm. Her inner muscles clamped around his fingers.

"Oh, you are close, baby," he mumbled. "Deep breath. Don't moan. Definitely don't shout my name. But let go. I've got you."

Her head fell back. Her lips parted. She reached behind her back to brace a hand on each of his knees and bowed her spine, pressing his hand, his erection, his fly.

He curled his fingers.

Her breath exploded from her chest, along with a whimper. The rhythm of her release pulsed. He could only feel it on his hand, but it didn't matter—he nearly lost control himself. Breathing deeply, he waited until her body relaxed before sliding his hand away and coaxing her to rest on his chest.

She melted against him.

"You know…" A few, panting breaths followed.

"I don't, actually."

"I would normally hate being called 'baby.' But when you have your fingers in me and you use it, it's like…*argh*, it's so perfect."

He smiled against her cheek. "Noted."

"Sparingly."

"Gotcha. On very special occasions."

She paused. "You think it'll be rare for us to manage to have sex?"

"No," he said, kissing her softly. "I think it'll always be special."

"Oh, my God, you can't just say stuff like that," she mumbled, her lips brushing his neck.

"Why?"

"Because I'll never be able to get off your lap and go to bed. Which, I shouldn't yet. I might have come, but you didn't."

"Nah, it's bedtime. Adulting strikes again."

"I'm leaving you high and dry, though."

"I—" he cupped her jaw and brought her head up enough

to make eye contact "—unlike you—" he kissed one corner of her mouth, then the other "—am wholly incapable of finishing without waking up the neighbors. No backyard sex for me."

"You're missing out," she whispered.

"Oh, I have no doubt we'll make up for it."

Four weeks after the night Clara returned from delivering Daniel to school, Lawson was ready to test his first three GF beers. Isla was done work for the day, and willing to be his beta drinker.

"Moment of truth," he said.

"Bottoms up." She lifted her glass.

He held the liquid up to the overhead light. They were starting with the one where he'd added molasses for depth of flavor and to up the alcohol content a bit, to try to match the ABV on an imperial stout. The color was close to a dark chocolate, but not quite as deep as his barley-based stouts.

He sucked a quick sip across his tongue.

Isla followed suit.

Hmm. Nutty, for sure. A hint of bitterness. Holding off on a second addition of hops had been the right call. Maybe a little heavy on the molasses, but he'd avoided it turning out funky.

His sister's face went thoughtful. "Well, it *resembles* beer."

"Bare minimum. Cool, cool," he said, taking another sip.

"And it tastes…"

"Be honest." He took a larger drink, nodding to himself. He'd nailed the mouthfeel he wanted.

If it got Isla's seal of approval, he'd run it by Matias.

"Uh, it's complex." His sister was failing to hold back a wince.

His heart sank. Different was fine, but unpalatable wouldn't fly. Hers was only one opinion, but she had a fairly educated palate, what with how much she worked with food.

"That's vague, Isla."

She put down the tasting glass. "Law, can I be honest with you?"

"Please. If I need to toss this batch, so be it. We have two more to try."

Isla's face was all apology. "No, it's not about *this* beer. I'm sure some people might like it."

"Some people?"

She shook her head. "Not me. I don't like beer."

"Uh, what? You've been drinking my beer for years."

"*Choking it down* would be closer to the truth. I've really tried. It's important to you, and I want you to feel supported. But in this new era of honesty and truth, I have to say—if I never drank another beer, I would be a happy camper."

His jaw was on the floor.

"If it helps, I can tell yours is better than some of the others I've had over the years. And I almost liked the pilsner you made with Matias. Almost."

"Almost."

She shrugged. "I wish it were different."

"For crying out loud. What is it with the women in my life *not* liking beer?"

She nudged him with an elbow. "You know Mom loves it. She hasn't been pretending. And I got the impression from Clara that the gluten-free stuff she's tried hasn't been her favorite, but she wishes it were otherwise. She's mentioned to me before that it's too bad she can't try your summer and fall releases. Why isn't *she* your tester? She'll be surprised, no matter what."

"Yes, one day, but for the first batch, I want it to be perfect, first."

Fingers crossed, he hadn't completely messed up.

Chapter Thirteen

Clara inhaled to the bottom of her lungs, savoring the umami smell of the stew Kellan was crafting in The Cannery's kitchen for his October pop-up Friday dinner.

"You are a genius, Kell, I swear."

"It's simple comfort food for a rainy autumn night, love."

"I know, and it smells good enough to bury my face in it."

"Which you could, safely. I used tapioca starch as a thickener, not wheat flour like the recipe calls for."

"I know. I can't wait to dig in." She'd have to forgo the biscuits, but the stew was the main event, anyway. She peered into the pot. Potatoes and parsnips studded the thick, glossy gravy. "One of these days, I'll have to make sure I'm not on shift for your monthly takeover, so I can sit and enjoy your creation rather than eat it over the counter in my corner of the kitchen. Maybe Lawson and I could come here for a date." She paused. "Then again, coming to a date at work is *not* romantic."

"You two have progressed to dates, then? Not solely sneaking from your house to his, or vice versa?" Kellan eyed her, a glint of curiosity in his dark eyes. Oof, he was handsome. Talented, too, and so very kind. Sam had struck gold when the Irishman had decided to stay on Oyster Island.

Would she be able to cobble together enough of a life here to make the same choice?

"We haven't managed much time to ourselves. Our schedules don't always align, and he's even busier now with the girls in day care and Charlotte babysitting less."

Kellan nodded, and tested his stew with a clean teaspoon.

"Tomorrow, though, he's got something planned. He asked me to book off the whole morning and afternoon."

"From one recent transplant to another—these Oyster Island boys are a right menace," Kellan said. "You come looking for a little peace and quiet and then fall right into a trap of 'Aw, shucks' charm and wind-tousled hair and Gore-Tex. Impossible to break free. No use fighting it."

"I'm not sure I'm staying, Kellan."

He smiled. "Mmm, yes, I said that, too."

She sighed. "Lawson doesn't feel like a trap."

"No, I reckon it feels like magic," Kellan said with a wink.

It did, sometimes. Their quiet moments on the porch filled her soul. The minute he left her bed, she was itchy to get him back in it.

But none of it felt settled. Was he truly ready for a relationship?

She chatted about inconsequential things with Kellan for a few more minutes, and then excused herself to duck into the back hallway. Noise spilled from the doorway to the brewery. Lawson would be busy slinging flights, from the sound of it.

She pulled out her phone to text June. After their time together, her friend had enough context to be the right sounding board.

Before she had time to start typing, the screen lit up and the device vibrated, startling her.

Daniel.

And an actual call. In the six weeks he'd been gone, he'd reverted more to texts than calling, and when they did talk, he wasn't exactly baring his soul to her. She supposed he had Charlotte for that, but it still worried her.

"Hey honey, happy Friday night," she said, answering on the second buzz.

"Maybe it is on the island," he grumbled.

Oof. And here he'd seemed happier the past couple of weekends.

"Pretty quiet around these parts," she said.

"It's quiet here, too. Everyone on my floor left for the football game."

Her stomach twinged at the thought of him choosing to be alone tonight.

"Why are you calling to talk to your mom instead of joining your floormates for their shenanigans?"

"I'm trying to do my laundry," he said. "But the machine stopped working halfway through the cycle. It's got all my towels and clothes in it, and they're just sitting in the water."

"Laundry on a Friday night?"

"Better than rewearing clothes."

"I guess, but—"

"I've only ever used front-loading machines," he complained. "This one top loads, and it's ancient."

"Maybe it got off balance from having a big load?"

"Yeah, that's what YouTube said."

"YouTube for laundry hints. It's a whole new world from when I was in school."

"Mom?" His voice cracked. "I miss home."

Ah. *There* it was.

"I bet. It's a big change."

"If you still lived in Portland, I could come home to do my laundry."

Guilt stabbed.

"It's normal for some of the moments after leaving home to feel lonely. And it's okay to want a quiet night to yourself. The football game didn't sound like your jam?"

"I don't know. The guys on my floor are super outgoing, always trying to one-up each other in a crowd. It's weird to be there solo, when a bunch of the girls assume I'm single…"

"Too popular for your own good," she said. Unsurprising.

Her son was a good-looking guy, and she had a feeling some of the people who'd find him attractive might like the fact he wasn't into the *one-upping* behavior. God knew she'd been attracted to Eddy because he'd been comfortable in his own skin and gainfully employed, rather than grandstanding his way through one of her nutrition lectures or English seminars.

"I wish I wasn't," he lamented. "I feel like I'm the only person with a girlfriend back home who isn't planning to break up with her over Thanksgiving."

"So you're doing laundry instead of fending off flirtatious first-years?"

"My English professor would like your alliteration," he said.

His tone wasn't as sad.

Her worry lightened a fraction, at least.

"Did you eat dinner?" she asked.

"If you can call it food. Rumor has it the caf serves squirrel."

"Yeah, my campus had the same rumor. A classic urban legend."

"I'm almost out of your cookies."

"The ones left must be stale. I'll FedEx you more." She'd have to take the ferry to San Juan. Maybe Lawson and the girls would come, make an adventure out of it.

"And muffins?" he said hopefully.

"It's a possibility." She totally would. "Not sure what I'm baking this weekend."

"The ones from Hideaway Bakery would be fine if you're not already making something."

She fake-gasped. "Traitor."

"Yours are great, Mom, but—"

"I see how it is. All those bakery dates with Charlotte, and you lose your appreciation for my gluten-free recipes."

"It's more her company than the muffins."

"I know. Pippa and Harper will be in bed by eight. Then you can call *her* to keep you company in the laundry room."

"Yeah."

"You okay for the next couple of hours? I'd better go check on the pub."

"I just…"

She let the pause hang for a bit, until it was clear he wasn't finishing. "You just what, honey?"

"Nothing, Mom. Have a good shift."

"Call anytime, Daniel."

They hung up.

A pair of hands slid around her waist.

She shrieked and nearly hit the ceiling.

But those hands…strong and becoming so familiar…they kept her steady, tethered to the ground.

"You startled me." She slumped against Lawson and waited for her heart rate to return to normal.

She really did need to return to the dining room, but indulging in his strength for a minute or two was irresistible. He should have smelled like malt and hops, but he wore enough of his warm, clove-and-salt cologne for it to drift around her, another kind of comforting hug.

"Sorry," he murmured into her hair. "I thought for sure you heard me. I wasn't trying to sneak up on you."

"I was so focused on Daniel that I didn't hear."

"Everything okay?"

"I'm not sure. I think the shine has worn off. Heck, I don't know if the shine was ever there."

His arms banded around her arms and chest. "He's bound to have some off days."

"Yeah, I know. But I can't help but wonder if I've made too many changes for him all at once." She cupped his crossed wrists with her hands. "Maybe I should have only stayed here for the summer."

"In that case, you'd already be gone. Back in Portland, in front of a classroom again."

She held off a shudder.

"Not what you want?"

"No. For my sake, leaving that life behind was the right choice. But it feels like I'm messing up on the mom front."

"Would having you closer truly make him happier? It's not like he'd be living with you. You'd still be hours away from each other."

"True. He just... I mean, I promised myself I'd create stability for him."

"He'll let you know if he needs something."

"Cookies, apparently." She paused. "Do you and the girls want to take a ferry ride with me soon? I'm going to ship him a care package from Friday Harbor."

"Sure, we'll tag along." He nipped at her ear. "And the girls are staying at Isla's tonight. A test run for when I go to Oktoberfest next weekend. My sister and I figured we should see how they do with twenty-four hours before I spring four days on them."

"Oh?"

"Yes." His voice was dangerously low. "Invite me over for a drink, Clara."

"The pub's closing at ten, though. I'll already be in bed when you get off at eleven." Glancing at him sideways, she shot him a playful look.

"Oh, darn."

"I mean, you *do* have a key to my place."

"I'm legally required to give you notice before using it."

She spun, desperate for thirty more seconds of staring into his smoke-gray eyes. "Consider this an emergency request. I mean, my kitchen sink could be leaking. Who knows."

He smirked. "Worth checking."

At 11:05 p.m., he shifted his feet on Clara's back doormat, a tall bottle gripped in each hand. It was about time he copped to his project. One of the three was unsalvageable, after not bottle conditioning properly, but he had high hopes she might like one of the other two. His pulse skipped in his chest as he knocked.

His beautiful, rosy-cheeked woman answered. Her smile held all the secrets of the universe.

Her sweatshirt fell from one shoulder and was loose enough to almost cover the bottom hem of her sleep shorts. She had on thick, hand-knitted knee socks.

Grabbing a fistful of his "I Do Crafts" T-shirt—right over the graphic of six different kinds of beer glasses—she pulled him into the house and nudged the door shut with her toe.

"Those are some socks," he said. They were a soft pink and cabled in an intricate pattern all the way up her gorgeous calves.

She locked the door. "Winnie knitted them for me."

He let out a low whistle. "Well, you know you've been accepted into the fold now."

"I've been told that's what they mean."

He still hadn't gotten his requisite knitwear item from the bakery owner. Maybe he'd earn one this winter if he kept taking them spent grain to turn into cookies and bread. They'd agreed to a partnership, selling the items at the brewery and the bakery, and the baked goods were flying off the shelves in both locales. He frowned. Another thing Clara couldn't try. Maybe on his next batch of gluten-free beer, he'd bring the discards home and they could bake some cookies in her oven.

"You have a very serious face for someone carrying two large bottles of beer, sir."

Sir.

He shot her an imperious look.

"Oh, no, we're not going down *that* road tonight," she scolded.

"You sure, baby?"

The flare of her pupils said "Maybe another day." He was kidding anyway. The only role he needed to play in her bed was "Lawson pleasuring Clara."

She shivered and backed away, then grabbed a fat brandy snifter from the cupboard. "Will this work?"

"Yes. It'll hold the aromas in. But we'll need four. We're doing a tasting."

"I'll have a cider from my fridge."

"No, you can have this. It's safe," he said. "I mean, if you like it. If not, feel free with the cider."

"It's gluten-free?" she asked, taking down another curvy, short-stemmed glass.

"Yes. Special delivery."

"From another one of your friends? You didn't have to," she said softly, sitting on one of her kitchen stools. She crossed her legs. The stretch of skin between the bottom of her shorts and the top of her socks was damn perfection.

He opened the first bottle and poured a few inches into each glass. He wasn't going to correct her about where he'd gotten it from. Better she be honest about it.

"Ooh, it's dark," she said.

"Give it a try."

She sniffed delicately, then took a small sip.

Her eyes widened. "Is that…molasses?"

He nodded. Sitting on the other stool, he drank from his own glass. "Yeah. I'm liking how it gave it rum notes, but it might be a little sweet."

Her second drink was longer. "Man, it's *complex*. And interesting. I agree about the sweetness, though."

If he used this recipe again, he could tweak it by cutting down the molasses or using a lighter type. Or maybe not including it in the cook and using it as a priming sugar instead—

Focus. He'd brought this over to make her happy, not to make a to-do list for his next brewing steps.

She stuck her nose in the glass and inhaled. "Sweetness aside, it's so smooth. And am I getting chocolate?"

"A hint. But more from this one." He poured her a serving from the second bottle. The brew swirled in the glass, a beautiful dark espresso with a toasted marshmallow head. "It won't be quite as sweet, and you'll get more chocolate and coffee notes."

She made grabby hands, and he faked out passing it to her, leaning in for a kiss.

"Gotta pay the tax." He found her lips with his.

The little moan at the back of her throat made him want to toss the beer and taste her all night instead.

Patience.

He'd waited nearly two months for this moment.

Pulling away, he held up his glass to clink with hers.

Her eyes fluttered shut the second the beer passed her lips.

Pride jolted through him. God, that look right there... It made every second of hard work worth it.

After a quick sip so he wouldn't tempt bad luck by cheersing without drinking, he put his glass on the countertop. "You like it, Clara?"

"Oh, yeah, *this* one. The other one was good, but this one tastes like fall nights cuddled up in an oversize camp chair, toasting our feet by the fire."

"Can I use that in my marketing?"

Her gaze shot to his. "*Your* marketing?"

He nodded and took her free hand, toying with her fingers. "I've been making it at Isla's since August. Do you like it?"

Plump, raspberry-pink lips parted.

Cocking an eyebrow, he waited.

"Shut the front door. You made this for *me?*" She froze. "Or not for me. Talk about being presumptuous. Obviously, it's for Hau'oli. But it's still so awesome if you're making something local that I can drink—"

"Of course, it's for you," he interrupted. "*Not* the brewery. I know you're not a huge beer drinker, but it's a significant part of my life, and I wanted to at least *try* to make something you'd find palatable. You share food and baking with me all the time. I wanted to give something back."

Her eyes brimmed with happiness. "This is *not* the same as a plate of cookies. You've been making it since *August?*"

He lifted a shoulder. "That's part of the fun of it. Bit of a gamble, every time."

"But this had to be even more so—you'd have needed new equipment and ingredients and the space..." She flung her arms around his neck and launched into his lap, twining her ankles around his back. "I love it. *Thank you.*"

"You're amazing," he murmured into her hair. "You deserve to feel special."

"Well, mission-freaking-accomplished." She pressed her face into his neck.

The skin there dampened.

He tightened his embrace. Her reaction validated every hour he'd spent at his sister's, fussing with unfamiliar malts and checking thermometers down to the tenth of a degree and cleaning Matias's old stainless equipment until he could see his reflection.

"I'm glad you love it. Didn't mean to make you cry, though."

"They're happy ones," she said, her words muffled against his shoulder.

"That's a relief." He kissed her hair and stroked her back. "And this is only part one of my plan. We get to wake up together tomorrow. And then I have a few other surprises in store."

Leaning back a little, she grinned. "I can't wait."

"I want to wow you."

Her sweet mouth kissed a line along his jaw. It was his turn to shiver. "Lawson?"

"Yeah?"

"You already do."

The next morning, he woke up holding Clara. God, it was everything he'd hoped it would be.

Her warmth clinging to his side. The light fragrance of her hair, and the even sound of her breathing.

Instead of rousing her and putting his plans for their date into action, he slid away, went to the bathroom and brushed his teeth and then returned to bed. He tucked her closer against his side and soaked in the pleasure of this precious, utterly common moment.

When her beautiful eyes opened a half hour later, she unknowingly did the same thing he'd done with a visit to his en suite, and then came back to cuddle.

Goddamn. He could get used to this.

"These schemes you have for me today—when do they start?" she asked.

"As soon as I've made you gasp and moan a couple of times."

Her fingers stilled on his chest. "A couple?"

"Fine, three."

She laughed.

"Oh, not enough? I mean, I wouldn't say no to four."

"Lawson." She kissed him.

And they didn't bother counting.

Hours later, he pulled his car into Archer and Franci's driveway and watched confusion spread across Clara's face.

The house had a gorgeous ocean view, but faced the open Pacific instead of toward Mount Baker, like Lawson and Clara's yard.

"When you said we were going to the far side of the island, I didn't think it would be here," she said. "Taking me out to a friend's place?"

"You'll see."

"I don't think they're home. Their car isn't in the carport."

"No, they're out with Matias and Violet on their sailboat today. Mati mentioned something about Violet feeling antsy, given she's two weeks away from her due date."

Envy spread across her features. "I've been nagging Matias to take me out on the *Albatross* again since the end of the summer."

"I know. And I considered going with them. But I thought we should do something more private."

They got out of the car, Clara slinging her backpack over her shoulder. He'd told her to dress casual, in layers, and to bring sunscreen, sunglasses and a hat. He thought she might have some snacks tucked in her bag, too. A habit from repeated situations where hosts made mistakes concerning what she could and could not eat, no doubt. He was confident the picnic he'd packed was all on her safe list.

He took the basket out of the trunk, put his own backpack on his shoulders. Going over to her side, he smiled. Surprising her was fun. Especially since he'd had to get one of her best friends in on the secret, too. Archer was part of Lawson's friend circle, too, but he and Franci were family-levels of close to Clara and Daniel.

Hopefully, the added layers of subterfuge made her feel special. God knew he felt like he could scale one of the sheer cliffs off Buoy Point whenever she smiled at him.

He linked fingers with her. She tugged him in the direction of the front door, but he shook his head and led her around the other way.

"Where are we going?"

"The dock," he said.

She cocked a pale eyebrow. "You're sure we're not going out on Matias's boat?"

"No, we're taking Archer's out."

Her jaw dropped. "His Chris-Craft?"

"Yeah."

"He babies it like a freaking Monet."

"And yet, he's trusting us with it."

Fine, Lawson's purpose for today was making Clara feel special *and* making sure he brought the antique vessel back in one piece.

Hand in hand, they followed the lawn around the side of the house. The architecture of the navy blue–stained, shingle-sided house spoke to the '50s or '60s, though from the tour Archer had given him once, Lawson knew the interior had been updated and modified, in large part to Archer needing accessibility for when he used his wheelchair or crutches instead of his prosthetic leg.

In fact, with how close Clara was to her late husband's friend, she'd likely witnessed a lot of said renovation.

"Were you around for when he had his house renovated?" he asked.

"From afar, mostly. I was moving myself at that time. While he was healing from the accident, and adjusting to both living with a disability and leaving the Coast Guard, I was moving to Portland to be closer to my parents and trying to hold Daniel together. We helped each other where we could. I gave him some decorating suggestions. But really, he depended on his contractor a lot, in terms of the house. Neither of us had experience with the design specs for a wheelchair-friendly floor plan."

"If I've learned anything from taking on the guardianship, the most important part is the emotional support. And you're a hell of a listener."

They reached the paved path connecting the downstairs side door to the gentle ramp of the long, narrow pier. Her sandals slapped on the cement.

"We both needed a sounding board," Clara said. "And as much as I knew he was coming back to the community where he'd grown up, I worried about him being so far away from medical care and Veterans Affairs services. But he made do. Got back into diving, which seemed to bring him back to life. I was so happy for him. And when I came to visit for the first time… I could see why it was so special here."

"Weird to think of what life would have been like had you

come to visit while I was still living here. Before the accident, that is."

"Well, we were both with other people, so I don't think meeting earlier would have changed anything. And even if you and I had run into each other in the past five years, after the accident and after you breaking up with Violet, I wouldn't have been open to a relationship. I've only considered it more recently."

And how much of a relationship do you want now? One with no end in sight?

His pulse jumped at the thought.

The boat he'd begged Archer to borrow shone in the sun, teak paneling glossy with what looked to be a recent coat of varnish. The front bench seat was tucked behind a protective windscreen. Another row of seating backed the stern, separated from the front by the engine, which was hidden under a wood cover.

"Sharing the bench will be cozy," she said, mouth tipping up at the corner.

"That was my plan," he admitted.

It came to fruition seconds after they untied the boat and he steered it away from the dock, the engine rumbling low. Clara sat in the middle of the bench seat. The breeze teased a few strands of pale hair from her braid.

Sun glinted off the water, and he pushed his prescription sunglasses up. The sea air stung his nose as he breathed in, shifting the throttle forward to increase their speed.

"You've never talked about boating," Clara said, voice raised over the accelerating engine. "I didn't know you felt comfortable driving one. Especially not this one, given how old it is. I think Archer's grandfather bought it in the '40s or '50s."

"Don't remind me," he replied. "I'm amazed he lent it to me. If we don't bring it back in one piece, I'll have to flee in disgrace again."

She nudged his side with an elbow. "Don't say that."

"I'm kidding," he said.

He put his arm around her and she snuggled close.

One thing about cruising—it wasn't super conducive to conversation. But Clara didn't seem to mind, smiling and cozy under his arm. With one hand on the steering wheel, he hugged the island's coastline and took them toward their destination, a tiny mound of land known for creating a protected cove off the neighboring, uninhabited Mussel Island. A few permanent buoys were anchored on the leeward side of the islet, and he thought it would be the perfect place to tie up and enjoy their picnic.

Witnessing the change in seasons from the water was a special gift. Deciduous yellows and oranges dotted the dominant deep greens of the firs and pines along the granite cliffs and rocky beaches. This side of the island wasn't as inhabited as the inner coast, so only the occasional house and cleared property broke up the wild expanse of nature.

Mindful of the worth of the vessel he helmed, he slowed down as soon as he caught a glimpse of Littleneck Channel.

"I promise, I will take you out for dinner one night. But for today, being alone seemed like a great idea."

"I love it," she said. "Any chance to get out on the water. It's way more of a thrill!"

The boat cut through the shallow waves, a rise and fall he hadn't felt in a while, but it was like yesterday. Something about being out on the ocean brought back memories of his own grandparents' boat. They had both passed over a decade ago, but it seemed more recent when he was getting a bit of spray in the face. Maybe Isla had their childhood albums close at hand and he could show Harper and Pippa what life had looked like on the island when he was little.

"Isla and I used to come out a lot with our grandfather," he explained. "He had a Double Eagle. One of our favorite things to do was hike into the Mussel Island hot springs."

"Oh, I've heard of those!" she said. "We should explore them one day."

"Sure," he said. "I was just thinking, I should pull out some of the old pictures from when we were kids."

"Were your early 2000s as awkward as mine? I cut my hair super short, which looks awesome on some people, but not at all on me."

"My frosted tips in my senior year were a sight to behold," he joked.

"I'd love to see a picture," she said, face dancing with mischief. Twisting slightly, she reached up and mussed his hair. "Though I'm betting this style is an improvement."

"I don't think anyone's going to mistake me for a singer in a boy band."

"Did they then?" she asked, cracking up.

"It was always my sincerest hope." He kept his expression solemn, but knew the corners of his mouth gave away the unavoidable mix of humor and humiliation. "You know, that's one thing about Daniel. He's way more settled in his skin than I ever was at his age."

Her expression turned thoughtful. Not sad. But she was definitely replaying something in her head.

"Did you and Eduardo get out on the water much? Or the three of you?"

"Not as much as you'd expect, given we were always living near a Coast Guard base. And Eddy—he lived for the ocean, being on it and below the surface. But life was hectic. We were like any other parents. The nice-to-dos got taken over by laundry, soccer practice, swim meets, cramming in family visits."

"So, you're saying the low-level sense of forgetting something at any given moment is normal?"

"Um, yeah. I still feel that, and my kid is hundreds of miles away. It's what makes days like these so important."

She turned her face to the sun. Her mouth softened into contentment. Not a full smile. Just relaxed, happy.

One of the thousand faces of Clara he was learning.

He planned to discover at least five more by the time he docked the boat back at Archer and Franci's.

He steered them into the cove and they tied up to one of the pink buoys, tucked in behind the shelter offered by the islet fondly known as the Pearl. Trees scattered the top of the looming rock, which was big enough to protect the cove from the wind.

He switched the engine from Neutral to Off.

"It's even quieter than sitting on our porches," she said.

"Even louder, you mean."

The chatter of birdsong, the lapping of water against the hull, wind moving through the trees.

Sliding his hand around her cheek, he leaned in.

She closed the rest of the distance, tasting his mouth.

"Fine," she said, drawing back. "It's not quiet, but it is peaceful."

"Perfect place for a picnic."

They set up in the stern area, where there was more room to move around. After they ate, he lounged sideways on the aft seat, with Clara snuggled along his front.

"Big week ahead," she mused, toying with the hair behind his ear. "Need any help organizing the twins' birthday on Tuesday? Or for their Halloween costumes?"

He shook his head. "They both want to be cats, so I ordered ears and tails online. And everything's set for their birthday. Maybe next year I'll do a big party with friends from day care and such, but for this year I'm glad I decided to keep it small. You're still up for picking apples and making their cake with them?"

"I've been perfecting my recipe for weeks."

I love her.

The truth sang in his veins.

But what did he have to offer her? She was supposed to be

enjoying her empty nest, not looking to fill it with him and his nieces.

Her breathing was slowing, as if she was starting to doze, when a huffing *pshhh* sound filled the wide cove.

She shot to sitting. He did, too, craning his neck to see what animal had made the noise. It had to be something big, but—

"Oh my *God*," she whispered, pointing behind him.

He turned in time to see a shining, black dorsal fin arcing through the water.

"An orca." He could barely hear her. "Since when do they come into coves? And this late in the year?"

"Water's been warmer than normal," he murmured. "And I bet the fishing's good behind the islet."

Pshhhh.

A bigger animal, and a bigger arc.

"Look at those eyespots. What a showoff," he joked.

"And its belly is so white. It's *huge. And magnificent.*" She covered her mouth with her hands, her eyes tracking the movement of the two whales as they took turns breaching, about a hundred feet from the port side of the boat.

He'd seen similar shows a few times in his youth and twenties, but her excitement was contagious. The wildlife around Oyster Island would always be a privilege to watch.

Tears glistened in her eyes and she wiped her lashes with her thumbs. "My phone is under the bow!"

He took his from his pocket, unlocked it and passed it to her. "Record away."

The animals swam around in the cove for a few more minutes before leaving from the opposite side where they'd entered.

"I can't believe that happened." Clara was still whispering, despite the whales being out of sight.

"You said you were jealous of Daniel's sighting this summer, so I ordered an even better one for you," he teased. "I promised you today would be special."

"Mmm, yes, your hotline connection with the resident orcas. I appreciate you calling in the favor."

She kissed him, all eager lips and roaming hands. "And you've followed through on all your promises today."

Fear struck him.

It must have shown on his face, because she froze. "What?"

The truth was impossible to hide. "What if I make promises I can't keep? I don't want to hurt you. Or Harper and Pippa."

She was very still. "We choose what promises to keep and not to keep, Lawson."

"Yes, and I'm far more careful with making them than I used to be. But it's hard not to be tempted by your charm, Clara. How much I l-like you, and wanting more."

Her brows drew together. "What do you mean? I get why you need to keep things consistent for the girls. It's complicated for you to parent and to have a relationship with me. But we seem to be finding a balance?"

"Is this what you want your life to be, though? You're getting ready to climb mountains again, and I'm stuck on flat, flat land for a long time."

She stared at him.

"Parenting," he continued. "You're releasing an adult into the world, and I'm only getting started. You aren't looking to begin again."

She stiffened. "That's a big assumption."

His gut churned. His honesty had not cleared things up at all. More like made it worse.

The boat ride back to Archer and Franci's was quiet, but this time, it had nothing to do with the roaring engine and everything to do with him having said the wrong thing.

Chapter Fourteen

"I'm sorry," Clara apologized to Archer, trailing her friend on a last-minute paddle. Two days after her boat trip with Lawson, and she was still on edge about his assumptions. "I'm not great company this morning."

"Don't worry about it. We're all entitled to our quiet days. I'm just happy to have someone join me for an early-morning kayak."

Clara sent him a puzzled look. "Don't you and your sister go out a few times a week?"

"We did, but once Violet hit month eight, she decided she needed to take a break." Archer's smile was bemused. "I suspect my wife is partly at fault."

"Ohhh, the infamous near-tumble into the water?"

"Yeah. Last winter, Vi and Franci were out kayaking. Franci was close to full-term with Iris, and then Violet got called for a delivery. My darling wife decided she was fine to return to the dock alone and get out without a hand or the accessible kayak ramp we have for anyone who needs it. I was in the parking lot when I heard her shout. I've never run so fast. It was the beginning of it all, really."

His expression turned the kind of fond only distance from an emergency could bring.

"I remember you calling me after you delivered Iris. I *knew* she was the one for you, even if you were in deep denial. Your voice—you were wrecked."

"Never to recover," he agreed jovially.

She wasn't feeling particularly cheery about her own romance, not after Lawson had laid out his doubts on their boat ride, but she had no problem mustering some joy for her friends. "I love it for you. And Franci and Iris."

Archer paddled for a few strokes, then turned a knowing look on Clara. "I had my tent set in the will-defend-little-sister-against-evil-ex-for-life camp for a while—but Lawson's *actually* managed to make amends with her and Mati. And it seems like you're getting more serious. I hope he understands how lucky he is to have you in his life."

She stared at her friend for a second. With how close Archer and Eddy had been, he could have been weird about Clara pursuing love again. But he was as supportive of her exploring a second chance at love as he'd been of her first.

Archer's support might be moot, if her stubborn boyfriend didn't decide to see the possibilities.

"He's having a hard time believing I'd want to get more serious with him. As if I don't love his nieces. Love h—" She cleared her throat. "There are lots of people my age who are starting young families. Look at you, adopting Iris. Or Violet and Matias, getting closer to parenthood by the day. Mati and I are the same age. Just because I started younger, doesn't mean I couldn't do it again. Especially since Daniel loves the twins, too."

"I wonder if he's shifting his own insecurities onto you." His voice was cautious. "He left my sister because of something similar."

"He's been open about their breakup. It's for sure on his mind."

"Well, that's something," he said. "He *didn't* talk to Violet."

"He's been open about his lack of communication, too." Whether or not he trusted himself to choose differently this time was still uncertain, though.

"Also good."

"For sure. I was just taken aback. When he was worried about balancing parenting and dating, I understood. It's no small feat. But turning it on me, and assuming the girls can't fit into my life? He made space for them. Why can't he see I could do the same? Daniel having graduated doesn't mean I can't consider being with someone who has a young family."

"People end up falling for single parents all the time," he said, a knowing smirk on his face.

"*Exactly.* When we're with each other, it feels right," she said. "When I wake up in the morning, I want to pour him coffee, and go through the hassle of toasting him a bagel wrapped in tinfoil in the oven, because I know he doesn't like my gluten-free ones, but his can't go in my toaster. The little stuff. But I don't want to be the only one falling in love. And he's said he struggles to trust himself. Should I be listening to his self-doubt, instead of to the way my heart's urging me to cling to him and not let go?"

"He's not giving you what you need?" Protectiveness edged her friend's tone.

"If it turns into a perpetual cycle of wondering if he'll be willing to be vulnerable, then no, it won't be what I need." And as much as she found it easier to recognize where she was needed—by Lawson, by the twins, by Daniel—she did need to attend to her inner voice, too. "It doesn't have to be *now.* I get these things take time. But if he doesn't see the possibility *ever*... Maybe he's right. Maybe he and I aren't at the same stage."

"Give me five minutes with him."

"Oh, no. None of that latent-protective-military-officer posturing, thank you."

His jaw tightened.

"There's always the public declaration route. Marching right up the dock and announcing your love."

She pictured standing on the boardwalk in front of the tasting room and shouting her lifelong devotion for one Lawson Thorne. His cheeks would turn the color of his raspberry sour, no doubt, and he'd shove up his glasses all awkward-like. And given this was her daydream, damn it, he didn't shy away. He strolled, those long legs eating up the boards, and lifted her off her feet for a kiss that went down in the Hideaway Wharf annals.

Her stomach went hollow and yearning at her trip down fanciful lane.

"I couldn't do that to him," she lamented. "I might have committed to being more daring this year, to taking more chances, but I don't think this falls in the category of times to run in, sword held high."

He flicked a small spray of water at her. "I was teasing. Embarrassment isn't the way to go. Honesty is, though. If the 'more' he's asked for feels hollow, tell him what's missing. Franci did with me, and it's what I needed to hear."

She had to keep hoping they could slowly meld their lives.

Her heart wouldn't be able to wait much longer for her to admit she loved him.

Something heavy catapulted onto Lawson's bed, jarring him from sleep.

It wasn't the cat, was it?

Giggles ensued.

Also: "Apples!"

Phew.

"Morning, girls." He pressed the heels of his hands into his eyelids. Four tiny knees dug into his legs and stomach. Opening his eyes, he squinted at the dual messes of hair. They both wore tie-dyed pajamas, though not matching. Without his glasses on, and halfway down the bed, they were smears of color to his blurry vision. Pippa, in swirls of blue, was like a partly cloudy sky. Harper, in pink and purple, was like the horizon at dusk.

Fumbling for his glasses and the necessary clarity to face

the day, he grinned and opened his arms wide. A second later, and his embrace was full of wiggling twins.

"We're *four*," Pippa announced.

"No, you're two," he teased, dropping a kiss to the top of both their heads. "One, two."

"No, Unca Sonny. Four *years old*," Harper corrected.

"*What?* When did *that* happen?" he said, feigning surprise.

Giggles ensued.

"To*day*," Pippa said.

"Well, then we'd better celebrate," he said. "Party dresses. A suit for me. A three-course dinner at the fanciest restaurant in town."

"No," Pippa said, dissolving into more laughter. "Us and Clara are apple picking. And making apple cake."

"And chicka nuggies. You promised," Harper said over her sister, far more indignant than Pippa, who seemed to have caught his joking tone.

"I did promise," he said solemnly. "Celery with ranch dressing, and then chicken nuggets and Tater Tots."

"*Can* we wear party dresses?" Pippa asked.

"For dinner? Yes," he replied.

She shook her head, messy strands flying like an electric halo. "For apples."

His knee-jerk reaction was "no."

"Your dress will get dirty," he pointed out.

"But I want to sparkle," Pippa said.

Who was he to fight the desire to sparkle on her birthday? Clean laundry was not the hill to die on.

He turned to Harper. "Do you want to sparkle, too?"

She shook her head. "I want a cape."

"Okay. After birthday pancakes, we'll pick the perfect apple-picking dresses and capes."

When the girls tumbled into the yard an hour and a half later, they weren't the only ones dressed up. Harper had clipped a dozen glittering butterfly barrettes into his hair and had made him put on a tie. With a T-shirt, mind you, and shorts. At least he wasn't going to get anything from his meagre collection of business-appropriate clothing filthy.

Ignore what I'm wearing, he texted Clara, who had asked for an alert when they were ready for apple picking. She'd been…quieter…with him since their boat trip. Not distant, exactly, but he could tell she was thinking. Which—fair. His point about them being at different places in their lives wasn't a small one, and he appreciated her taking the time to think.

His phone dinged.

You're ready for apples?

With bells on. And by bells, I mean barrettes.

When she descended from her porch into the yard, she did a double take. Her smile softened around the edges.

"I haven't forgotten how to dress myself, I promise," he said.

"Oh, I can tell you had expert help."

She came over to him and began to play with a few of the hair clips, nudging them into place.

He wanted them all out, mainly so she'd be able to dig her fingers into the mess.

Couldn't deconstruct the girls' hard work, though.

"I picked the colors," Harper said.

"I barretted them," Pippa followed up. "Aren't they pretty?"

"Oh, yes," Clara said, bending down and taking them both in her arms. "But you two are even prettier. Happy birthday, sweethearts. I didn't know we were going with formal wear for apple picking."

"And superheroes," Harper added.

"You need a sparkly dress, too, Clara," Pippa said.

Amusement danced across Clara's gaze. "Oh, do I?"

"You look very pretty to me," he said. Her navy blue T-shirt was pulling across her breasts a little, irresistible tugs in the fabric. He couldn't think of a thing she could wear that would look hotter.

"Mmm, I can do better." She winked at the girls. "Go have a swing for a few minutes, and I'll see what I can do to match what you're wearing."

The girls took off.

"Can I come watch?" he murmured.

She gave him a chiding look and jogged back into her house.

After a few minutes, she reappeared in a floaty, long sundress. She carried a wide, shallow basket with a thick handle. A tea towel lined the wicker. It outdid the plastic bucket he'd planned to use to collect fruit.

"Hey there, Red Riding Hood."

"I was thinking more 'Princess Buttercup.'"

He nodded. "As you wish."

Her laugh was genuine, warming him to his core.

"And here's my loyal steed," she announced.

Français plodded behind her, a gold, glitzy bow tie attached to the front of his collar, and a small square of velvet fabric pinned opposite, draped over half his back.

Huh. It appeared dogs could, indeed, sulk. Not something he'd noticed before, not having ever had a dog as a pet, but Français was certainly making his opinion known. His nose scrunched even more than usual.

"I think your dog is mortally offended," Lawson said.

Clara's smile danced. "Everyone needed formal wear. Human and canine."

Her dress wasn't the end of her costume. She'd somehow affixed a ribbon to a beach towel, and had it wrapped over her shoulders a bit like a shoulder holster. It must have been tied in the back.

"I didn't want it to choke me," she explained, watching him as he puzzled out what she'd done.

"You're wearing a towel cape," he said quietly.

"You have a metal butterfly garden in your hair," she whispered back.

He crooked his finger toward her.

She came right up to him, a fraction of an inch of grass separating her silver flats and his flip-flops.

With his back turned to the swing set, there was no way the girls could see what was happening.

Or he'd tell himself that, anyway, because he absolutely had to kiss Clara right now, and wasn't ready to explain it to Harper or Pippa.

Bending his head, he slid his hand around the back of Clara's head, his fingers luxuriating in the long, soft strands.

A taste of fruity tea, or maybe lip gloss, lingered on her plush mouth.

She kissed him back, five, ten, fifteen seconds of losing his head.

She was the first to pull away.

"I didn't know we were at the *kissing in front of the kids* stage." She touched the fingertips of one hand to her lips.

"They can't see."

"You're willing to risk it? They're speedy," she said, peeking around him.

"I think I am," he said.

She chewed on her lip.

"What?" he asked.

She shook her head. "Let's pick apples."

For whatever reason, his stomach sank.

They approached the tree, where the girls were rapt with something at the base. They were both on their hands and knees, examining the trunk.

"Look, a mushroom!" Pippa exclaimed.

"It has pope-adots!" Harper added.

"'Pope-adots,'" Clara echoed, glancing at Lawson. "Are

you writing some of these things down? Their mispronuncia-
tions? It's worth recording."

Damn. He should be doing that. "Hadn't thought of it."

She paused. A whole raft of regret crossed her face. "It's
okay. It's impossible to do it all. Especially when you're just
one parent."

Stacking his hands on his head, he exhaled. His pulse was
thrumming. As soon as he'd start to feel like he was doing
something right, something simultaneously small and enormous would sideswipe him.

"One thing at a time," Clara said quietly. "Take a few pictures of the day. It'll be good enough for now."

"I want to be better than 'good enough,' Clara."

"You are." She reached over and squeezed his hand. "I
promise."

For you, too.

Good wasn't close to enough for Clara.

"Take a minute," she said, before focusing her attention
on the girls, getting on her knees between them. "Show me
this mushroom!"

Three heads bent together, the brown of the girls' matching braids stark against the pale blond of Clara's loose waves.

She spoke quietly to them, weaving a tale of tiny, fantasti-
cal creatures sheltering under the spotty fungus.

It was…love.

A mother's love, freely given.

She'd chosen every moment of her participation this day.
Would she keep choosing it?

And did he have enough to give in return?

His throat was full. Of worries, of his own feelings of love
swirling in his chest.

Damn it. He needed to get himself together.

But before he redirected everyone back to picking, he
opened a new note page in his phone and typed "Harper:
pope-adots."

Soon after, the girls lost interest in the mushroom. The two of them took turns on the ladder. Lawson stood at the base, arms at the ready in case of a tumble. Clara stood to the side, accepting each picked apple and placing them in the wide-bottomed straw basket she carried.

Before long, a glossy heap of pink-streaked apples filled the basket.

"We have way more than we'll need for a cake," he commented. "Too bad they're not the right strain to make cider."

"We could give them to our neighbors," Clara said. "Or I could make a dessert for the pub."

Lawson peered up at the still-teeming branches. "Bet it's enough to do both."

"Auntie Isla could make cheese." Pippa puffed up proudly at her suggestion.

"Cheese is not apples," Harper countered. "Cheese is milk."

"Auntie Isla has *berry* cheese!"

"It's delicious with apples, Pippa," Clara said, playing referee. "If your aunt can't use it in her cheese, it can go beside it."

The little one shot her sister a smug smile.

Harper burst into tears.

Pippa followed suit.

One twin attached herself to one of his legs, and the other to Clara's.

Français blinked up at them all with ennui.

They each hoisted their sobbing child, twin spider monkeys.

"Cake time?" Clara asked dryly.

"Well, we've got the added salt taken care of."

To Lawson's relief, the remainder of the day was tear free. They baked the apple cake, played fairies on the beach, opened presents and had the promised dinner of chicken nuggets. They'd cooked at Clara's to make sure they didn't accidentally cross contaminate, and the girls hadn't even noticed the nuggets weren't their usual wheat-battered kind.

Right before bed, Clara had read the girls a book about filling their buckets.

After so much joy and busyness, his bucket was somehow overflowing and empty at the same time.

He sprawled on the couch, savoring the quiet in his living room. "Hopefully, having a day like today will help while I'm away this weekend."

"Oh, my goodness. Who's more nervous—them, or you?"

"Right now? Me, I think."

This weekend was going to be the first time he was alone in so long. He did have a laundry list of festival tasks—he needed to talk up Hau'oli for Matias like no one's business—but he would only be responsible for himself for four days. Well, himself and James, one of the bartenders from The Cannery, who was coming as his second set of hands.

"I'll be alone, but the girls won't be," he said, more of a reminder to himself than anything. "They're excited about staying with Isla. They'll, uh, they'll be fine."

"They *will* be fine," she assured him. "They're resilient."

"They are. You know what was great about them crying today?"

She eyed him. "We have different opinions about *great*."

"No, no, it makes sense. It was a big day. They were crying. But not about Quentin and Kiera. I mean, them being upset about celebrating without their parents would have been totally normal. But they weren't, which is okay, too. Like you said, they're resilient."

"Most kids are. More than adults, sometimes."

He rubbed a hand over his sternum. "I remember really feeling my dad's loss on the milestone days."

"Daniel would agree with you. He still struggles on holidays."

"And what about you? With Eddy, I mean. Not your very alive dad."

She let out a *ha*. "The day-to-day is when it sticks out more.

I tend to prep myself mentally and emotionally before holidays, having strategies in place and stuff. The small moments tend to shake me more."

"If that happens, I want to support you."

"Thanks," she said, biting her lip.

"Is there something you tend to need in particular?"

"It depends on the day. I'll let you know if there is."

Something in her tone suggested she had more to say.

"Is there something you need now?" He was afraid to even ask it. What if she replied with something he couldn't do, or be?

She exhaled, slow, the kind of breath a person let out when they were trying to steady themselves.

"Yeah, about that. I… I don't want you to feel rushed to make a commitment right now. There's no set amount of time in terms of adjusting to your new reality. And you're also saying you want to be closer, and are *feeling* closer. Which I love. I want it with you. I see the possibilities we could have together. But you got something wrong."

"Oh?"

She nodded. "I do like being independent. I'm getting to do things I never felt free to do, which is fantastic. And yet, I gravitate to you and the girls more than those other things. I genuinely enjoy them, Lawson. I enjoy *you*. And me being independent is less about me being free of any commitments and more about me choosing what I invite into my life. I *want* to invite you and the girls in."

Even knowing everything she did about the mistakes he'd made in the past, she was willing to choose him?

"Lawson? You look…shocked."

"Well, yeah. Your courage blows me away, Clara. You want to explore what being together could look like, even though you're completely aware our life wouldn't be easy."

Her mouth was turned up at the corners, but her eyes were sad. "That's what love is, Lawson. Knowing it's hard—being scared as hell to put your heart in someone else's hands—but doing it anyway. Going forward together."

"Which is something I failed to do," he said.

"Okay, but it doesn't mean you'd fail this time."

"Maybe. But if I did?"

She studied her hands for a while. "You say that as if I don't worry about the same thing. Making myself vulnerable again means opening up to the possibility of being eviscerated one more time."

"The thought of being the one to destroy you is intolerable, Clara. But I don't know if I can handle living without you, either."

The breath she let out seemed to go on forever. "I was so freaking young when I fell in love with Eddy. Eighteen. *Daniel's* age. A damn kid, really. And she had *no idea* what she was getting into. But if you went back to that eighteen-year-old girl and told her what would happen, how she'd fall in love with a Coastie and then proceed to have years and years of excellent times with him, and with the son we would make together, and then would lose him..."

"Would she still choose him?"

"Without a doubt. Every ounce of love I had with Eduardo was worth a thousand days of anguish."

"And you'd be willing to make the same choice with me?"

"Every time I see you hesitate, whether to protect yourself or the girls, it reminds me how strong that self-preservation instinct is. And it reminds me that finding something exceptional, *making* something exceptional, takes a knock-down, drag-out fight between fear and courage. So even though my heart loves to point out how it would be safer to wait to tell you how I feel until I had a thousand-percent guarantee of you returning my feelings, I can't let that be my guide. I want to say yes to this, Lawson."

Yes. Thrilling, coming from someone who made him feel

the things Clara made him feel. And also terrifying. "I want to agree."

"But you're not there."

He shook his head slowly. "The girls aren't settled enough, yet."

"Okay. I can be patient."

He exhaled. "Seems unfair to you."

"Not if it's a matter of giving Harper and Pippa more time."

"Oh."

"Except it's still more than that, isn't it?"

The words almost got stuck in his throat, but he forced them out. "I've believed I'd be alone. Getting out of that mindset is a challenge."

"Which is fair."

"But?"

She frowned, deep enough to crease her cheeks. "I'm willing to face the unknown with you. What I can't do is be in a half-on, half-off relationship because you're anticipating the myriad ways you might screw up. You're in charge of your choices, Lawson. You can trust yourself to make better decisions, knowing you've been making a whole lot of them for years now."

He didn't know what to do with her honesty.

"I don't know if I have an answer," he said.

"I understand. But while you figure it out, we have to stick to friendship. It's too confusing, too easy to fall for you when we're sleeping together. Sex with you…it's amazing. And my heart's getting too tied up in it to be able to share a bed and be casual."

"Right. Of course."

It ripped him in two, left him in a bloody heap on the floor, but he couldn't blame her for trying to protect herself.

Not when he was doing the exact same thing.

She leaned in, but dropped a kiss to his cheek, not his mouth. "I had so much fun celebrating the girls' birthday."

Regret made his bones ache. "I'm sorry."

"Me, too." She bit her lip as she rose from the couch.

Every cell of his body urged him to reach up, to pull her toward him, to assure her he could do this.

"You were easy to fall in love with, Lawson Thorne."

She loved him.

His heart wanted to throw confetti.

I love you, too.

But until he knew he was capable of loving her properly, he couldn't say the words. Not even if it meant she walked away.

The next morning, his chest still felt hollow.

Harper was bouncing in the back seat on the way to Isla's, chattering about Cashew and showing her aunt the giant stuffed dog he'd given her for her birthday, an exact, magnified replica of the small one she was so close to.

She'd slept draped over it last night.

He should have felt victorious, having picked the right gift.

Feeling *anything* was hard. He was numb.

Two seconds after he parked, Harper unbuckled her booster seat, hopped out of the car and began pelting his sister with questions about Cashew.

Pippa was slower, sticking close to Lawson's side, clinging to his hand as he went around to the hatch and hoisted out their overnight bag. She clutched her well-worn bunny in her other hand.

"Bunny can't sleep in a different bed," Pippa said solemnly.

He squeezed her hand. He'd been expecting this. Last weekend, Pippa had found it harder to go to sleep in an unfamiliar bed than Harper had. "And what is going to stop Bunny from falling asleep, do you think?"

"Shadows," she said.

"Did you remind Bunny you brought your night-light from home? And your special blanket?"

She nodded. "He's not sure it will work."

"Hmm. Has there ever been a night where Bunny has been awake all night long? Or does he fall asleep after a while?"

She pouted. "He always falls asleep. But sometimes it is really late."

Lawson could relate. He'd almost seen the sun come up before he finally managed to stop cycling last night. Clara had fallen in love with him. His inability to accept that gift was a knife to the chest. Why was he so frozen?

Pippa stared at him.

Oh, damn, he'd asked her a question, and she'd answered, and then he'd spaced out. Not cool.

"Bunny falls asleep late, huh? Well, that's okay. Sometimes, sleeping is tough. If he wakes up in the morning and is still tired, you can put him in bed for a nap. Naps are *great* here at Auntie Isla's."

"Do you nap with the goats?"

"Not with the goats. But I did live here for a couple of months, remember?" They'd talked about this numerous times, but Pippa seemed to need the repetition. "In the same bedroom where you'll be staying. I mean, you're a pro. You fall asleep every night. You can help Bunny fall asleep, too."

She paused for a second, then whispered, "I'm scared."

Me too, Pips. Me too.

Of the weekend and the success of Hau'oli, of his feelings for Clara and losing her forever.

And yet, you're expecting a four-year-old to face her fear.

He lifted Pippa with his free arm, encouraging her to snuggle against his side.

"It's okay to be scared," he said. "That's your body telling you something is new, and to be careful. But you can trust that Auntie Isla will take care of you while I'm away. We can talk on the phone every day. And you'll have so much fun with the goats. I'll be home before you know it. Okay?"

"Okay," she whispered.

"I love you," he said, hugging her tighter.

"I love you, too, Uncle Sonny."

Oh, *damn*. Why was he going away for the weekend, again? Was it truly necessary?

His sister came up, wearing her usual hat and a big grin.

"Looks like someone needs to come along and test out recipes for apple cheese," Isla said.

"Harper says apples are not cheese," Pippa complained.

"Ah, but we should still experiment." Isla held her arms out. "Come. Let's try a few different recipes and decide which one we like best."

Lawson transferred his clingy niece into his sister's loving embrace. She shifted Pippa onto her hip and then took the bag, too.

"Shoo," she said. "Go put Hau'oli on the map."

"Yes. Yes, right. Mati needs that."

"So do you," she said under her breath.

"It's not mine."

"It could be." She was so damn cheerful about it. "Just reach out."

He sighed.

"You're trustworthy, you know."

He shot her a look. "Do we need to get into this?"

"If it's holding you back from asking for part ownership in the brewery you're dying to share with Matias, then yes. Not to mention, you're doing the same thing with Clara."

"Auntie Clara looked sad today," Harper announced, sidling up to Isla.

His sister raised an accusatory eyebrow at him.

He could barely take it in. His stomach was on the ground at Harper's words. He blinked at his niece. "Auntie Clara?"

Her lip wobbled. "Am I in trouble?"

"No, sweetheart. I was surprised. I love that you love Clara."

No matter if she stayed on the island or went back to Portland or wherever else, he knew she wouldn't break contact with Harper and Pippa. She was the epitome of trustworthy when it came to the girls.

And with my own heart.

"You know what Auntie Clara goes with?" Isla was downright singsonging. "Uncle Lawson."

"Could we not?" He gritted his teeth. "We have an audience."

"Of course, of course." She looked somewhat chagrined. "Later, then. Have fun at the festival. And Lawson... I love you. And I'm proud of you."

Chapter Fifteen

A glitter bomb had detonated in the farmhouse kitchen. None of the three occupants—Isla, Harper and Pippa—had escaped unscathed.

Clara stood in the doorway with her lips pulled between her teeth, trying not to laugh. "Wow, it's looking creative in here."

She had time before her Friday afternoon shift, and had decided to stop by Isla's under the guise of saving Isla from having to deliver The Cannery's current cheese order. Really, she wanted to see how the girls were doing on their second full day with Lawson out of town.

"We're making slime!" Harper announced. Her expression darkened and focused on her sister. "*Not* apple cheese."

Oof, the little girl was still on that? She needed a T-shirt printed with #1 GRUDGE HOLDER.

"Hey, now." Isla stepped in gently. "There's room for cheese *and* slime in the world. Cheese is delicious, and slime is super fun."

Pippa held out a glob of neon pink slime dotted with purple glitter. "Try it, Clara! It's not sticky."

The goat cheese sounded even more up her alley, but she took a seat at the kitchen table and accepted the offered lump.

"It's cold," she said. "Feels like gelatin."

"Jelly-tin?" Harper asked, poking at the glob she had on the table in front of her. It appeared she'd put some sort of beads in hers. Green lumps bulged from the yellow goo.

"It's what makes Jell-O firm," she explained. "It's not what's in your slime, though. It just feels the same."

Both girls nodded sagely, as if they'd been let in on a trade-marked secret.

She played with the girls for ten or so minutes, until it was time to think about getting to work. "I should grab that order, Isla."

"Oh, yeah, it's in the fridge in the tasting shop," her friend said. "Girls, should we go get it with Clara?"

Pippa's face crumbled. "You're leaving?"

"I need to run the pub tonight," she explained.

"You will leave, and Uncle Sonny leaved, and Mommy and Daddy leaved—"

"Mommy and Daddy *died*," Harper corrected.

Clara's heart lurched. She and Isla glanced at each other, silently agreeing to divide and conquer.

She took Pippa by the hand and guided the little girl into Isla's cozy living room. They took a seat on the squishy teal blue couch. Pippa cuddled close, and Clara held her tight.

"Want to talk about your worries?" she asked. "It sounds like you don't like it when people leave."

Pippa sniffled and shook her head.

"It hurts when people leave, doesn't it? Because we love them so much, and sometimes it feels harder to love them when they're far away."

She'd had a similar conversation with Daniel a few days ago, trying to stop him from cycling in his thoughts about being so far from Charlotte.

"Far away. Or gone," Pippa whispered.

"Or gone." A wave of her own grief took her out at the knees. Always a sneak attack. "Like how I miss Daniel's daddy. Every day."

The small, pigtailed head cocked. "But you are friends with Uncle Sonny."

"I am. I can do both things at the same time," she said, then clarifying with, "I can miss Daniel's daddy *and* be friends with your uncle."

No matter what happened with them romantically, she wasn't going to cut him from her life. Even so, his inability to take a chance on her would hurt for a while.

A *long* while.

But she couldn't imagine going without seeing him at all. Especially without seeing his girls. They'd just need to create a new normal.

One where her heart ached on the regular.

She could live with that kind of pain, though.

She couldn't give up moments like this, holding Pippa and drying her tears.

"Oh." Pippa scrunched up her face. "When will Uncle Sonny get home?"

"Sunday, my love."

"I want to tell him my slime is pink with purple sparkles."

"I could send him a text," Clara offered. "With a picture of you and me waving, even. Would you like that?"

Pippa nodded.

"Okay. Let's see what we can do."

She pulled out her phone and opened the camera, then instructed Pippa to wave.

"Looks good?" Clara confirmed.

"Yup."

She sent the picture, along with a message: Pippa would like you to know her slime is pink with purple sparkles.

"Feeling a bit better?" Clara asked.

"Yes."

Her phone buzzed. Not a text, a video call from Lawson.

She accepted the call and adjusted the screen to center both Pippa and her in the frame.

Lawson's face filled the screen. A Hau'oli banner, in reverse, stretched behind him.

"Hi, there," Clara said. "You're not busy?"

"We're getting set up for the tasting event tonight," he explained. "Look, we won a medal."

He held up a growler with a gold medal and blue ribbon hanging around the neck.

"That's amazing!" Clara said. "Congratulations."

He grinned. "More importantly—what's this I hear about pink-and-purple slime?"

Pippa nodded, brightening. "I'll go get it."

She ran off, leaving Clara alone with the breaker of her heart.

Okay, so maybe it was going to hurt a lot.

I can do this.

His mouth gaped for a few seconds, as if he was deciding what to say. After clearing his throat, he said, "Visiting my sister's?"

"Thought I'd stop in and say hi to the girls."

His gaze turned wistful. "You're too good to us."

"No," she said. "You underestimate how much love you all deserve."

He shook his head. "Are Harper and Pippa okay?"

"They had a little bit of a sibling squabble, and were feeling some feelings about you being away, but they got through it."

"I'm wondering whether coming here was the right decision."

"You and Matias won a medal," she reminded him. "That's important, too."

Pippa tore back into the living room, her sister on her heels. They were both brandishing their slime. They landed in Clara's lap, narrowly missing getting the goo in Clara's side braid.

"That is very pink, and very yellow, and very glittery," he said.

"So is Isla's kitchen," Clara said, shifting the girls in her lap so they could all be seen on the screen.

"She's the best aunt," Lawson said.

"Damn straight!" Isla called from the other room.

He chuckled, his amusement clear on his face. "Hearing of a bat, too."

"We played fetch with Cashew," Harper announced.

"Terrific."

"Can you come home, please?" Pippa said. She lowered her voice. "Bunny couldn't sleep until he had warm milk."

"Well, that's okay. Warm milk is a great idea. And I'll be home in two days," he promised.

Harper's lip wobbled. "No, come home now."

"What if you can't ever come home?" Pippa said.

His jaw slackened, as if pulled down by the weight of his nieces' worries. "Oh, honey. Pippa. Nothing I'm in control of could keep me from coming home to you three. I promise."

Three? Clara's own mouth hung open.

"You *promise* promise?" Pippa asked.

"Triple promise," he vowed. "A very smart person told me I get to choose what promises I keep. And I will do everything I can to keep the promises I make to you."

"Okay!" Pippa said. She and her sister darted off Clara's lap and headed for the kitchen.

"You *three*?" Clara whispered.

"Clara, I didn't mean—"

"Don't. Don't make excuses. Let it be."

He pressed his lips together before nodding. "How upset were they just now? They looked like they'd been crying."

She was impressed he managed to notice over the small screen. "A bit upset, but nothing critical."

"I don't want to remind them of Quentin and Kiera being gone."

"I know. And it's on their minds, but they aren't consumed. You've done the right things, Lawson. They're attached to you."

So am I.

She didn't say it out loud, but it hung between them anyway.

"Right. Well…"

"You should get back to work. Have fun with the tasting."

"Thanks, Clara." He wiped his hand down his face. "I did mean it. About coming home to you. It's where I want to be right now."

Coming home to you three. Coming home to you three. *Coming home to you* three?

Argh.

Lawson spent the entire tasting with the slip running through his brain on repeat.

He was still distracted when he video-called Matias at the end of the night.

"Any baby yet?" Lawson asked.

"No."

"Still a good thing you stayed home, though."

"From the looks of things, you didn't need me there," Matias said. "You charmed an impressive number of beer drinkers."

"I can do that in my sleep." Lawson sat in one of the chairs behind their tasting display. "I want this to go well for you."

Matias rubbed the back of his neck. "Do you want to start calling it ours at some point?"

He froze. "What, Hau'oli?"

"Yeah. It was always supposed to be you and me."

"You're doing fine with it being you."

"Except, it's not only me. Some of the recipes? You. Reputation? Partly you. Look at why we got the invite to Oktoberfest in the first place—it was because you're involved in Hau'oli. A lot of it's me, sure. But it's getting hard to tease it out."

"Kellan is your business partner."

On the screen, Matias took a drink from a bottle of water before replying. "So, funny story. I was sharing your gluten-free experiment with him the other day—"

"You what?"

"The sample you brought me was good. Kellan lives for new food and drink. It was a natural progression."

"But…"

"He thinks the market for gluten-free beer in Washington is still growing. Says Colorado's a hotbed, and a bit in Seattle, but there's room for an up-and-coming brewery with a boutique gluten-free branch attached to it."

Lawson was reeling. "I made it for Clara. Really."

"Well, you should think bigger." Matias smirked. *Think bigger* was advice Lawson had given Matias almost a decade ago.

"Where?"

"Don't see why we couldn't wall off part of the warehouse to make a dedicated space. We'd need a new brewhouse… Might be able to use one of the existing five fermenting tanks, maybe not. We'd need to see. And we'd need to keep bringing in milled grain."

"That's mighty expensive." He'd priced it out already. Hadn't been able to help at least crunching the numbers. The challenge of trying something completely new to him, and less tested and established—talk about tempting. Two of the batches he'd made *had* turned out decent. Could he perfect them, and at a larger scale? Starting up his own place was more than he wanted to take on, though.

Matias's expression turned dry. "Starting a brewery? Expensive? You don't say."

"What are you suggesting, here?"

"Didn't you get a buyout from Mill Plain for the continued ability to use your name and recipes, et cetera?"

He nodded, caution tickling his neck.

"So, pour it into Hau'oli."

"It can't be that simple, Matias," he murmured.

"Why not?" His friend's voice held all the confidence his own lacked.

"Because…because—I don't know what to say."

"Take a page out of Clara's book—say yes."

"I… This feels like a conversation we should be having in person."

"Tell you what. Think about it. Figure out what's going on with her first, if you're even going to stick around Oyster Island. Hell, maybe you have plans to leave again, and you're trying to let me off easy. It would make sense to take the twins back to Vancouver after you've finished your commitment to me."

"No. God, no. Oyster Island is home, and I want it to be *their* home."

"They certainly seem to think it is."

"Yeah. It's hard to be away from them." He pinched the bridge of his nose, dislodging his glasses. "I miss them like there's a hole in my heart. Clara, too. Though, she asked for space."

Matias groaned. "What did you screw up?"

He wasn't going to pretend he hadn't. "I'm not sure I can commit. The girls…they need so much."

"They need love. Something Clara gives them."

"And if I can't give enough to her?" Lawson said.

"Our brains lie to us, man. Sounds like yours has been for a while now."

"I love them. All of them."

"The twins know it."

"They do, don't they?"

"No, listen to me. Think about what it means," Matias said. "You're not messing this up. You know how to love fully. There's no reason you can't do the same with Clara, other than fear. Think about all the things you've done this year. Asking Isla and Violet for forgiveness—"

"And you."

"Yeah, me too," Matias agreed. "And navigating an unimaginable tragedy. Stepping up. Becoming a parent. All I'm saying is telling fear to piss off was worth it."

He wished it hadn't involved that tragedy. God, he missed

Quent and Kiera, and there wouldn't be a day in his life where he went to bed and felt it was fair he was the one who got to raise their little girls.

But with them in his life, seeing he couldn't dwell on mistakes was so much easier. He could grow around his past choices. Grow with them.

Even invite others along on the journey.

Because I broke the pattern.

He had.

Time to start acting like it.

"Does Clara know you love her?" Matias asked.

"Haven't quite told her."

"You're as much of a mess as Violet was when she and I were falling in love."

He winced. "She needed to get over being hurt. I need to move past being the one who did the hurting. It's not the same."

"I am in no place to question how it all turned out, because that would mean changing my present, which I wouldn't for any reason in the entire world. But here's the thing—if Violet can move past being hurt, and if Clara can be resilient after losing Eddy, don't you think there's space for you to try loving someone again?"

He had an amazing woman asking him to take a chance on her. How was it even a question?

"You're right. I know you are. Looking forward, I can see all your wild designs with the brewery. I can see watching the girls grow up. And alongside all that, I see her. Clara."

Matias waved his hand, a silent "I rest my case."

"I should finish cleaning up," Lawson said.

"She'll listen, you know." Matias sounded so damned convinced.

"I know. And I'll tell her. She needs to know she's at the center of my world."

"Yeah, and it'll take time to show her, but I think she'll give you the chance."

"I've been falling in love with her since she met me on the beach and gave me her blanket to wipe my eyes. At the library, and in the pub, and with my sister's ridiculous goats. Especially in our yard. I wish she could see it. All the moments of *her*."

Matias shook his head and signed off.

Lawson got back to cleaning up, rolling up the backdrop with James.

Ten more minutes of work, and they were ready to load everything up to James's hotel room.

They each grabbed a dolly and wheeled toward the door, James in the lead, chattering about the after-party he planned to attend.

The lobby was cooler than the packed event room, which had been sticky with warmth from the jovial crowd.

Lawson inhaled, feeling on the way to settled for the first time in a long time.

James halted, right beside the front desk. "Uh, Law?"

"What?"

The bartender tilted his chin at one of the groups of armchairs near the lounge. "Isn't that Clara's son?"

A hooded figure sat, face shadowed, arms wrapped around a backpack in his lap. There was no mistaking those lanky shoulders.

Lawson fumbled with his own dolly, just managing to keep it from crashing to the ground.

"Daniel?"

Chapter Sixteen

Lawson stared at Daniel, trying to make sense of having the kid standing here, in Salem, when he should have been snug in his university dorm almost an hour's drive away.

James lifted a brow and tilted his head in the direction of the elevators.

"Go up without me," Lawson said. "I'll bring my load to your room in a few."

"Okay. I'm going to take off right after I get changed." The clap on the shoulder he gave Lawson was a clear "Good luck."

Once James was out of earshot, Lawson focused on the teen.

"Something tells me you're not here for the beer festival," Lawson said.

Daniel shook his head. "Uh, no. I need to talk to you."

Lawson tilted the dolly to rest on its base. "Me?"

"Yeah. I was hoping… Well, I'm having a hard time getting through to my mom. And I thought she might listen to you."

Record scratch.

"Oh. Daniel. Man, there are layers of issues with this."

The teen shot him a questioning look.

"To start, we have to tell your mom you're here."

Daniel crossed his arms. "I'm an adult. She doesn't know what I'm doing most of the time."

"True, but that is not this. This feels dishonest. I can't hide having met with you from her."

Daniel's face fell. "You won't talk to her, then?"

"Whoa, whoa, whoa. I don't even know what you want me to talk to her about."

"Okay. Fair."

Lawson pulled out his phone.

"Wait. Can you give me an hour, at least, before calling her? Hear me out?"

Lawson had spent so much time thinking about Clara's relationship with the girls. But a life with Clara meant being a stepfather to this young man, too. He wished he'd known Eduardo, could know what the other man would do in this situation.

No way could he hide any of this from Clara. But Daniel wasn't in danger. He could give the teen an hour before he put the call in.

"Best I can offer you is to bring you up to my room. We can talk a bit, call your mom and then I'll take you back to school."

Daniel deflated, then nodded.

Ten minutes later, Lawson had dropped the dolly off in James's room and had put in a room service order of his own, for both him and Daniel, who hadn't managed to eat when he'd hitched a ride to Salem with a classmate.

Daniel sat in the chair and braced his elbows on his knees, as if staring at the floor was the only way he could gather the courage to say whatever it was he needed to say.

"Hey, Daniel?"

The teen lifted his gaze. He didn't look much like Clara, but a familiarity still lingered somewhere in the angles of the young face. "Yeah?"

"We'll figure this out. Whatever 'this' is. Want to tell me what's going on? Is it school related? Health? Oh, hell, Charlotte's not pregnant, is she?"

"*No.* Jeez. We're careful. Mom practically jammed condoms into my pockets this summer." Embarrassment splotched his light brown cheeks. "It's not about Charlotte. Well, I guess it sort of is. But not really. Charlotte or no, I'd feel the same."

"About what?"

A sigh the strength of a typhoon gusted through the room. The kid was all baggy hoodie and sprawled legs and bubbling frustration. "I hate school."

"Ah. You, uh, don't think your sample size is a bit small? It's not even Halloween yet."

"I should have known you'd take her side," Daniel grumbled.

"Hey, now. It's not about sides. I have a bit more perspective than you do, is all. And, like your mom, I'm pro college. I finished my degree, and my life wouldn't be the same if I hadn't."

"I don't need a degree to dive."

"No, but having a marine biology degree *with* your dive certifications would open more doors for you. Or getting a business degree and doing something like Sam does."

The suggestion earned him a jutted chin and another sigh. "Not if I have to be here for four years while I'm doing it. I want to be like my dad and Archer and get to dive for a living."

"But where do you want to work? Teaching? Industrial sites? Do you, uh, plan to enlist in the Coast Guard like your dad?"

"No. God, no. He was amazing, so was Archer, but I've heard enough of the stories. I'm… I don't want to be around explosives, you know?"

"I can imagine." He could also imagine Clara would be mighty relieved. She was nervous enough about Daniel being under the water, let alone doing it in military situations.

"I… I guess I like my biology class." Daniel's mouth twisted.

Lawson had been in conversations more fraught than this one over the course of his life. He'd broken off an engagement, for Christ's sake. This one was up there, though.

He decided to go with honesty. "I'm not sure what advice

to give you here, Danny. I want to support you. I also feel loyalty to your mom. She's—obviously—really important to me, and I don't want her to feel like any advice I give you is working against her own priorities."

"She won't listen to me."

"Seems unusual. She's listened to me a ton over the past while." He was about to say it was more than he deserved, but no. That wasn't true. Clara gave to him freely, and he wasn't going to turn away the precious gift of her time and care.

"I know. She usually does. But she's so insistent about school."

Lawson laced his fingers together. "Now, I'm not saying she's right or wrong. But consider why she might be digging in her heels. Her degrees kept a roof over both your heads since your dad died."

Daniel's jaw hung open, and his eyes were looking a little damp.

Panic streaked up his throat. "I'm not trying to make you feel guilty or anything. Every parent wants to be able to provide for their child, and your mom is no different. I just wanted to point out why she's having a hard time seeing any other path for you."

"If it's so important, why is she now deciding to do a job she doesn't need her degrees for?"

Oh, the stark thinking of teenagers. "Even though they aren't a requirement, doesn't mean she isn't benefiting from having them. She uses her experience every time she manages her staff or does something in the kitchen or even helping out with scheduling. It's all skills she built when teaching. As much as a degree is important, knowing when you're doing something you don't want to do anymore matters, too. And your mom got to that point."

"Uh, *exactly*."

Shit.

Lawson raked a hand through his hair. "Guess I didn't craft a great argument there, did I?"

Daniel lifted a shoulder. "Actually, I guess what you said about my mom's perspective made sense."

That was something, at least.

"So what is it you want me to do?" Lawson asked. "Try to convince her to let you quit school? I don't intend to. It's not my place. I want to be clear on what you're asking."

"I guess I was hoping you could—" Daniel shook his head. "Could mediate on your behalf?"

"Yeah, but you know what? If I want her to take me seriously, I need to be the one to make the argument. It won't work if I use you as an intermediary."

Pride filled him. "Good choice."

"Can you, uh, break the ice for me, though? Let her know I'm here?"

"Sure, Danny."

He needed to show her he was in for all the times—the easy, the difficult, the everyday. And he wanted her to know he loved her son, too, not just her. More than ever, he knew the reality of a "package deal."

He could only hope they'd manage to meld into a family.

Clara had her hair pushed back with a headband and was washing her face when her phone buzzed on the bathroom counter. She dried her face with a towel and grabbed the device.

"Lawson. Hey. How did the tasting go?" She took a seat on the closed toilet lid.

"It was successful. Good to feel in the game, again. Tons of familiar faces." He cleared his throat. "One in particular. Uh… Daniel made his way to say hello."

Her ears started buzzing. Daniel had done what?

"Uh, Clara? Say something, baby. Please."

"*Daniel,* Daniel? My *son* Daniel?"

"That would be the one."

"Is he safe? Hurt?"

"Yes."

"What?" Her heart was in her throat. "How. *When?*"

"Oh, damn, no. I meant yes, he's safe. He's not hurt."

She swore in relief.

"I'm sorry. I didn't mean to scare you. He's just going through some things and wanted a second opinion. And a bit of help with talking to you about it."

Her son was going to Lawson instead of coming to her? Heat raced through her body, but her fingers also went tingly, as if anger and panic were fighting it out for who got to control her limbic system.

"Why does he think he can't talk to me? He's *always* talked to me."

"I know. He loves you so much. He's trying to pick a path he loves. Though it might not be the exact one you envisioned for him."

Was this about school? It had to be. Why did Daniel not understand the importance of getting an education?

Wait. She took a deep breath. Any time she'd ever jumped to conclusions, she'd regretted it.

"Can you put him on the phone, please?"

"Yes. But hang on, Clara. He'll figure this out. Promise. The whole reason he came here was because he wanted me to put a pitch in for him with you, but then he realized he needs to be the one to talk to you. That's growth and maturity, and it counts for something. You raised one hell of a son."

"He was planning to use you as an intermediary?"

She might have screeched a little.

"I, uh, took it partly as a compliment, to be honest," he said. "But we've never talked about me being involved in raising Daniel, so I get why you're surprised."

He sounded wounded.

Damn it.

"No, you *are* a good listener. And it is a compliment. I want him to respect you and consider you a role model. Also, it's good he recognizes I would hold your opinions in high regard."

"But you're choked he didn't come to you right away."

"Yes," she said. Him seeing it helped.

"I think he was trying to find a way *not* to hurt you."

"Noted. Assuming best intent." She hauled in a massive breath. Her stomach was rolling like a boat caught in a flash storm.

"Okay. Here he is."

"Mom?" Daniel's voice was so small.

Ugh. She never wanted him to feel diminished.

"Honey, hey."

"I'm sorry."

She wasn't exactly sure what for, but she didn't want to put words in his mouth by guessing. "Okay. I'm listening."

"I want to quit school. I mean, I'm *going* to quit school."

Every nerve in her body flared.

Listen, listen. He'd taken the time to get to Salem to involve Lawson. A clear cry for attention, which meant she needed to wake up. She couldn't get him through this one on encouragement alone. "Tell me more."

"I know you're going to assume it's about Charlotte, and me wanting to be back on the island with her, but it's not. I miss her all the time, obviously. But that's not why I don't like it here. It's just...college isn't my place, Mom. I like learning, but big lecture halls are overwhelming. I miss being able to do modules like I did for my diving courses, when most of the learning happens in the water. I miss *being* in the water. I dove, like, every day for four months, and now I haven't in weeks and it's killing me. Everyone in my dorm is either studying all the time, or gaming or going to parties. And I miss... I miss going to work at the dive shop. Even doing the ecotours and the nondiving stuff."

She waited a few seconds to make sure he'd gotten it all out.

"Okay," she said. "I hear what you said. And it's complicated. It's also your life and career path, and you get to make the ultimate decision, even if it's not the one I would make. I'm hoping you don't throw away the idea of school entirely. I do understand you loving diving and wanting it to be part of your career."

"And…"

She scrunched her toes in the bathmat and squeezed her eyes shut. "We'd be better off having this conversation in person, Daniel. If you're going to be making big decisions, I want to be in the same room."

"Can I come home with Lawson and James?" he asked.

"Oh, honey…" She almost said yes. But she didn't want to write off him finishing the year, or even the term, and suspected that once she got him back on the island, it would be impossible to get him off.

He sighed, clearly sensing the no. "I thought you wanted to listen."

"I do. I want to help you find a solution, in fact. But I don't think you coming home for a weekend is the answer, not when the drive is that long and you have class on Monday."

"I don't care about class."

God, he didn't sound like her son when he talked like that. He'd loved most of his high school subjects, and had always striven to do his best.

No, this was on her to go to him. For a mental health check, if nothing else.

"Let me see what I can do," she said. "Can you pass the phone back to Lawson?"

"Sure," he said, voice back to small.

"I love you, so, so much," she said.

"I love you, too," he said.

She heard him mumble something to Lawson, but didn't catch what it was.

"You okay?" Lawson asked quietly.

"Yes. No." Her throat ached. "Ugh."

"It was a ridiculous question. Of course you're not okay." He paused. "You will be, though."

"C-could Danny stay with you for a night?" she asked. "I know it's a big favor, but I don't know how he'd even get back to his dorm, and I want him to be safe, and I think I'll catch a ferry and come to him tomorrow—"

"Clara. Hey. Easy. It's not a big ask, not at all. I'm invested in keeping him safe and happy, too. I have two beds, even. He'll be fine. He won't be able to come along for the seminars during the day tomorrow because minors are a no-no, but he can chill in the hotel room. What are you going to do about the pub?"

"Beg Kellan to step in."

"He will. It's an emergency."

Her stomach rolled. "It is, isn't it?"

"Yeah, but it's solvable." He paused. "If you want my input or support."

"I really, really do."

She needed him. *We* hadn't sounded that good in a long time.

Chapter Seventeen

Few drives had felt as long as the hours-long one down the I-5 today, knowing her son was in a bad place.

Guilt swamped her—was she responsible for this? Had she pushed him into a choice he hadn't wanted to make?

By the time she got to Lawson's hotel and stood outside the room number she'd been given, her insides were in knots.

She knocked.

The door swung open.

Daniel wore a Hau'oli Brewing T-shirt—Lawson's?—and jeans. Pillow creases marked his cheek.

But he was intact, and holding out his arms.

She embraced him, feeling a measure of peace for the first time all day.

"It's a good thing for you I drove alone for most of the day. Gave me time to think of all the reasons you *might* have called me. And let me tell you, a mom alone in a car can catastrophize like no one's business. Knowing you were thinking of changing your major, or maybe schools, or career paths seems positively tame now."

His face crumbled. "I don't want to disappoint you, Mom. Dad was never about quitting. And he was so proud of you for finishing your degrees, and I want to feel like he'd be proud of me, too, but I know this isn't right for me—"

"Hey. Let's go sit."

A few things around the standard hotel room gave away

the identity of its occupants. Daniel's backpack on the ground next to the desk parallel to the window. The '90s rock star biography Lawson had been reading all month. Two big-eyed, purple stuffed unicorns, each lent to him by a twin, were propped against the lamp. The covers were straight on one bed and wrinkled on the other. Daniel sat on the edge of the discombobulated covers, facing the other bed.

Clara toed out of her shoes and sat cross-legged on Lawson's mattress, opposite her son.

"Let's start with your dad," she said. "It's impossible to know what he would have thought. He never got this far with parenting. And I know he was big on following through on promises. He also loved seeing you explore. He went through his own arguments with his own parents when he enlisted—family lore claims your grandmother was unhappy as anything. He did it anyway. And it was the right choice. He was excellent at his job and adored doing it. So, I think, if it came down to it—" something she'd spent long hours contemplating as she struggled to fall asleep last night "—he would have wanted you to find your passion."

"There are online biology programs I could take."

"Legit ones?"

"I know, I know, some online schools aren't rigorous, but a few are. There's a top-ten one in Canada with an online life sciences degree, and even though it would be international tuition, with the exchange rate and the cost of college here, it wouldn't be much different. I'd be saving money on living expenses, too."

"I'm glad you've put some thought into details. Let's make a plan for this term first, okay?"

"Okay," he said warily.

"You have less than a month until Thanksgiving. Can you handle getting that far?"

He paused, then nodded.

"Are you sure? If this is a mental health situation, you know I take that more seriously than any course."

"So, you mean, finishing the term and then withdrawing?"

"For your sake, there are benefits to finishing. You'll get some credits out of it."

He stared at his tented fingers.

A knock sounded, and then the door to the hallway opened, breaking the stillness.

She turned.

Lawson. Had it only been two days since she'd seen him? It felt like weeks.

He strode toward her and gathered her up before she even had the chance to uncross her legs.

He smelled like a hint of cologne and hops.

She returned his tight hug. "I didn't expect you to come up."

She could do this alone. She had been for years. But having him at her side made life better. Hopefully, Daniel felt that way, too.

"It's happy hour," Lawson explained. "I taught two seminars this afternoon, so I get to relax for the rest of the evening. Unless you'd rather deal with this mom-to-son only."

Clara chanced a glance at her son.

He regarded them with teenage weariness. "Like Thanos, you're inevitable."

Lawson reached a hand over and high-fived him. "Nice Marvel insert."

Clara took the opportunity to sit down again, as she had been before. Lawson sat next to her. With the extra weight on the mattress, she tipped toward him and had to adjust. Sprawling all over her boyfriend while trying to have a serious conversation with her son would not do.

"I'm good if you stay, Lawson," Daniel said. "You majored in chem. You might have some ideas."

"Maybe," Lawson said cautiously.

Daniel studied them. "You guys are like, together now, right?"

"Don't change the subject," she said, before filling Lawson in with "We'd gotten as far as the benefits of Daniel finishing out the semester."

"It'd be good not being out time and money. Those aren't the only important considerations, though," Lawson said. "What's your bottom line, Danny? The nonnegotiables?"

She wanted to say everything was negotiable, but Lawson was right—just like she had done when she had decided to stop teaching, her son was allowed to draw a hard line about his life.

"Not starting a new semester here," Daniel said.

"And finishing this one?" she asked. He still hadn't given her a definitive answer on that one.

"I guess it's only a month until Thanksgiving," he mused.

"And exam period a few weeks later?" Lawson asked.

"Yes."

"No matter what, you'll be home by mid-December," Clara pointed out. "You can spend Christmas entirely underwater. Maybe Sam would even let you captain the *Oyster Queen* for the island's holiday-lights boat parade."

He laughed.

It had been too long since she'd heard her son laugh.

"I wonder if I could get my job back starting in January," he said. "And if Sam would be willing to do my advanced cert. Also, when I'd need to apply for online programs. I might have to take a term off. And I wonder if I can transfer my credits."

All questions pointing in a specific direction.

"Do all those possibilities feel exciting?" she asked.

"They—yes. They do." He glanced at Lawson. "What's your unbiased advice?"

Lawson shook his head. "If you think I'm unbiased about anything involving your mom, you're reading me wrong."

Daniel rolled his eyes. "Fine, as someone who hasn't known me my whole life."

Lawson took his time before answering. Every second of care he was putting into his advice made her love him a little bit more. "Not everything we do in life is going to make us happy, nor will it always be thrilling. And sometimes, we have to persevere through hard things. But dreading four years of your life in order to do something you think you have to do? Sounds extreme. I'm glad you're not thinking about ditching school entirely. I also don't blame you for looking for other options."

Relief spread across Daniel's expression.

"I… I have to agree with Lawson," she said.

"I didn't think you'd be this cool about it, Mom."

"I haven't been until now."

"But still. I know it's hard for you when I do things differently than you."

She barked out a laugh. "Unless you and Charlotte became very young parents within the next year, you're already doing things differently from me, honey."

Daniel blanched. "Uh, no thank you. We want to work abroad together. No offense, Lawson—she loves Harper and Pippa—but babysitting turned her off being a parent anytime soon."

Lawson chuckled. "I love them, too. And parenting is the most rewarding thing I've ever done. But I wouldn't have been ready for it at your age, either. Borrow them whenever either of you needs a reminder."

"I love them, too, you know." Daniel's voice went raw. "And I think you're a great dad. To them," he rushed to clarify. "But I'd be good with you being my stepdad, too."

Lawson locked eyes with her. So much yearning gray.

Daniel's gaze darted between them, narrowing by the second. "I… I didn't say something wrong, did I?"

"No, Danny, not at all," Lawson said. "Your mom and I still

have some things to figure out of our own. And even if we do that, I still think we'd be a ways off of marriage. But that's a big compliment, and it means more than you could know."

Her son slapped his hands on his knees and stood. "I need to text Charlotte, maybe get some fresh air. I won't come back until you text me it's safe."

"Daniel," Clara warned. "I came down here for you, not Lawson. We're not going to do anything 'unsafe.'" She made quotes with her fingers.

"Sweet, whatever you say." He darted for the door and was gone.

He'd disappeared so fast, she nearly had to do a double take. She leaned into Lawson.

He pulled her into his side. Strong arms banded around her. "You're amazing, you know that?"

"I should drive him back to school," she said. "And check into a motel there. Maybe he and I could get in with an academic adviser on Monday."

"No. It's so late. Stay here."

She cocked an eyebrow. "Three's a crowd."

"I'll crash in James's room."

She buried her face in her hands. "This is a lot."

Leaning back against his pillows, he made a V with his legs and pulled her into the space. He cradled her to his chest. "It's so much."

"Doing it with you made it easier."

"Ditto with helping the girls adjust to me being away for the weekend."

Holy crap. She blinked. They'd *parented* together.

"Lawson. Being a team with you like this—it's not making me love you less."

His smile was lopsided. "I was going to bare my soul to you when I got home. Some sort of harebrained scheme where I impressed you. I had visions of a scavenger hunt all over the island."

"With you as the prize?"

"Not exactly. More to show you all the places where I fell in love with you."

"I think I fell a little more for you tonight, in this hotel room. You impressed me more by supporting my son than pretty much anything else you could do. You caring for Daniel proves you're the man I want as mine, ten times over."

"What about this right here?" He tightened his embrace. "It's about you and me, too. It's how I wake up in the morning, and your face is the first image on my mind. About how I lie there for a few seconds, wondering how many minutes I'll have to wait to see you. What the trick will be to earn my first smile of the day. How many I can eke out by the time I go to bed. They're better than caffeine, your smiles. They fuel me, Clara. Because I know in those moments, you're satisfied and loving life. Making sure both those things are happening is quickly becoming one of the main goals of my existence."

"Pretty simple request, wanting to see me smile."

"It's not simple, not at all. You *know* how much I've doubted my value in a relationship, my ability to meet someone's needs. But I can see it with you. And for a while, being *able* to see it scared me. I couldn't trust it. I worry I'm getting greedy, demanding so much from life. Success at work, sure. I honestly expect it at this point. And making sure the girls are safe, healthy, loved to the moon and back. If I *had* to choose, I'd have to choose them. But the beauty I'm finding is *not* having to choose. I can have all that, *and* you. I want this to be my life, Clara. You, in my heart. Hell, you *are* my heart."

Wow. She could get used to dissolving into nothingness on Lawson Thorne's chest.

"I promise you, you're in mine," she said. "I love you."

"We don't have to make each other promises yet."

"Yes and no. I want you and the girls in my future. Of course, we're going to need to finesse out the details as we go along. But I want to work on making a family together, Lawson."

His face fell. "You mean with the kids we have, right?"

"Of course. I meant it when I said I didn't want to be pregnant or have a baby again. And I respect you not wanting to go through trying to have one."

"And you're sure you want two four-year-olds? It's not like with me and Daniel, where I'll be more of a friend and mentor. The longer we're together, the more you'll become…well… like their mom. Or at a minimum, Auntie Clara."

"I want that with my whole heart, Lawson. I know the math of it all doesn't make sense. Giving all my love to you, and to the girls, and to Daniel. And yet, it's possible."

"Heart math is exponential, I think."

Thank goodness that was true.

Sunday morning, she drove Daniel back to school.

"You're sure you don't want me to stay and meet with your adviser with you?"

"As soon as I get all the details, I'll let you know what I need your help for. But it's important I do it myself. If I'm going to make major changes like this, I need to be the one to do the work." He rubbed the back of his neck. "You showed me that. Lawson, too. I'm… I'm glad you worked things out with him."

"Me, too."

"I always figured I'd have a stepdad one day. And man, when all my dormmates find out he makes beer, they'll be hitting me up for a hookup constantly."

She made a face at him. "Adult doesn't mean legal age for *that*."

"I know, Mom. I'm kidding. Well, not about liking having him as a stepdad. I meant that."

"We're not engaged yet," she said. "We need to ease the

girls into the idea. Ease ourselves, quite frankly. But we are going to move in together when the time is right."

"Hand me a sledgehammer, and I'll start knocking down walls. Can you imagine how big the duplex would feel if we joined some of the rooms together? It would be wicked. Or maybe we could wall off part of it like a suite, and Charlotte and I could live there together—"

"Daniel Eduardo Martinez. Did you just suggest you're going to move in with your girlfriend of three months?"

He blinked at her.

He also managed to stay alive for another day by *not* pointing out Clara's situation wasn't much different.

"You'll note Lawson and I are not moving in together, either. And as for you and Charlotte, we will talk about what would be appropriate there once you are home. I'm not naive enough to think you aren't going to have sleepovers sometimes. But it would be nice if you'd hold off on living together until you're paying your own bills."

If he worked for Sam come the winter, he might be able to be financially independent earlier than she'd expected, but they'd ford that river later.

"You'd better go, Mom. Long drive with Lawson before catching the evening ferry."

"I know. The girls might even be asleep when we get home."

He shook his head, amazement crossing his features. "Stepsisters."

"Daniel," she warned. "Slow down. Lawson and I are still learning how to blend a family."

"What are you talking about? You've been intertwining your lives together since we moved here, and with it, my life and Harper's and Pippa's lives, too. Those kids already think you're family."

"Huh. Look at you, being all wise." She sobered. "You're sure you'll be okay?"

"Small chunks, Mom." They'd agreed he'd spend the Veterans Day weekend in Portland with his grandparents, and would catch a ride with them to Oyster Island for Thanksgiving.

He swamped her in a hug.

"Hey. I believe in you. And once you've checked off this box, home will be waiting for you."

By the time Lawson and Clara were on the last leg of their ferry journey, a brilliant fall sunset painted the sky and the water. They were passing the tip of San Juan Island. The oranges and yellows of the leaves matched the sky.

"It's like the world is aflame," she mused, snuggling in closer with Lawson, her back to his front. The weight of her against his chest made him feel like he could take on the world.

They were outside on one of the passenger decks, tucked into a corner of the railing together. Wind whipped through her hair. It kept tickling his nose. His breath kept fogging up his glasses. They'd both forgotten gloves, but their hands couldn't get cold when they were linked together.

"I got a text from Isla," he said. "Harper and Pippa are already stalling with bedtime."

"I bet they want you to tuck them in."

"Which I'm going to do whenever I can. This weekend was a reminder—one of these days, I'm going to sneeze, and I'll discover they're eighteen figuring out their own lives."

She laughed. "You have a few scraped knees and lopsided birthday cakes and tooth fairy visits between now and then. And your first trick-or-treating tomorrow."

"Want to come with us?" he asked.

"Yes."

"I cannot wait to watch them grow," he said.

"You'll never be able to predict what they want to do. Oh—school drama aside, Daniel was full of ideas himself. He wants to start knocking walls down in the duplex," she said. "I think he has visions of renovating it into a big unit with the primary bedrooms and living rooms combined, and then keeping the other kitchen and the two spare bedrooms on my side for himself."

He rolled the possibility around, picturing what Daniel envisioned. "You know, it has potential."

She made a face. "You're not ruining your house for the sake of my son's not-so-opaque conspiracy."

"It wouldn't be ruining anything. We'd be making space for a life together. Otherwise, we'd have to find a new place where we'd all fit." He tried to think of anywhere else on the island he'd want to call home. But all he could see were two sets of brown pigtails bobbing on a hunt for fairies around the playhouse, or little arms stretching to pick apples in the fall, both the tree and their hands getting bigger by the year.

Her gaze gleamed. "The only place I want to live is ours."

"Then embrace the sledgehammer, Clara."

"We'll see," she said. "You know, when I dropped Daniel off, I told him home would be waiting for him. It applies to us, too."

"Sure does."

Two sides of a duplex, with grand visions to make it one.

Lawson nuzzled his face into the side of her neck.

She squealed. "Your nose is freezing!"

"None of this 'we'll see' business," he said. "I expect unequivocal agreement from my lady of 'yes.'"

He nipped at her earlobe.

"Yes! Yes. Let's make something amazing."

"I plan on it," he said. "For the rest of my life."

Epilogue

Late May

"You would think it's my birthday, not my first anniversary of living on Oyster Island," Clara said, threading a fifth bead onto the silver charm bangle Lawson had affixed to the handle of her morning coffee. He'd also tied a handwritten riddle to the mug, the answer to which had started off the day's adventure.

They sat as a cozy group of four on a bench outside Otter Marine Tours, warm in the late spring sunshine.

"Put it on your wrist!" Pippa instructed.

"Read the clue!" Harper said.

The twins weren't as identical as they had been when they had arrived last summer. After Lawson had gamely perfected crown braids and Dutch braids using Clara as a guinea pig, he'd lost the chance to show off his new skills on Harper. His niece had decided she wanted to cut her hair like Dora the Explorer, and then had gained a new love for sparkly barrettes.

Both girls, one with butterflies and ladybugs clipped in her bangs, the other with her hair in two French braids, crowded around Clara as she fastened the clasp on the bracelet. Lawson watched from the other side of Harper, a bemused smile on his face.

"Okay," Clara said, spinning the beads one at a time. "We

have the house charm, for me moving in next door. Then the blue wavy glass for the beach."

"Uncle Sonny said you helped him when he was sad," Pippa said.

Lawson had hidden the tiny box with the bead and clue on the log where they'd sat the day he found out about the twins' parents' accident.

From there, the riddle had directed them to Isla's farm, and a cheese-wedge charm from his sister in her tasting shop. The next clue pointed to Hideaway Wharf, where she'd collected a book charm from Charlotte at the library, and a mushroom charm from Kellan and Sam, who'd been waiting for her behind the counter of the dive shop. The dangling silver addition was a hat tip to how much foraging she'd been doing with the chef through fall, winter and spring. She'd even joined in with the couple to guest cook for a handful of their Forest + Brine foraging-and-dinner tours.

"Read the clue!" Harper repeated.

Clara unfolded the slip of paper.

At eight, I am one
At fifteen, I am three
At nineteen, I am five

"Huh?" she asked. "Something to do with their kids' ages?"

But it didn't match the gap between the twins and Daniel.

As he'd been doing all morning, Lawson shrugged, his mouth equal parts smirk and excited smile.

"Numbers…ages, or distance…" Her years of using a twenty-four hour clock to mark Eddy's schedule popped into her head. "Or *time*."

"Getting warmer," he said.

"One at eight, three at three in the afternoon, and five at five… Oh! That's how many people are in the kitchen of the pub at those times."

She was still doing the early prep shift, so she was the solo one there in the morning hours.

He shot her a finger gun. "You got it."

The girls led the way to The Cannery, skipping along the boardwalk and then down the alley to the side door. They made it all the way into the currently quiet kitchen before running into another person.

Matias and Violet were leaning against one of the prep counters, grins on their faces. Matias carried their six-month-old daughter, Lilia, in his arms. She clapped her hands and reached for Lawson, who held out his hands to take her.

The baby snuggled into his neck. The twins each latched onto one of his legs, never fans of having to share their uncle with the new addition.

Violet chuckled at Harper and Pippa before gesturing for Clara to come closer. "How's it looking so far? The bracelet?"

Clara held out her wrist, earning a long *ooooo* from her friend.

"You did good with the ocean bead, Lawson," Violet said. "It looks bottomless."

"And yet, it's not my favorite," he said mischievously.

"Which one is?" she asked.

"Maybe you don't have it, yet."

"You went for a cheese wedge instead of a goat?" Violet asked.

Lawson made a gagging face. "I wanted to *want* to look at her bracelet when she wears it."

"Don't be mean to Cashew!" Pippa said, crossing her arms.

Before it could turn into a full, two-twin, goat-related defense, Clara redirected them all. "I take it there's another box around here somewhere?"

Matias plucked the sixth instalment off the stainless steel counter and passed it to her.

Clara lifted the lid, and grinned. A three-charm collection, attached to a round spacer, lay on the folded tissue inside. The miniature whisk was especially impressive, alongside a spatula. The pair of utensils were only to be outdone by the tiny frying pan, studded with two yellow stones, like tiny fried eggs.

"This is adorable," she said, adding the charm to her collection. She kissed Lawson on the cheek. "Thank you."

Violet handed over a slip of paper.

"More?" Clara said to Lawson. "It's too much."

"Nah." He winked. "Keep reading."

Not your first ride, but the most black-and-white.

Clara read the line out loud.

"I don't get it," Pippa announced.

"I'm not sure I do, either," Clara said. "A ride? Neither of our cars are black-and-white."

"Whales are black and white," Harper mused. "I like whales."

"I do, too, sweetie, and your uncle and I saw them last year when we went out on—oh! Archer and Franci's boat!"

Violet and Matias gave a round of applause.

"Are we driving to their house?" Clara said.

"No, I pulled some strings," Lawson explained. He was still swaying with Lilia, who was blissed out, teetering toward sleep.

Clara shook her head in amazement and motioned to their friends. "Seems like you did with everyone we know."

"Yeah, everyone wanted to help celebrate your anniversary," Lawson said, kissing the baby on the top of her dark curls and passing her back to her dad. "Plus, I've been planning it for over six months."

Wild. She pressed a hand to her chest. "So, where's Archer's boat, then?"

"Tied up next to the *Oyster Queen.*"

They said goodbye to Matias and Violet and left for the dock. Right before they got to the ramp, Sam jogged out from the dive shop and handed them matching life jackets in Harper and Pippa's size.

"Are we going out on the boat?" Clara asked.

"No, but safety first. This way, they can roam free," Lawson explained.

They made their way through the rabbit warren of docks, until they got to the fork where the Otter Marine boats moored. On the end of the pier, Archer and Franci were lounging in the cockpit of the Chris-Craft. It looked like a tight fit, given both Iris and their black Labrador, Honu, were sharing the bench seat. Clara understood the look of contentment on Archer's face. She felt that same feeling herself, whenever she was with her whole family.

"You made it!" Franci said The sun glowed off her red hair. "We thought you'd be along soon. Charlotte texted to say you visited the library about forty minutes ago."

"We've been *everywhere*," Pippa emphasized.

Clara glanced at Lawson. "This *must* be all." She held out her wrist and jingled the six charms. "I'm going to run out of space, soon."

"Don't you worry," he said.

Archer climbed out of the boat, yet another small cardboard box in hand. "I think you're looking for this?"

She took it and lifted the lid. "Oh, an orca. *Lawson.* It's perfect."

"Mmm, getting there," he said.

She put the lid back on and then tucked it into her cross-body purse. "I'll wait until we're on solid ground before I add this one to the bracelet."

"Smart. Many a thing has been lost in this water," Archer said.

"Nearly me, from the dang kayak when I was pregnant with Iris," Franci joked from her seat in the boat.

"Well, that one turned out okay," Archer said. "This one will, too." He held his arms open and beckoned Clara forward for a hug. "Happy anniversary."

Her friend absorbed her in his strong embrace. For the first time today, a lump formed in her throat. Both their lives had changed so much since the accident, and yet they'd both managed to find love, family, home. Truth was, without Archer having grown up here and choosing to move back, Clara wouldn't have found any of this.

She hugged him harder. "Thank you."

"Eddy'd be happy that you're happy," Archer murmured in her ear.

"I think so, too. And he'd be so proud of you."

"Took me a bit, but I figured things out." He glanced over his shoulder, aiming a loving look at his wife and child.

Sniffling, she let go of her friend.

"Auntie Clara, are you sad?" Harper asked.

"No, honey. I'm the happiest right now."

Archer pulled a slip marked with a seven from his pocket and handed it to Clara.

"This one's for the little ones." Clara wiggled her eyebrows at Harper and Pippa. "Are you ready, girls?"

They nodded

"Branch then flower then fruit then cake."

Pippa's face screwed up.

Harper clapped her hands. "The apple tree!"

"Should we take the path?"

They skipped ahead.

Waving goodbye to Archer and Franci, Clara took Lawson's hand and pulled him along, following the joyful trail forged by the twins.

The minute they got to the beach, Harper grabbed a ten-foot-long piece of giant kelp and started dragging it behind her, the thick bulb bouncing along the rocks in her wake. "It's my doggy. I'm walking him!"

Lawson laughed. "Make sure he stays on his leash!"

Clara had walked down the boardwalk, through the trees and along the beach hundreds of times now. The route would never get old. Comfortingly the same, but always a bit different. What didn't change was holding hands with Lawson.

Her bracelet rolled on her wrist, pressed against his. One of the dangling charms tickled the top of her palm.

"This is too much," she said. "There can't be many more."

"Only two, promise."

"No beer charm?" she asked, studying the collection.

"That's more my thing than yours," he said. "As much as you were an inspiration for the gluten-free line."

His GF creations were on the menu at Hau'oli now, as well as a few other pubs in the San Juans and on the Olympic Peninsula. This summer, they were planning to bottle and distribute to select liquor stores, and if all went well, they would expand the warehouse with a dedicated GF space starting in the fall.

When they got to the yard, Daniel and Charlotte were waiting in the gazebo, playing fetch with Français.

A giant pink ribbon frilled off one of the apple tree branches.

"I think I'm supposed to go there," she whispered to the twins.

They nodded, all seriousness.

"An apple from the apple tree?" She plucked the box hanging from the bow and opened it. "Or not."

Lawson smirked. "Not. It would look too much like a teacher charm, which is your past, but not this past year. But *this…*"

She lifted the dangling silver heart and held it up for the girls to see. Three smaller hearts hugged the point of the bigger one, two in yellow gold and one in rose gold.

"The children, Lawson," she breathed.

"Yeah. Our children."

In the corner of her eye, Daniel sat cross-legged with the girls, who piled into his lap. Français got in on the fun, sprawling in between Harper and Pippa.

She took Lawson's hand and squeezed.

Daniel shifted Pippa around and reached into his shorts pocket. He held another box to Clara. "Here, Mom."

"Is this one from you?"

"Uh, *no*. But I think it's a good idea."

She opened it. A boxy heart sat on the center, bearing the name of the bracelet brand.

"Is this one *your* heart, Lawson?" she asked. It made sense, given the last charm had four hearts in total. "That's sweet."

His expression was cautious. "Sort of. Open it."

She cocked a brow.

"There's a latch," he said, motioning to her hand.

"Ooh, a locket?" She stuck her thumbnail in the tiny divot. The picture inside was...

Her jaw dropped. *Not a picture.*

A miniscule *diamond ring*?

Was it? Did it mean...?

She stared at the charm. "Lawson?"

"Yes, Clara?"

She glanced at him, just as he got down on one knee. He held a small olive-colored velvet ring box. Vintage, maybe.

He flipped it open.

She covered her mouth with her hands. "I think I'm the one who's supposed to say *yes*, not you."

"I haven't even asked a question yet."

"Please. Please ask."

He lifted the ring out and held it up. The oval diamond glinted in the sun. A halo of diamonds ringed the center stone.

She gasped. "Oh, my god, Lawson."

"Don't tell me I went overboard again. It needs to last a lifetime."

She nodded.

"There you go again, agreeing before you know what you're saying yes to."

"I do know, though," she said. "I'm getting you. And this family, and our home."

"You're saving me from having to make a speech," he said with a wink.

"Oh, don't let me derail you."

He chuckled. "You derailed me from the day you arrived on this island. And I don't ever want my life to go back to what it was. Will you marry me, Clara? Have me for life? With this family, and our home?"

Her heart thrilled. The word had never been easier to say. "Yes."

* * * * *

Look for Laurel Greer's next book,
Coming soon to Harlequin Special Edition!
And catch up with the previous books in
the Love at Hideaway Wharf miniseries
by USA Today *bestselling author Laurel Greer!*

Diving into Forever
A Hideaway Wharf Holiday
Their Unexpected Forever

Available now!

Harlequin® Reader Service

Enjoyed your book?

Try the perfect subscription for Romance readers and get more great books like this delivered right to your door.

See why over 10+ million readers have tried Harlequin Reader Service.

Start with a Free Welcome Collection with free books and a gift—valued over $20.

Choose any series in print or ebook. See website for details and order today:

TryReaderService.com/subscriptions

RSBPA2409